the
schemer

Entangled Publishing, LLC
2614 South Timberline Road
Suite 105, PMB 159
Fort Collins, CO 80525
Visit our website at www.entangledpublishing.com.

AMARA is an imprint of Entangled Publishing, LLC.

Edited by Liz Pelletier
Cover design by Liz Pelletier
Photography from Wander Aguiar

ebook ISBN 978-1-64063-195-3
MMP ISBN 978-1-64063-442-8

Manufactured in the United States of America

First Edition February 2018

AMARA
an imprint of Entangled Publishing LLC

the schemer

A HOT ROMANTIC COMEDY

AVERY FLYNN

Chapter One

Jet-lagged and so tired his brain was leaking out of his left ear, Tyler Jacobson jerked to a stop in the narrow hallway of his apartment building, barely avoiding getting crushed to death by eight feet of boxes.

So this is how it's all going to end. He was going to die getting run over by a stack of boxes moving straight at him, seemingly all on their own power. Well, it was a pretty unique death, even if being dead would really get in the way of his plans to take over the world.

"Hey, I'm walking here," he called out as a joke, using a line from one of his favorite movies and using a fake blue-collar accent. His normal accent was much more refined, thanks to six months' worth of voice lessons to get rid of his natural working-class inflections when he'd first graduated college.

The stack of boxes halted and tilted forward slightly, followed by the muffled sound of the metal dolly clunking against the carpeted floor. But no one appeared. Okay, he'd been kidding about the whole ghostly boxes thing. He owned the building, even if he didn't handle the day-to-day management of it, and knew it wasn't haunted even if he'd been the kind of person to believe in that kind of bullshit—which he wasn't. He may not sound like it, look like it, or act like it anymore, but some parts of growing up across the harbor from the glitz and money of Harbor City didn't go away, and a skeptical worldview was definitely one of them.

"Sorry, didn't see you," said a woman's disembodied

voice from behind the boxes.

"I'm not surprised." The woman needed help. Times like this, he wished the building had a doorman to assist with moving boxes. He really needed to look into renovating so there would be room for a small lobby. When she didn't make a move to go around the boxes, his curiosity got the better of him. "Are you hiding back there?"

A woman peeked around the boxes. A pretty woman. Scratch that. A gorgeous woman—with large, expressive eyes that were too big for her face and the kind of hair a man could wrap his hand around in bed.

She narrowed her sharp brown eyes, taking a full summary of him in a nanosecond from her rather impressive height, assessing the situation with a calculated ease that told him without her having to say a word that there was more to this woman than her looks. She had the kind of perfectly smooth hair, perfectly applied makeup, and perfectly sexy set of legs encased in designer jeans that screamed "contained"—but just barely.

"Why would I hide?" she asked, her thick Riverside accent as real as the attitude she was copping. "You don't scare me."

Tyler had the feeling very little did. He liked that. And from her accent he could tell her roots were as blue collar as the ones he did his best to hide. Jury was still out on how he felt about that.

He held out his hand. "Tyler Jacobson."

"Everly Ribinski," she said as she shook his hand, quick up, down, and release. Her gaze had widened ever so briefly when their skin had touched, but she'd caught herself. Could be mutual attraction or she was shocked he'd not tried to use the moment to linger. Jury was still out on that, too. He imagined a woman as beautiful as she was got a lot of unwanted extra touching by men when strictly business should be the name of the game. His belly tightened for a moment at the thought of any man sexually harassing her, but she met his gaze with such confidence, he figured they'd been treated to a verbal kick to the groin had they tried it. He found himself grinning at the mental image of her putting some man in his place.

And then he realized he was standing in the hallway, blocking her from finishing her move-in, and grinning like an idiot at her. When she simply raised one brow, he shook his head. *Get it together, Jacobson.*

He tried to get his fried brain to work. Gorgeous women weren't new to him. They liked him. He liked them. Win-win. However, for some reason, Everly made his very fast brain stutter to a near stop. He blamed the fact that he'd had to take the red-eye from Hungary with a teething and very angry baby on board and a seatmate who loved to talk.

"Nice to meet ya," she said when he didn't move. "But I gotta get these up to my apartment."

The sexy way she dropped her A's was doing crazy things to what was left of his addled brain.

"You're 3B." Of course, his mind picked that moment to actually start working. The gallery owner who was leasing the street-level commercial property in the building. "I'm 2B, but don't worry. I don't mind being beneath you."

What the fuck did you just say, Jacobson?

In his sleep-deprived mind, he'd meant that because he owned the building, he didn't mind not being on the top floor. But she didn't know he owned the building, and now he wasn't sure telling her wouldn't seem like he'd said that just to work in he owned the building. Remain rude or look pathetic? Either option left him looking like the asshole he'd just acted like.

And to think he had used his brain and communi-cations skills to put millions of dollars in the bank in the matter of only a few years. *Come on, Jacobson, think of something to say that isn't an innuendo or bragging. Something helpful. And then get the hell out of here while she still lets you.*

His mind jumped around from pivot to pivot, each follow-up potentially life-threatening in the minefield he'd just created.

"I can hook you up with a great guy I know; he helps people get rid of accents." Okay, not his first choice of topics upon just meeting someone, but it qualified as helpful.

She planted a hand on a round hip and narrowed her eyes. "Accents?"

"Yeah." He nodded, realizing too late what fuckery his jet-lagged brain had just gotten him into.

"And what's wrong with how I speak?" Everly asked, her tone hard. No A's were dropped suggestively that time, as each word came out like bullets from a machine gun.

He thought he heard the faint ringing of a bell before a boxing match began in the distance of his subconscious, and his gaze darted around for a way to get to his apartment quickly. She deserved an apology, he was sure, but he was afraid he'd just dig the hole even deeper, he was so jet-lagged and off his game. "Umm. Nothing?"

Tyler could read anyone, know their weaknesses in a moment, and use them to his own advantage. It's how he had turned his consulting firm into the one organization in Harbor City guaranteed to make businesses successful. Part coach, part drill instructor, part Machiavelli, he brought whatever was needed to the table to transform companies and take them from good to great. But for the second time that day, his scheming mind was drawing a blank. As the shock of that settled into his belly and set up shop, he had no choice but to throw her a self-deprecating half smile he'd seen his friend Frankie do all too often, which always charmed the ladies and got Frankie out of sticky situations. Hopefully he wasn't as rusty at trying to charm his way out of a mess as he felt.

She pursed her cherry-red lips together, her intelligent eyes narrowing as she picked up on his change in tack. This woman was far too clever, and she was having none of it. She nodded as if she were actually considering what he'd said. "But I should change it?"

Minefield. Minefield. "Forget I said anything." Really. It would be a blessing at this point, since they were going to be neighbors. He sure as hell wasn't going to let her know he actually owned the building after acting like such an ass. *Thank you last-minute red-eye flight from Budapest.*

Normally, Tyler was the one in any situation analyzing the room, looking for the best angles. But as he watched her options flash behind her eyes while schooling her features to remain calm, he was impressed by the plotting going on behind those big, dark eyes of hers. She seemed to consider smiling. He could see the corners of her eyes almost crinkle. But, from how he imagined her perspective, if she played it flirtatiously, she might get a neighbor who constantly cornered her for more attention. Her mouth started to turn down. She could try anger that he was in her way, that he had insulted her, but they had to share the same building, so that was unnecessary stress, especially with her business downstairs. Finally she seemed to settle on a guarded but friendly persona that shut down any opportunities on his part for help or further conversation. Damn. She was good.

"Okay," she said with a smile that looked almost genuine if a little annoyed, then waited, staring at him. "Tyler?"

"Yeah?" he asked, stuffing his hands in his pockets and gracing her with another of what he hoped was a charming smile.

"Can you move?" she asked, her tone teasing. "I don't want to run you over."

"Oh," he said, moving like lightning to get out of her way. "Sorry."

She just nodded, disappeared behind the stack of boxes loaded on the dolly, and moved past him down the hallway. Okay, this entire interaction had been a dumpster fire of jet-lagged idiocy on his part, but watching her heart-shaped ass move as she walked away was pretty damn good.

Forty-eight hours later, and Everly was breaking down the last moving box. The rent on her new apartment was obnoxiously high—nothing new for Harbor City—but she couldn't beat the commute. The Black Hearts Art Gallery was in the same building on the ground floor. Since she put in a ton of hours trying to keep the gallery in the black while covering her nunni's expenses at the nursing home, that three-minute commute was worth the extra rent.

Moving all her stuff from her old, small apartment had been a pain in the ass, but it was done now. That deserved a celebration. She shot off a quick text to her friend Kiki, inviting her out for drinks, and then headed to the hall to drop the boxes in the recycling area. She made it two steps before the smell of smoke hit her.

She ran to the stairwell. It wasn't tire-fire thick black smoke, but there was still a gray haze floating up to the third floor along with the smell of charbroiled something to make her whip her phone out of her back pocket as panic squeezed her lungs. She didn't see smoke yet or hear an alarm, but she was sure that was just a matter of seconds away.

"9-1-1, what's your emergency?"

"There's a fire in my building."

After giving the operator her address, she hustled down the stairs with only one thought in mind—getting the hell out of there before she got stuck in some sort of towering inferno situation.

"Fire!" she hollered on her way down, knowing her voice was loud enough to carry back to Riverside.

She made it to the second-floor landing when someone called out her name. Acting on instinct, she turned and immediately regretted the too-fast movement. Her four-inch heel caught in the carpet, and she flailed forward, gravity yanking her downward at the same time. Moments before she could stop her fall with her nose, a strong arm wrapped around her middle and yanked her back against something unyielding and—she sniffed—smelling of burned baker's chocolate.

"You okay?" Tyler asked, letting her go once she'd regained her balance.

"We gotta go." She grabbed his hand and yanked him toward the stairwell—well, she *tried* to yank him, but he was too solid and muscular for her to move an inch. "The place is on fire!"

"What? No. I was cooking and set the heat too high in the oven," he said, as if it were no big deal to almost burn down a building. "It was smoking up my whole apartment when I got out of the shower."

She looked around, noticing that the smoke was indeed lessening. That's when the first blare of the sirens sounded, barely louder than the fear pounding through her body. "The fire department."

"Tell me you didn't call them," he groaned. "They've already been out three times this month."

"For your cooking?" she asked, not thinking about her question, just concentrating on calming her breathing before she hyperventilated. After the apartment complex next to hers had burned to the ground when she was a kid, even the idea of a building fire freaked her out.

He crossed his arms across his chest. "Yeah."

Any other time and she would have checked out the way his biceps looked in his short-sleeve shirt and the sinewy lines of his forearm. Arm porn was usually her weakness. As it was, she was too busy giving herself a pep talk to do more than barely notice. *In. Out. In. Out. Don't lose your shit. Stay in control.*

"Ever think of cooking lessons?"

His jaw squared and the vein in his temple bulged. "Ever think of checking things out before you over-react?"

"Overreact?" And whoosh, the panic came roaring back along with the memory of the screams coming from that burning building. "I came out of my apartment and the hall was filled with smoke."

He looked up the stairwell, and even with the anger dueling with her panic, she couldn't help but take advantage of the perfect opportunity to take a long look at his face without being observed. The man was too good-looking for her taste. Square jaw. Model-perfect nose. Dark hair that could work in a shampoo commercial. And his eyes? That shade of blue should be outlawed for what it did to a woman's heart rate—not to mention her panties—when he stared right at her.

They hadn't run into each other since the day she'd moved in. When she'd gotten over her annoyance at his rude suggestion for voice lessons, she'd remembered the fatigue she'd seen around his eyes. Another neighbor had mentioned he'd just gotten back from Europe, and she'd been prepared to let the mishap go and start fresh. She'd reminded herself that just because a man is rich and would go to the lengths of taking voice lessons to shed his blue-collar upbringing did *not* make him like her father. The fact that he'd wanted *her* to lose her accent too though was a red warning label in neon lights that she would do well to pay attention to.

But they were going to be neighbors for a while, so it was prudent to not create avoidable situations. Nothing to do with how his hand had felt holding hers or that ridiculously sexy half grin he'd tried to use on her. Of course, her second impression of him was not faring any better than the first.

"I barely see any smoke," he grumbled.

She jerked her gaze upward and saw…nothing but air. "It must have dissipated."

"Sure it did," he said, sounding exactly the way her nunni had whenever she'd called Everly out in a lie without actually using the words "liar, liar, pants on fire." The sound of sirens blared outside, followed by the thunder of booted footsteps on the stairs. "Tell that to the firefighters."

She did. They weren't convinced. By the time the firefighters had checked the building, specifically Tyler's apartment, and left, she was more than ready for that drink with Kiki. Before she could head back upstairs, though, Tyler appeared next to her with a bakery box that he handed to her with an apologetic grin.

Inside was a plate of burned-to-hockey-puck-hardness brownies. And that solved the mystery of what in the hell had been smoking up the building.

"**A**nd then he just left?" Kiki asked a few hours later while they were tucked away in a corner booth of their favorite wine bar.

"Yep," Everly said, still trying to wrap her brain around it. "He walked back into his apartment and closed the door."

Peering at her over the top of her wineglass as she took a drink, Kiki gave her friend a questioning look. "This is the hot one you talked to in the hallway who made the crack about your accent?"

"Yep." God, she got sick of people thinking someone with her accent needed to change it or she wouldn't be taken seriously. All through college that had been the number one piece of advice from people in the art department. She'd told them to take a flying leap then, and she would now, too. She was proud of where she was from, and even people from Riverside could appreciate art.

"And today he gave you inedible brownies?" Kiki asked. "Do you think he's crazy?"

She shook her head. "Just pissy."

"Look, you're gonna have to live in the same building as the guy. I say you make a peace offering."

It wasn't a bad idea. Who wanted to go to war with their neighbor as if they were urban Hatfields and McCoys? "Suggestions?"

"Here." Kiki reached into her purse and whipped out a gift certificate for her company, Be Merry Catering. "The guy obviously can't cook. I can provide a week's worth of meals. All he has to do is call and tell me what he wants from our at-home menu."

It was brilliant. "You're the best."

"True story." Kiki lost some of her teasing humor. "So how did your last visit with Nunni go?"

A heaviness invaded Everly, and her limbs felt like concrete blocks. "About as well as could be expected with the dementia. She thought I was my mom again."

Kiki winced in sympathy. "So you got the lecture?"

"Yep." Just like nine out of ten visits. It wasn't unusual for dementia patients to pick one life event to circle back to over and over again, but that didn't make it any easier to hear—especially when it always cut straight through to Everly's heart. "Every time I thought she'd let go and move on, she circled back around to warning me about all the evils of men who promised heaven and delivered hell."

"Your dad sure was a piece of work."

"That's putting it mildly." The man was a narcissistic, lying, abandoning asshole of the highest order.

Kiki raised her glass again. "To getting over your daddy issues."

"What daddy issues?" she asked, but clinked their glasses anyway, ignoring the little voice that told her she was full of shit.

"Girl, don't even pretend." Kiki rolled her eyes. "You judge every guy who even looks at you like he has to pay the sins of your father."

That may be true, but who could blame her after what her father had done, what had happened to her mother after, and the fact that the whole episode had so scarred her nunni that it was the one thing she fixated on most as she spent her days in the assisted living center. The whole thing was a shit show, and Everly got to live it every single day of her life. Still, there was no denying one very important fact.

"Just because Nunni has dementia," she told Kiki, "doesn't mean she's wrong about self-entitled rich assholes."

T he next day, Tyler woke up without a trace of jet lag to find an envelope had been slipped under his door. Since it wasn't ticking, he opened it up.

Be Merry Catering

Gift certificate for one week's worth of at-home meals. Please call for more information.

It was signed Everly Ribinski.

What. The. Fuck. A guy burns one tray of brownies—okay, it was like his millionth time he'd failed at cooking, but she didn't know that—and he gets told to just give up? If he'd given up, he never would have made it out of Waterbury. He'd be in some boring dead-end job instead of raking in millions doing what he loved.

He glanced down at the paper in his hand. He'd never had salt poured in a wound via gift certificate before. So that's how it was gonna be, huh? War by passive-aggressive gift certificate?

He tossed the paper on his kitchen island and paused, considering his options. Was he overthinking this? He'd been making brownies for her to apologize for his shitty comment about her accent, and she'd called the Harbor City Fire Department. Then, she'd followed up by telling him he was so bad at cooking he needed to hire a caterer. Okay, he did suck in the kitchen, but he was learning. Plus, even after only talking to her twice he *knew* that woman never had a simple thought in her life. She was layers of intelligence and motives—like a fucking parfait.

The *clip-clop* of the passive-aggressor in question's heels made its way across his ceiling. He listened to her catwalk her way from one end of the apartment to the other, each step sounding as self-satisfied as he was sure she was feeling.

Fine. Two can play this game.

Grabbing his phone off the island, he shot off an email to his assistant.

Fuzzy pink foot-shaped monstrosities with googly eyes glued to the top looked up at Everly like a deranged stalker. She held them to her phone so Kiki could see what had arrived in the package along with a note from Tyler wondering if her high heels hurt her feet as much as they hurt his ears.

"Slippers?" Kiki asked, pressing her face closer to her camera as if she really wanted to get a better look at the hideous things. "He sent you ugly-ass slippers?"

All Everly could do was nod. She took another look at the slippers, shivered involuntarily, and dropped them into the trash.

"Just how cute is he?" Kiki asked.

Drop-dead gorgeous. "Not enough for this."

"So what's your plan?"

Her best friend knew her so well. She *always* had a plan. "Avoid him as much as possible."

"And when that's not possible?"

It was a small building with only a handful of apartments and a small parking garage. Total avoidance was probably a fantasy. It was best to be prepared. "Not give him an inch."

"So you're going all Riverside all the way?" Kiki asked with a laugh.

Growing up poor and in a shitty neighborhood meant growing up with a code. "We don't back down. Ever."

"Girl." Kiki shook her head in amusement. "I love you, but not everything in life is a competition to the death."

"Of course it is." What would her life be if she just gave in to every asshole who crossed her path? Not one in which she owned her own gallery, that was for sure.

Kiki giggled. "This is going to get interesting."

Interesting was the last thing Everly needed in her life right now, but backing down from a fight just wasn't in her nature.

Chapter Two

"**Y**ou've *got* ta be kiddin' me."

Tyler kept his attention on his copy of *Investor's Business Daily*. He didn't need to look up to identify the speaker or her car, which was why he'd kept his eyes on the words he wasn't reading as she'd driven closer. It wasn't like he needed to actually watch her. Much to his annoyance, he *never* had any trouble picturing the woman who went with that thick Riverside accent, with its dropped Ts and Gs at the ends of words and saying *cawfee* instead of *coffee*. Everly Ribinski was a high-heeled addict who clip-clomped her way across the apartment above his loud enough to wake the dead.

But that had been just the beginning of their little war two months ago, which explained why he was sitting in a folding lounge chair parked in the building's primo parking spot in the middle of a Tuesday, waiting for his evil upstairs neighbor to come home and try to park there. That wasn't going to happen. He'd make sure of it.

"Are you gonna move so I can park, or do I get to run you over?" she asked.

He looked up. It was a mistake. From his spot on the lounge chair, gazing up at her as she stood next to the open door of her car, she was all curves and attitude. Hell, who was he kidding? Everly looked that dangerous no matter where he was sitting. Jet-black hair that ended in a curl that barely brushed her shoulders and that lush body encased in a form-fitting ebony dress and leather jacket, full lips begging to have the red lipstick kissed off them, and a heart-shaped ass that made his cock take notice every damn time he saw her. Right now was no exception, even though he couldn't see her ass from this angle. Pity that.

Slowly, Tyler lowered his gaze, closed his paper and folded it in half, then laid it on his lap. He picked up the longneck bottle of beer next to him and looked back at her. Everly didn't seem happy to see him. That wasn't a shocker. She never was—not that he gave her a reason to be.

He took a long sip from the cool bottle, watching as she narrowed her dark-brown eyes at him. He could practically see all the ways she was considering offing him running through her mind. Of course, she never would. He knew people. Knew how they thought. Knew all their plots and plans. Knew how to outmaneuver them and come out on top. Always.

Well, except since he'd met her. But where they'd been locked in a draw, he was sure this latest maneuver would put him on top once and for all.

He set the bottle back down on the concrete and forced himself not to imagine all the things those cherry lips of hers could do. "You wouldn't run me over."

She jiggled her keys. "Guess again, 2B."

"Well, 3B," he said, playing along with her we-don't-know-each-other's-names game. "They don't allow high heels in prison."

"I have faith in the penitentiary black market," she said without a second's hesitation.

"Speaking from experience?" he asked, knowing that she wasn't.

Everly Ribinski might come from a shady side of town, but she wasn't a mafia princess or a badass looking to make her mark in a very rough part of town. She was an art dealer with a shoe fetish and a killer ass.

She raised her chin even higher with arrogance. "You have *no* idea."

"We need to settle this."

"Your thing for gas fumes and shadowy parking garages?" she asked. "I totally agree. It's weird."

Getting up from the lounge chair, he opened his arms to encompass the eight and a half feet wide by nineteen feet long area marked by yellow paint nearest to the resident elevator entrance. Also, it happened to be directly next to where Mrs. MacIntosh parked her ancient Chevrolet, usually taking off a layer of paint from whoever had the bad luck of being parked in the next spot, which was why his car was three blocks away in the garage of another building he owned. That's why he'd kept everyone out of this spot. Although he'd never tell Everly the real reason. He preferred to let her think he just liked to harass her. Which just happened to be a real fringe benefit. "This parking spot is mine."

She gave him a squinty look as if he really was on her very last nerve, only the laughing gleam in her dark eyes gave her away. "It goes to whoever gets it first."

He stood and swept his arms out. "And I'm here."

She laughed, a loud, astonished sound that echoed in the garage. "You're sitting on an ugly pink lounge chair. Where did you even get it?"

The building's lost and found, but she didn't need to know that.

"You don't even park here," she said, her voice bleeding with exasperation.

"I do now. I decided to buy a bike. I've had my eye on this Harley, and today I pulled the trigger. They're delivering it later this afternoon, and I'll need a place to store it near the building, where it'll be less likely to get stolen. So see, I need the spot more than you." True story. Well, except the part where he'd been eyeballing a bike. He didn't even know how to ride one, hence the need to forevermore store it in this spot. He refused to examine the fact that he'd bought a $50,000 bike to save his nemesis from getting her pride and joy dinged up on a regular basis. He'd seen her financials during the review process to rent the art gallery space, and he knew she was cutting it close every month. He also knew what it was like to work hard for a symbol of that success and to see someone else take shots at it. He shook his head. No, he dropped fifty large because he liked to win, plain and simple. If he also saved her car, well, that was a fortunate side benefit for her.

"I'll flip you for it. And when I win, you lose the heels when you're in your apartment." It was a game he played often enough to take the emotion out of certain decisions. Of course, him being him, he'd learned just the right technique to increase his odds of it landing heads or tails because he wasn't a guy who ever really left things to chance. And as much as he enjoyed their war of wits, he was dying to get those shoes off her one way or another. She really was keeping him up all hours of the night, and he was positive it was those clip-clopping fuck-me heels and not images of her fiery gaze and her wearing them and nothing else. So considering the current circumstances, he wasn't above finessing a flip to find out.

"I'm calling building management." But she didn't make a move for her phone. "You're nuts."

"What's wrong?" He arched an eyebrow, issuing the challenge without saying the words. After the back and forth for the past few months, he didn't have to. "You don't trust fate?"

She crossed her arms and cocked out one hip. "I'm from Riverside," she said, matching her streetwise pose with a deliberate thickening of her accent so it sounded like Riva-side. "I don't trust anything."

They both knew the game they were playing, neither giving an inch. He burned his food and stank up her apartment. She stomped on his ceiling. He claimed the best parking spot with a folding chair. She threatened to run him over. If she knew he owned the building, she'd back off. And while at first he'd have liked nothing better, well, now it would take all the fun out of things because the queen of the high-heel promenade made moves he couldn't predict. And that was a total oddity in his world. One he wasn't ready to give up, and if judging by the heat in her gaze, neither was she.

"One flip of the coin and the winner gets the parking spot. Otherwise, I'll just sit here and drink my beer until my bike arrives. Your call. At least with a flip, I'm giving you a fifty-fifty shot at the spot."

She held up her keys. "You do realize I've got the keys to Germany's second-most impressive export, and it has enough horsepower to squash you like a bug, right?"

Glancing over at the Beemer, he decided it fit her. Black. Sleek. A little mean-looking but with a massive purr when you turned the motor right. "What's the most impressive export?"

"Anselm Kiefer."

His brain skidded to a stop. "Who?"

"Only one of the most thought-provoking German artists of the post–World War II era," she said, challenge filling her voice as if she was just daring him to disagree.

Gauntlet picked up. "And here I thought you were going to say black forest cake. I was thinking of baking you one, too."

She cut him a glare. "Funny."

He shrugged. "What can I say? Art doesn't do it

for me but cake does."

"Of all the idiotic things to say." Her eyes went wide and she pulled herself up to her full height, indignation coming off her in hot sparks that burned his skin. "Art is better than cake. Art is as necessary to living as breathing. And if we're honest, no one can breathe when you bake anything."

He took the hit on the chin. Well played. "I do like some art, like those old-school velvet Elvis paintings or the dogs playing poker," he said, goading her.

The curse that flew out of Everly's mouth sounded Italian, but he couldn't be sure. "You're an animal."

"News flash, all humans are animals." He pulled out the quarter he'd swiped years ago out of his dad's dresser from the special pocket in his wallet and held it up for her to see. It had been with him for decades, and the choices he'd made with it had gotten him out of Waterbury. Some might call it a lucky coin. For him, it was so much more. "Heads or tails?"

"You're not serious." She shook her head, making her dark hair dance against her shoulders.

He held up his hand, making the Boy Scout salute. "Like a book nerd at the library."

"You mocking the book nerds?"

"Honey, I *am* a book nerd." Growing up, the library had been his refuge during his parents' many fights, especially the ones where the screaming was followed by plates breaking against the walls.

Everly glanced down at the dingy quarter in his hand. "One with a Two Face obsession?"

Oh yeah, here was a talk-nerdy-to-me conversation he could have. "Batman or Superman?"

She smirked at him. "Wonder Woman."

Yeah. He could see it—maybe a little too well. The mental image of Everly in Wonder Woman's outfit flashed in his head before he could stop it, and he had to adjust his stance to accommodate his dick's oh-I-like-that reaction. "Heads or tails?"

"Tails for the parking spot."

She made the choice, and Tyler felt no qualms about tweaking the flip. He was saving her car either way, even if she'd never see it that way. And he'd get to watch the spark in her eyes set ablaze when she lost. Win-win.

"Sugar," he said, tossing the coin with a hard flick at just the right angle, "get ready to park at the end of the garage for the foreseeable future."

Everly dropped her keys the moment the coin went airborne. It flew up into the air, flipping end over end several times before she snatched it out of the air, turned it, smacked it down on the top of her hand, and held her palm over it. 2B—okay, Tyler Jacobson, she knew his name—just stared at her bug-eyed and slack-jawed.

Boys. They are so fucking easy.

Well, he hadn't been up until now, anyway. The dark Adonis who looked like a rich woman's David Gandy with his black hair, blue eyes, and perfect body—my God, how much time did he spend in the gym getting hot and sweaty? She could picture his biceps flexing with every curl. His thighs straining with each weight-bearing squat. His back glistening as he—*Girl! Focus!* Where was she? Oh yeah, shocking Mr. Cocksure Know-It-All by not following his playbook. *Deal with it, 2B.*

"What? You don't flip so it lands on the ground like some kind of heathen, do you?" she asked as he stared at her like she was a Rubik's Cube that needed to be solved. "You toss. I catch. That's only fair, right?"

Tyler recovered quickly, she had to give him that. The black-haired, blue-eyed devil snapped his mouth shut, ending the motion with a cocky smile that didn't affect her at all. *Liar.*

"Tit for tat, huh?" He held out his hand, palm up, obviously wanting his quarter back.

She shrugged. What could she say, she was Italian via Poland, and she'd picked up the eye-for-an-eye habit from her nunni.

"Holding a grudge isn't good for your health," he said, taking a step closer, his stride as sure as a man who was always six moves ahead on the chessboard.

She nodded her chin toward the chair behind him. "Neither is sitting in my parking spot."

Determined to ignore the delicious scent of his cologne teasing her senses and just how sexy his forearms looked in that navy-blue button-down rolled up to his elbows, she went through a few of Tyler's greatest cooking misses. Burned curry. Scorched grilled cheese. Blackened eggs. Incinerated popcorn.

"The spot's not yours," he said. "I believe you called tails."

Her stomach did a shimmy as she lifted her hand. She didn't have to glance at the coin. The look on the smug bastard's face said it all. It was heads.

Everly glanced over her shoulder at the dim gloom of the rest of the small underground parking garage. It had only six spots in the long narrow garage, each spot requiring parallel parking except the front two, one for each of the six large apartments above Black Heart Art Gallery. She'd learned from Mrs. MacIntosh that Clyde Fester in 1C had spent a fortune two years ago to buy the rights to three of the spots for his classic GTO he took out only on special occasions. That left the spot by the door next to Mrs. MacIntosh and the one in the rear of the garage. Everly had heard tales of Mrs. MacIntosh dinging the cars parked beside her from time to time, but Everly had ding insurance and a soft spot for anyone older than sixty. That's what happened when your grandma, along with her circle of cutthroat bingo partners, practically raised you from seventh grade on. So Everly would squeeze her aging German metal baby, Helga, as close to the line away from Cecilia's land yacht as possible and cash in on her insurance policy one week at a time. She'd also save herself from the mile-long hike from the back of the garage in her four-inch stilettos. As any woman with sense would agree, what's a ding compared to walking a mile in high heels?

"Aww. Too bad. Best two out of three?" Tyler asked, his smooth voice pulling her attention back to the matter at hand.

She picked up the coin off the top of her hand and looked at both sides. It was grimy, the kind of coin that had been through a million vending machines, but the weight was good. It had a heads and a tails side. There wasn't anything off about it that stood out. Still, she couldn't shake the nugget of disbelief in the pit of her stomach. Of course, Tyler always jumbled her up that way. It was part of the reason why she got so snarly around him. He made her nervous—no, she self corrected, he made her excited, hopeful, aroused. Three things she couldn't afford to be if she was going to keep her focus on making her borderline failing gallery a go and keeping her dementia-suffering nunni in the well staffed, caring senior residence instead of a state-run nursing home.

What would Nunni say at the moment? To pick her battles. "Nah, I'm good." She gave her building nemesis an evil smirk. "Anyway, carrying all my extra heels from my new parking spot will be good exercise."

The grin slid off his face. "I won. No heels inside your apartment."

"I never agreed to that part. Anyway, everybody's got a vice." She flipped the coin to him, relishing the small victory.

He swiped it from the air and shoved it in his pocket. "Your vice couldn't be underwater basket weaving?"

"And miss out on my salsa practice to the beat of you pounding a broom against your ceiling? Where's the fun in that?" Yeah, she was taunting him, but he deserved it after this stunt.

"I expected an answer like that from a woman who believes in the healing power of art and always wears head-to-toe black probably right down to your panties that are always in a twist," he scoffed.

Walk away, Everly. Just walk away.

It was great advice she was giving herself, but there was no way she was taking it. Challenges, thought-provoking art, and the smell of a bingo card marker were her kryptonite—and Tyler Jacobson, Mr. 2B, was a walking, talking, panty-melting challenge.

She lifted her chin and looked him in the eyes, not backing down an inch. She may have lost the coin toss but she wasn't going to lose the battle. "You're wrong."

"No. I'm not," he said, cocky as ever. "I'm *never* wrong."

"You are this time."

They stood so close together that she could see the varying shades of blue in his eyes and feel the electricity coming off him in waves that fried her badass circuitry and turned her hot and expectant. This was why she should have walked away—because fighting with Tyler felt *a lot* like foreplay. And she liked it.

"You don't believe in the healing power of art?" He didn't step back. He didn't touch her, either, but he didn't need to.

"No," she said, barely over the sound of her pulse thundering in her ears. "I'm not wearing black panties."

She shouldn't have said that. She shouldn't have even put the idea into his head. But it was too late. His bright-blue eyes darkened a few shades, followed by the slow upward curl of his lips. "Soft. Girlie. Pink."

She leaned in close. "Nothing." Her lips were only millimeters from his ear. "At." A delicious shiver ran up her spine. "All."

Satisfied she'd taken his game board and shaken all the pieces into new positions, she took a step back, but not far enough. The raw heat in his gaze, all semblance of cockiness or confidence wiped clean to reveal nothing but honest, naked desire, was like a tractor beam to her clit. Her heartbeat galloped in her chest as her body realized exactly where it wanted to be. And for once in her life, without thinking, she took a step forward. Quick as lightning, he moved forward to meet her, his mouth crashing down on hers. It was like touching a match to an oil painting—*everything* caught fire. The next thing she knew, her ass was pressed against her used BMW's hood, her hands were in Tyler's dark hair, and she was still using her tongue to duel with him but in a totally different way. She'd thought she'd been hot before—she was wrong. This was the-face-of-the-sun hot and all she wanted was *more*.

Her legs were spread as far as they could in the form-fitting stretch jersey dress, and he stood between them, the hard length of his cock rubbing against her stomach as he kissed her dumb. The temptation to wrap her legs around his hips and hook her ankles together just above his perfect ass was nearly overwhelming. It would feel so good. She wanted it. Bad. Which was exactly why she couldn't do it. Man-size frat boys and moneymen like Tyler ate up women like her and spit them out. They promised the moon and stars but delivered only tacky glow-in-the-dark stickers you stuck to your bedroom ceiling. She knew firsthand. She'd grown up staring at the pale-yellow stars, one more cheap gift from a man who never could tear himself away from work to cross from the fancy part of Harbor City to Riverside, where beat-up, older model cars lined the streets, to see someone as unimportant as his bastard daughter.

It didn't take any effort to push Tyler away—well, at least once she was able to force herself to put her hands to his muscular chest and shove. He backstepped, stopping just out of arm's reach, his chest heaving, his hair messed up by her fingers, and his bright-blue eyes dark with lust.

"We can't do that again," she said between harsh breaths, sounding to her own ears as if she'd finished a marathon. Nunni had warned her one or a billion times how that way lay danger and trouble and all the bad shit in the world.

"That kiss was…" The words faded out, and he shoved his fingers through his thick hair. "You can have the parking spot. I'll get the building super to repaint the lines to make the space bigger so it's not so near Mrs. MacIntosh's car."

That was a bucket of ice dumped right into her nonexistent panties. Transactional. That's how guys like Tyler saw passion. She may have fucked up fighting and foreplay in her head, but at least she didn't mix up a bad idea with payment for services rendered.

"Fuck you," she said, strutting from the hood to

the driver's door and yanking it open.

As she turned to slide behind the wheel, she caught the confusion making the corners of his eyes crinkle. Yeah. He'd probably never thought anyone would tell someone like him to fuck off. Life was always a shock to the system for the privileged. Without another word, she got into her car and guided Helga into her new parking spot in the back. By the time she'd given herself enough pep talks to walk across the parking garage to the residents' elevator, Tyler was gone, taking his pink lounge chair, beer bottle, and cocksure attitude with him.

Good. He was the last man she needed to be dealing with right now. Her life was enough like a trailer park in the middle of a tornado as it was without adding a man like Tyler into the mix.

Chapter Three

Four very long—and often uncomfortably hard—days later and Tyler was making his way into the lion's den. Or lioness, in this case. The Black Heart Art Gallery took up the street-level floor of the small but pricey building that had been his celebration purchase after he'd earned his first real money, the kind the folks he'd grown up with called "fuck you money" because that's exactly what it said to everyone around him.

The building sat right on the edge of the art district and the financial district. He'd known the rough-around-the-edges neighborhood had possibilities even when everyone told him it was a lousy investment. When the neighborhood took off a year later, though, he'd started turning away buyers offering triple what he'd paid. By his calculations, the area was only beginning to grow into what it could be and wouldn't peak for another decade at the least. That was always the problem with people. They were so hot on immediate results, they failed to play the long game—but not him. That was exactly why he was about to face the woman who'd haunted his late-night dreams and shower-time fantasies for the past four days. He'd disregarded his long-term game plan of antagonizing but not fraternizing with his sexy and off-limits upstairs neighbor from the wrong side of Harbor City, but he couldn't avoid her any longer.

Luckily, his target tonight wasn't Everly Ribinski but Italian hotel magnate Alberto Ferranti, who had finally decided to expand his empire of high-end boutique hotels into the United States. Every business consultant in Harbor City had the Italian in his or her sights in hopes of being the one to guide Ferranti in his American business dealings and taking a very healthy cut of the profits, but Tyler was going to be the one to land him. He had the numbers, the vision, and the plan to make it happen. All he needed was some one-on-one face time with the man, and he was going to get it here tonight.

That would solidify Tyler's position as one of the city's key movers and shakers. After that, his days of hearing the whispers about being a pity scholarship kid from working-class Waterbury would be behind him for good. Then, he would have made it and finally become a part of the world he'd watched from the outside for so much of his life. According to Tyler's well-placed informants, Ferranti was going to be here tonight.

"Tyler," a familiar voice called out.

He turned in time to see Helene Carlyle, queen of Harbor City's social elite and his friend Sawyer's mom, wearing a designer navy dress, a necklace worth as much as the pricy art hanging on the gallery walls, and a name tag with the words "Art Adviser" printed beneath her name. This was a woman who instilled fear into some of the city's most powerful, made doormen shake in their shined shoes, and had enough icy reserve for those she didn't know or like to reverse climate change. What in the world was she doing here wearing a *name tag*? He hadn't heard anything about Carlyle Enterprises being in trouble.

"Is everything all right?" he asked, ready to reach for his wallet if necessary.

"Well," Helene said, her dissatisfaction obvious in the pinched look to her mouth. "The wine is horrible, but it always is at events like this."

"No offense," he said, his brain trying to catch up

with the visuals. "But it looks like you're working here."

So what was her play here? Everyone had one—including himself. Always. Was she planning on opening her own gallery? Had Everly brought her in as a potential investor? If so, how would that impact his current plan to get some face time with Alberto? Could Helene help out if she was in a power position at the gallery? Would she want to? What if this was something else entirely? Could she be looking to buy the gallery outright?

"I wouldn't call it working," she said as she eyeballed the crowd with a critical eye. "I get to educate the uninformed about their bad taste in art, correct it, and tell them what to buy—and they do."

The chuckle escaped before he could stop it. Here he was spinning out every possibility and its impact and Helene was just doing what she loved—telling everyone else what to do. When he'd first met her at the prep school his family never could have afforded on their own, she scared the shit out of him. "Formidable" wasn't the right word for the woman in her late fifties who managed to make ruling the Harbor City elite social circle look like child's play. She was as tough as dried-out beef jerky, sharp as broken glass, and—underneath it all—a devoted, if more than a little manipulative, advocate for the people she loved. It had taken him a while to figure out that last one. Most people never did.

However, Helene Carlyle had been his first and most influential mentor in how to navigate the shark-infested waters of Harbor City's elite. He'd be forever grateful and, no matter how many millions he earned, wouldn't be able to pay her back for it all. Still, working as an art adviser in a small gallery—even if it was with the stated objective to boss everyone into having better taste—didn't seem like anything he'd ever expected Helene to do.

"How did this happen?" he asked.

Helene gave a graceful shrug. "Hudson asked for a favor for his friend who owns the gallery during one of his shows. Of course the name tag's horrendous, but I couldn't change Everly's mind on that—and I thought my boys were stubborn. So." She paused, giving him an assessing look. "What are you doing here? I never took you for much of an art aficionado." She held up her hand before he could speak. "Don't tell me. It's for work."

Bingo. "I'm here for Alberto Ferranti."

He quickly scanned the crowd, milling in small groups and staring at the primary-colored blobs splattering white canvases lining the walls as if they'd find the meaning of life or even something that looked almost like art in the paintings. There were lots of expensive black outfits on bored rich people. Lots of pretentious expressions that reminded him of someone pretending they weren't smelling a fart. Lots of ignored waiters offering hors d'oeuvres. A handful of starving artist types stuffing their bags with the otherwise disregarded bacon-wrapped shrimp and pâté on tiny triangles of toast. There had to be nearly seventy people here, but none of them had Ferranti's signature shock of chin-length silver hair.

Out of the corner of his eye, he spotted Helene shake her head at him.

"You do know," she said, "that there's more to life than work."

Maybe for some people, but not for him—not yet. He had a plan, a scheme, that was going to change everything, and he'd go from being the kid in a donated prep school jacket to the man at the head of the table.

Finally. And yes, he was well aware how childish those dreams sounded to most. But what could he say? It was the first vision of success he ever imagined for himself. It was the drive that had gotten him this far, and it deserved to finally be realized. "And this from the woman who could buy most of Harbor City three times over and is *still* wearing a name tag because she's at work?"

"You care too much what others think, Tyler. Always have."

His breath hitched from the verbal kick to the ribs, but he recovered quickly. They were harsh words, but her gaze held kindness, if only for a flicker of a second before the mantle of haughtiness settled back into place. It wasn't anything he hadn't thought himself anyway. But it was a whole lot easier not to care what others thought of you when you came from old money. Waterbury had a stench that was hard to wash away.

Helene waved her hand dismissively. "True power, dear, is wearing a name tag and knowing everyone will *still* bow before you. Besides, this is more like volunteering to improve humanity's taste in art."

"Lofty goal," he said, just as a flash of silver caught his eye. "And there he is."

Pivoting, Helene turned in the direction Tyler was looking. The move revealed Everly standing next to Ferranti with her arm hooked in his. The smile on her face was genuine, her shoulders relaxed, her step light. Meanwhile Ferranti continued to talk. They were too far away to be heard over the chatting gallery show attendees, but there was no missing the excited gestures Ferranti was making with his free hand. The two were obviously close, but just how close was the question — and the possible monkey wrench — to be determined.

"They know each other." Saying it out loud didn't

ice the burning poker jabbing him in his gut.

"Indeed," Helene said. "Everly told me that they met in Italy some years ago when she was searching for art for a client. She made an offer on one of the paintings in his hotel. There was some kind of exuberant bargaining. She came back home with the painting and a new friend."

"Friend?" he asked, images of all the naked things he'd like to do with Everly if she was his friend flashing in his mind's eye. "Is that what they were calling it?"

"Not that kind." Helene pinched his arm, hard enough to make him start. "From what I understand, she's more like a very close family friend, sort of like how I think of you."

Well, that explained the Mom's-not-putting-up-with-that-kind-of-talk reaction. He caught a calculating gleam in her eye. He knew that look and didn't need to run through a long list of scenarios to know what it meant. Helene Carlyle was known to play matchmaker, as she had with her two sons recently. He needed to nip this line of thought in the bud. "Don't even think it. I'm not the least bit interested in Ms. Ribinski for myself. I am, however, very interested in Mr. Ferranti's business," he said.

She smiled, no doubt attempting for it to be less devious and failing miserably. "Whatever do you mean? I would never presume anything where you are concerned, Tyler. Honestly, I'm not convinced you've changed your idiotic ways enough to *deserve* someone of Ms. Ribinski's caliber."

"Why do you say that?" he asked, unable to peel his attention off Everly and Ferranti as he went through the million and one possibilities of what this little plot twist could mean for his plans and how he could spin it to work in his favor. He'd not expected Everly to actually be close friends with Ferranti.

"Because," Helene said, drawing out the word in that upper-crust accent of hers. "It's a Friday night and you're at an art gallery trying to snag a new client instead of out wining and dining a beautiful woman."

He loved Helene. Hell, she'd been as much of a mother to him as his own mom, and without the histrionics and melodramatic public scenes that had scarred him right down to his bone marrow. However, that didn't mean he was willing to be up next in the Carlyle matriarch's matchmaking project. Time to deflect and disarm.

He turned on the sly grin that knocked the knees off women half Helene's age and their mamas as well. "Have you taken a look in the mirror lately?"

She didn't roll her eyes—too old money for that—but her lips thinned into a flat line. "I'm a widow."

Michael Carlyle had died of a sudden heart attack more than three years ago, a loss Helene still seemed to carry with her—even if she'd gotten good enough at hiding it to make people forget that she'd all but disappeared into mourning after her husband had died. Over the past year, though, she'd come back, rejoined society, and maneuvered both her sons into solid relationships. It was obvious the woman was bored.

"You might be a widow," he said, wrapping his arm around her shoulders and giving her a reassuring squeeze, "but that doesn't mean you couldn't stand to have a little fun."

"Of all the ridiculous…" But the rest of Helene's denial trailed off as she clasped her hands together and looked around at the art lovers and pretenders, her regal attitude returning. "So are you going to go over there or spend all your time making me your verbal security blanket?"

Direct hit again. Damn, she was good.

He planned to walk over eventually, but first, he needed to rethink his plans for the evening a bit. Luckily, it took only a few seconds for the outline of a better idea to form, the best kind that would be a win-win for all involved. All he had to do was get the woman who hated his rice-scorching guts to agree to help—in other words, a total cakewalk.

Chapter Four

Mr. 2-fucking-B was headed straight for Everly. Obviously, it was proof that she'd been a very bad person in a former life—the kind who pulled wings off flies and stole children's baseballs. Or worse—wore Crocs. *Shiver.*

She'd spotted Tyler the minute he'd swaggered— yes, *swaggered* like a cowboy wearing a black hat in an Old West movie—into the Black Heart Art Gallery. She hadn't been avoiding him when she'd had to rush into the back room to check on the party caterers from her friend Kiki's company, she'd just been a good business owner determined to make sure everything for the show went off without a hitch. And then, when she'd come out, it had been of utmost importance that she touch base with the valets outside to make sure everything was in order. After that, she had to check in on the artist, Umberto Bradley, who was either puking or doing blow in the bathroom. Was it wrong that she was relieved to hear the sound of retching through the bathroom door?

So, when Alberto Ferranti—patron saint of starving artists and antacid-addicted gallery owners—showed up to see the work of the artist she'd been raving about to him for a solid week, she didn't have any choice but to stroll over as he gazed at the piece entitled *The Thrill of It All* and find out what he thought. None of it had been done to avoid her annoying downstairs neighbor—or to block out memories of that knee-knocking kiss in the parking garage two weeks ago.

And now Tyler was heading straight for her. Sure, he was having to weave through the healthy crowd at tonight's show, but there was no question about his destination. This didn't bode well. The closer he got, the wobblier her stomach became and the higher her blood pressure spiked. By the time he was only a few steps away, she was primed for an argument or another kiss or a bare-knuckle, God-you're-annoying brawl— metaphorically speaking, of course. Her nunni wasn't gonna get to stay in that upscale facility if the cops hauled Everly away, so she'd keep her anger locked on the inside.

Steeling her shoulders and clamping her molars together tight enough that her dentist would be giving her a firm talking-to, Everly turned in her four-inch heels ready to engage the enemy and looked Tyler directly in the…chin. The man was too damn tall.

"2B," she said, the nickname coming out weird because her jaw was clenched.

Tyler winked at her. "3B."

Next to her, Alberto looked from her to Tyler and back again, his head cocked a little to one side. "Why are you calling each other numbers?"

For…reasons…each of which sounded dumb in her own head and saying them out loud wasn't going to make them any better, so she zigged instead of zagged. "This is my downstairs neighbor."

"Does he not have a name?" Alberto asked in a stage whisper, which was probably as close to an actual whisper as he got.

"Several that she's saying in her head right now, I'm sure." Tyler chuckled, his blue eyes crinkling at the corners. "Most of which can't be said in polite company."

A loud laugh erupted from Alberto. "I'm too old to

worry about being polite. Don't worry, Everly, someday you'll get there." The older man held out his hand for a handshake. "Alberto Ferranti."

"Tyler Jacobson or 2B, whichever you prefer."

The men laughed together, easy friends from the word go—of course. With Alberto, she believed it. He was as genuine as he was completely loaded. But Tyler? He was up to something. Ultra aware of him as always, she could feel the extra something in the air. The spark of trouble and the whiff of danger ahead were as identifiable as the smell of ozone on the wind after a rainstorm.

"What did you ever do to my Everly to make her scowl like that?" Alberto asked.

"I cooked. Badly," Tyler said, all appeasing good-old-dude bro. "But I'm pretty sure she has a soft spot for me anyway."

A look passed between the two men, one of complete understanding that left her on the outside. *Ugh. Men!* Alberto, she could make allowances for because of generational and cultural differences. Tyler? He was as close to being an ass as a donkey. Too bad he kissed like a god.

Determined to regain control of the conversation and her own mutinous mind, Everly exhaled a calming breath and yanked her thoughts away from her exasperating neighbor and back to what had brought Alberto here tonight.

"Alberto," she said, turning and taking a step toward Umberto's *The Ecstasy of It All*. "There's a truly fascinating piece I wanted to show you. Another buyer has already expressed an interest, and I wanted you to see it before they put in an offer."

The older man nodded, but before they could move away, Tyler made his move.

"I can't wait to get a look at it, too, if it's as exceptional as you say," he said, falling into step beside them.

She leveled a glare at Tyler, turning her head enough that Alberto wouldn't catch sight of it. "It's not of cake."

"Well," Tyler said, his gaze dropping to her mouth. "Perfection is hard to come by."

Heat slammed into her, smacking her on all four cheeks. She teetered, which, if she fell in her heels, would have been a timber of epic proportions. Tyler's arm shot out and he grabbed her, steadying her before she went down and holding on just long enough for her to recover. Sensation sizzled up her bare arm even without his touch, and her breath caught. Damn. The man was a fucking menace to her equilibrium in every way possible.

"You'll only find perfect in a good woman," Alberto said, seemingly unaware of the snap, crackle, pop going on around him. "Trust me. I've got decades more experience."

Since there wasn't any way to get rid of Tyler, she vowed to ignore him and her own body's reaction as she strode over to Umberto's most popular painting during the preshow when critics and high-end collectors made an appearance. It was fantastic. The bold use of color and exuberance of his technique made the rest of the world fade into black and white. It was like falling into a place where there was only joy. No memory loss, no disappointments, no fighting for every little scrap. Her chest filled, growing with an absolute crystalline joy that couldn't be measured. Umberto might be a nervous wreck who couldn't work a crowd if he tried, but the man was a phenomenal talent. Give him a few years and he'd be as well known as Helene's son, Hudson Carlyle's artistic alter ego, Hughston.

Heart half stuck in her throat, she turned to ask Alberto what he thought when what she saw made the largest beating muscle in her body drop to her toes. Umberto stood in the corner by the bar, a mostly empty bottle of wine dangling from his fingers and the sweaty, green-tinged face of a man about to spew all over his life's work. That couldn't happen. Her insurance didn't cover debut show nerves, and *The Agony of It All* had a one-hundred-thousand-dollar asking price.

"If you gentlemen will excuse me for a moment," she managed to get out before she slow-walked across the gallery as fast as she could without attracting attention.

She made it halfway there with what she hoped was not a terrified expression on her face—never let them see you freak the fuck out—when the ever no-nonsense Kiki swooped in, hooked her arm through Umberto's, and hustled him toward the bathroom while still managing to shoot Everly an I-got-this look of reassurance. If Kiki wasn't already her best friend, and had been since third grade when she pushed Sadie Almadore in the mud for calling Everly a daddy-less freak, at that moment Everly would have pledged her undying devotion to the woman.

Helene stopped next to her. Obviously the woman had the uncanny ability to know when danger was imminent—of course, raising two boys probably did that to a person.

"That was a narrowly avoided disaster," Helene said.

"I'll take the wins where they come." Especially tonight. Practically on autopilot, her gaze snapped back to Tyler, who was still chatting it up with Alberto. Helene might have a sixth sense for trouble, but Everly could smell a bullshit artist at a hundred yards—and

Tyler Jacobson couldn't cover his scheming stench with the woodsy cologne that made her pulse quicken. "So what's he doing here?"

Helene would know. From what Hudson had told Everly last week, Tyler's batshit insane fiancée tried to fuck his best friend, coincidentally Helene's eldest, Sawyer Carlyle, the night before she was supposed to marry Tyler. Sawyer had turned her down, but Tyler had walked away from the bitch fiancée *and* the friendship. Definitely a "cut off your nose to spite your face" move of tragic douchebaggery—the kind that showed what kind of loyalty-free dipwad her upstairs neighbor really was. And no, she wasn't the least bit upset to learn of his true colors *after* she'd stuck her tongue down his throat.

"Tyler?" Helene asked with a nonchalant sniff. "I suppose he's expanding his collection."

"He has an art collection?" Of stick-on-your-wall photos of old-time tycoons, she could believe.

"Why else would he be here?" she asked, her attention focused anywhere but on Everly.

The other woman might scare the Richie Rich set, but Helene and she had been like pepperoni pizza and crushed red peppers since Hudson had first introduced them years ago. Like recognizes like, and they were both horrible liars.

"You know something."

Helene leveled an imperious glare at her. "I know lots of things."

"Don't try the scary Harbor City matron thing on me," she said with a laugh, then planted one hand on her hip and narrowed her gaze. "Now, tell me what you know."

Helene seemed to consider her options, pursing her lips together and drumming her fingertips against her thumb. She opened her mouth, but before even a sliver of truth could escape, Alberto and Tyler joined them.

Alberto turned his most charming smile on Helene and made a deep bow before straightening and giving her a teasing wink. "Everly, you must introduce me to this vision."

If she could have spoken at that moment she would have, but all the words in the world deserted her as she saw a slight flush color the other woman's cheeks. Embarrassment? Enjoyment? Interest? Helene sure wasn't giving any of it away.

Helene held out her hand—her left hand with the glittering diamond wedding band adorning her ring finger. "Mrs. Helene Carlyle."

Seemingly oblivious to the message she was sending, Alberto accepted her hand, brought it up to his lips, and brushed a quick kiss across her knuckles. "It's a pleasure to meet you."

"I'm sure." Helene freed her hand, flexing her fingers as if she wasn't used to someone flirting with her—which she probably wasn't. "If you'll excuse me, Everly, I'll go check in on Umberto."

Doing her damnedest to suppress a grin as Helene strode away, weaving regally through the clumps of potential art buyers gazing at Umberto's work, Everly turned her attention back to the two men by her side. Tyler looked as surprised as she was. Alberto looked like he was up to something. Oh, *this* was going to be interesting to watch from a distance.

"I think she likes you," Tyler said, one admiring dude to another.

Alberto waved one hand in the air. "Of course. Women love me. I'm rich, happy, and I know how to make a woman smile."

Everly snorted. "And you're very humble."

"Never a day in my life," Alberto said without an

ounce of humility. "Now, do I have your yes for lunch on Saturday? Carlo's fiancée will be there, and I'm sure she'd love to meet you before the wedding. Anyway, it will give me the opportunity to show you a few of the pieces I've decided to sell."

Her gut twisted, her Pavlovian response whenever he spoke of splitting up the Ferranti collection that ranged from the old masters to the art world's up-and-comers. "You can't break up your collection."

Pieces of art were like family. Some belonged together; they complemented one another and strengthened one another. She'd had this argument with Alberto many times without getting him to budge an inch. She glanced over at Tyler for possible backup, but his attention was focused on whatever he was reading on his phone.

"There's a time for everything, *tesoro*," Alberto said, using the term of endearment, "treasure," he'd been using since they'd met in Italy years ago, as he patted her cheek with affection. "And now is the time for someone else to enjoy some of my treasures."

Ugh. She hated it when he made it sound so logical—when it came to art she liked to deal only in passion. "I'm not going to win this argument, am I?"

"Not in this lifetime," Alberto said with a grin.

"Everly, sugar," Tyler said, looking up from his phone. "We had that thing on Saturday, but I'm sure we can make lunch with Alberto work."

Her brain slammed to a stop. What the— "We?"

The smarmy snake slid his arm around her waist, pulling her in close to him and making it difficult for her to breathe because of the fury making her heart speed up—and nothing else. The quick pebbling of her nipples and butterflies in her stomach were obviously a side effect of her efforts not to go all Riverside on his rich-boy ass.

For his part, Tyler either lacked a basic sense of survival or thought he was badass enough to take her on. That was the only explanation she could come up with for how he had the balls to circle his fingertips over the small of her waist.

"Don't tell me you forgot about our cooking class," he said.

"Bah," Alberto said with enough authority to declare the matter closed. "Learn to cook another day. I insist you both come over for lunch. Saturday. One thirty. Now I must go see to that *fantastico* Helene Carlyle, who looks like she's about to disembowel the nervous artist. We can't have that. He has talent."

And with that, he strolled off through the gallery crowd, leaving her fuming beside Tyler.

She pivoted, put steel in her glare, and lowered her voice to a harsh whisper. "You are not going with me to lunch. And how dare you imply we're in a relationship to one of my closest friends and best clients."

"Come on, sugar," he said, leaning down so that his answer tickled her sensitive earlobe. "Don't be mad at me."

Just as her body said, "Hello," her brain said, "Goodbye." She went with the smart one and pulled away from his distracting touch. "As if there's any chance of that."

The teasing upward curl of his full lips did things to her stomach and her lungs' ability to function.

He reached into his pocket and pulled out his wallet. "I'll flip you for it."

"Forget it." Fool me once and all that.

He slipped the same quarter—or one just as beat up—out of the small front pocket. "You're not still upset that I won the parking spot, are you?"

Mad? No, not exactly. She'd lost fair and square. It's what happened after that had her fuming upset. At herself as much as him.

The upturn of his lips turned into a full-on sexy smirk. The bastard must think he'd already won. "Double or nothing? And if I win, you throw in lunch with Alberto."

Would he stick to his word? All signs pointed to no, but the stubborn optimistic side of her that she usually kept under lock and key had managed to escape. Thank God, that little part of her personality wasn't stupid either, though. "If I win, no cooking for two months."

A group of five that had been moving from painting to painting chose that moment to look at *The Agony of It All* next to where she stood with Tyler. To accommodate them, he took a step closer to her. She didn't move because a couple was in deep discussions behind her about *The Excitement of It All*, and she didn't want to intrude. It gave her a chance to be only inches from Tyler, close enough to smell his cologne and feel the electricity buzzing between them bounce off his body to hers. It was horrible.

Yeah, you'll just relive it tonight when you're under the covers alone, you big faker.

"Are you trying to starve me to death?" Tyler asked, lowering his voice so she had no choice but to shift so she nearly touched him in order to hear his words.

"Like I could get that lucky," she shot back.

"Fine." He held up the quarter, giving her a close-up view of his strong fingers and the unexpected calluses she never expected to see on someone who seemed like he had gotten his money the old-fashioned way—by inheriting it. "You win, no cooking for me. I win, we go to Alberto's and you pretend to have a good time with me."

Danger didn't begin to cover that. Running away was the smart plan. Too bad her body had stuffed her brain in a rock-filled bag and dumped it in the harbor. "All I'm agreeing to do is *accompany* you. Nothing more."

He nodded.

Oh hell. She gave in. One lunch for two months of nothing burned was worth the risk. "So flip already."

"Heads," he called as he flicked it up into the air.

He caught it and slapped it down on the top of his hand. It was heads.

The lucky little shit. "The odds were definitely in my favor."

"I have very talented fingers," he said as he put the quarter back in his wallet. "And the rest of me ain't so bad, either. Talk to you soon, sugar. We have date plans to make."

"Oh no," she said, holding up her hand in protest. "I only said I'd *accompany* you. This is most definitely not a date."

He slid his wallet into his pants, a self-satisfied cocky grin on his face. "To-may-to, to-mah-to."

"Of all the—" Her words died on her lips—or more like his lips blocked her words as he dipped his head down and kissed her.

It was as delicious as it was unexpected, and her body reacted before her brain had a chance to process. Demanding, firm lips that promised a million sinfully hot things. An insistent tongue that teased as much as it taunted when he drew it across the sensitive seam of her mouth. His muttered, desperate groan against her soft flesh that made it impossible not to open her mouth, seek out his tongue with her own, and return the kiss. And just like that, it went from a kiss to something more.

Then, he broke away and took a step back, his gaze never leaving her face. He ran a hand through his hair before squaring his shoulders and tightening his tie. "I'll be back after the show ends so we can figure out the details."

Lips swollen, heart racing, and reality beginning to sink in, Everly watched as her downstairs nemesis strutted through the crowd and walked out the front door of the Black Heart Art Gallery into the cool night while she roasted inside. Damn that man. She wasn't taking him to lunch. She couldn't. If she did, she'd end up either killing him or fucking him—neither of which was a good option. So when he came by later, she'd just tell him so. And she'd keep her lips to herself this time. Really.

Chapter Five

Three hours later, Tyler walked through the back door to the art gallery, accessible from the residential side of the building. The space was nearly deserted, with only a few of the catering staff cleaning up and a few art buyers lingering by the front door chatting with the artist, who looked like he'd just come down off a six-day meth binge. A quick scan confirmed Everly must be in the back office.

Since sitting on his ass and waiting for something good to happen wasn't what got Tyler out of Waterbury and into the rarefied air of Harbor City's elite, he wasn't about to twiddle his thumbs and wait for Everly to come up with a clever scheme to get out of lunch. Left to her own devices, the stubborn woman would probably feign a heart attack. What he needed was an ally to take this plot from plan to reality, one he spotted next to a table littered with wineglasses, a few crumpled napkins, and what could only be described as a very artistically folded show brochure. Helene held a glass of white wine in her hand, gave it a tentative sniff, and turned up her nose in revulsion.

Perfect timing, Jacobson.

Tyler crossed the gallery and, when he got close enough, lifted the bottle of Helene's favorite Sangiovese wine from Tuscany that he was carrying so she could read the label. It was expensive and—even more important—tasted fantastic.

"Oh, thank God." Helene dumped the offending Chardonnay into a mostly empty wineglass still on the table and held out her now empty glass.

"I take it you'd like some?" he asked as he poured one for her and then plucked a fresh glass from the table and poured one for himself.

"You know me so well." She lifted the glass, inhaled the bouquet, and her shoulders relaxed with a relieved sigh. She took a leisurely drink. "Instilling good taste in other people is just so exhausting. So what do you want help with?"

Barely tasting the wine as he stared at the closed door to Everly's office, he asked, "What makes you think I want anything?"

"Almost two decades of watching you work your brilliant schemes."

He stood just a little bit taller. "Brilliant, huh?" Okay, he had an ego. Shocker.

"As if you don't know." She shook her head. "The Singapore deal was quite impressive."

"That'll be nothing compared to when I land Alberto Ferranti." It really was the deal of the year. Nearly a billion dollars would go into setting up the Ferranti hotels across the U.S. The money was amazing, but the prestige of earning the commission as the project consultant was what he really craved.

"And what does that have to do with buttering me up?" Helene asked, cutting through all the bullshit as per usual.

"I've been trying for months to get a one-on-one with Alberto Ferranti."

Helene raised an eyebrow. "You and every other hungry consultant in town."

"Exactly," he said, relieved that she got it right away. "I could finally make that happen Saturday, but only if Everly doesn't murder me at lunch at Alberto's. I may have finagled an invite as her date earlier when she couldn't refuse."

She took a leisurely sip of her wine. "So how do I play a part in this little scheme of yours?"

"You should come, too. She'll say yes if it feels less like a forced date." Not that he wanted a date of any kind with his snarly neighbor. It was bad enough that he couldn't stop kissing her in the middle of their inevitable arguments lately.

"So I'm the…what do they call it?" Helene asked. "Third wheel?"

"Come on. We both know you're bored. Admit it." He waved his hand, gesturing to the gallery, now empty except for two waiters picking up the very last of the trash and giving Helene a wide berth, before turning back to face her. "If you still spent most of your days maneuvering your sons into doing what you wanted them to, then you wouldn't be here with bad wine and good art."

"*Great* art," Everly corrected, her voice strong and sure behind him.

He pivoted toward her voice—the one that did things to his dick—and watched her stride across from the nearby door of the staff break room where the caterers had set up. Damn. She never did or said what he expected her to. And he sincerely hoped she hadn't caught his entire conversation with Helene.

Don't stare at her mouth. She stopped within arm's reach. He kept his hands to himself and…looked right at her mouth. His cock approved. His brain did not. "Just the woman I was looking for."

"Lucky me," Everly said, sarcasm dripping from each syllable like bitter honey.

"Well," Helene said, stifling what sounded suspiciously close to a chuckle, looking from Everly to Tyler and back again. "I'll see you two Saturday at Alberto's."

Tyler managed—just barely—not to let his relief show. He was getting a case of this wine for Helene as a thank-you.

"That's great," Everly said. "I didn't realize he'd invited you, too."

Helene picked up her purse from the table and gave Everly a knowing look. "I've never had a problem getting invitations to anything."

Now that he could believe. He, on the other hand, spent years fighting for a place at the table.

The Carlyles' longtime driver, Linus, obviously using some kind of ninja magic, appeared at the gallery door right as Helene neared it. Tyler watched her leave—the other stragglers right after her—while he sipped his wine, determined to draw out the silence until Everly broke it. She wasn't the sit-around type any more than he was, but he'd had longer to perfect the facade.

She narrowed her dark-brown eyes at him and jutted out a hip, planting her hand on it in a full-on bad girl, somebody-hold-my-earrings kinda way. The girls he'd grown up with had a similar stance. It always meant things were about to get exciting. Of course, that kind of woman was the last thing he needed in his life. He needed someone with the ice-cold reserve that came with being born into Harbor City money, which was exactly why the next step of his plan after landing the Ferranti deal was to find the right kind of woman who would help him cement his legacy as far away from working-class as possible. Then, he'd finally prove the doubters—including his own parents—wrong.

Everly snatched the wineglass from his hand and set it down on the table next to a half-eaten toast triangle in a partially crumpled napkin. "What are you doing here?"

He shrugged as if he wasn't at least partially holding his tongue to make her nuts. "Staying quiet so you can think."

She tossed her head back and groaned. The sound shouldn't have been a turn on. It was.

"You." She pointed a long finger at him. "Are a giant pain in my ass."

The staff break room door swung open and a tall woman with enough curly long hair to make a mermaid jealous strolled out. She got a few steps into the gallery and stopped. "Need some help, Evs?" she asked as she flipped a dish towel over her shoulder and glared at him.

It didn't take a genius to figure out that the two women were close and that the other woman was ready to go to the mattresses for her friend. She didn't have the same tough-girl-from-the-streets body language as Everly, but the clues were there—feet hip-width apart, hands loose but ready at her sides, and the come-at-me-douchebag, pissed-off-Amazon-warrior-level glare that actually had him ready to take a step back.

"It's okay, Kiki," Everly said, waving off the other woman. "You're sure you're okay with finishing up?"

"The team and I will have everything squared in just a few," she said, continuing to give Tyler the evil eye. "Go on home, Ev. How you walked around as long as you did in those shoes, I have no idea."

Everly's shoulders dropped a few inches and the tired lines around her eyes softened. "Thanks, I owe you."

Obviously deciding that she'd delivered her warning to him, Kiki turned her attention back to Everly and chuckled. "I'll add it to your tab. You sure you're okay?"

"Oh, him?" Everly gave a dismissive wave with her hand. "This is 2B."

"This is Mr. Burn the Joint Down?" Kiki's glare disappeared, and she gave him an assessing up and down. "Huh."

He had no idea what to do with that. "You ladies know I'm right here, yes?"

"Yeah," they responded at the same time in the same totally unimpressed tone.

Then, Kiki turned her attention back to Everly. "Go on up. We've got everything down here."

"Thanks again." She hustled over and gave the other woman a quick hug, and then strolled over to the door leading upstairs to the apartments. She paused with her hand on the knob and looked over her shoulder at him. "You coming?"

It was an invitation he wasn't expecting but he sure as hell wasn't gonna turn down. He needed to get this lunch at Alberto's settled.

They were halfway up the first flight of stairs, their steps echoing through the stairwell, when she pivoted to look down at him two steps behind. "I don't know what you're up to or what you told Helene, but I don't like it."

So suspicious, rightly so, but still it turned him on that she wasn't the type to just accept the easy answer and had the instincts to know when something was off. Add to that the way her ass looked in that black sheath dress going up the stairs and he was starting to lose brainpower. She was just the type of woman he didn't need—the kind that made him think about sheets twisted around their naked limbs instead of his latest scheme. He'd learned his lesson the hard way with another sexy, dark-haired firebrand who'd sent him back to Waterbury defeated and humiliated. That wasn't ever going to happen again. If he didn't need Everly's connection to Alberto so badly, he'd treat Everly like the kryptonite she was. That, of course, wasn't going to happen, though. This deal meant everything.

"Helene and I were just talking about Alberto's lunch," he said, deciding it was time to push his luck before he broke and kissed her—again—because he couldn't stop his gaze from dipping down to her lush mouth that he wanted on his and locations much lower. "So what time do you want to leave for Alberto's place in Seaside?"

"A quarter to never," she shot back, not giving an inch. "I don't pimp out my friends, and believe it or not, Alberto is a friend."

Was it wrong that a little part of him—well, a big, thick, long part of him—wanted to be her friend, too? Yeah. Yeah it was.

Chapter Six

Everly meant every word of what she'd said. Loyalty wasn't just a thing—it was the most important thing. You didn't fuck over the people you cared about, and she wasn't convinced that taking Tyler to lunch at Alberto's wasn't screwing over the man who'd helped her get her start in this business and had become a mentor and friend.

Tyler's mouth tightened, and he let out a harsh breath as he shoved his long fingers through his thick black hair. "I understand about the importance of friendship."

"Do you?" she asked. "I know about how you turned on Sawyer."

Years of the silent treatment and even attempts to sabotage a business deal. Finding out that information had tipped the scales against him for her. Tyler Jacobson might be hot as hell with his dark hair, blue eyes, broad shoulders, and tight ass, but she wasn't having it. How someone treated other people was more important than what would no doubt be some amazing, mind-melting orgasms.

The vein in his temple pulsed. "I had my reasons."

She could become immortal, and she'd never understand how the male ego could be so big and so fragile at the same damn time. "He turned your fiancée away."

Tyler nodded, his blue eyes cold without even a hint of emotion. "He did."

His lack of reaction only sparked hers up, offending

her on her friend's brother's behalf. She may have grown up on the wrong side of town, but she sure as hell knew the right way to treat people. Righteous indignation flowed through her, hot and demanding. "And you gave him the cold shoulder for years like a total asshole."

He swallowed hard, his teeth clenched so tight the jaw muscle bulged, then let out a slow breath that forced all the feeling off his face. "I did."

"Why would you ever do that if you"—she held up her hands and made air quotes with her fingers—"understand the importance of friendship so much?"

Tyler didn't say anything. He just stared at her like no one had ever had the balls to ask him that before. Well, someone should have, because even if Tyler and Sawyer were friends again, they should have had some kind of come-to-Jesus conversation. Of course, these were two men. Anyone with a Y chromosome seemed to be at a distinct disadvantage when it came to talking through uncomfortable truths.

Finally, he started up the stairs again, sliding his hand across the small of her back and leading her toward the landing. She didn't mean to fall into step beside him, but his touch had set off the kamikaze butterflies in her stomach. Once again, fighting felt a lot like foreplay, and her body liked it.

"This is a conversation that requires alcohol and not being in the middle of a stairwell," he said, holding open the door leading from the stairwell to the second-floor hall. "Come over to my place, and I'll tell you the whole thing. I'll even make us some food."

That stopped her feet halfway through the door. "Are you trying to kill me?"

"Pasta," he said with a chuckle. "I'll boil some noodles, throw on some sauce. Even I can't mess that up."

Of course, her mutinous stomach picked that moment to growl. With a knowing smile making him look more relaxed than he had all evening, he reached into his pocket and pulled out a set of keys. Holding them up in the air, he jingled them. There was no missing the throwback to her taunting him in the parking garage.

"Unless you'd rather flip for it?" he asked.

She laughed despite knowing better. "Fine, but I haven't agreed to take you to Alberto's for lunch with him thinking we're an item. And if the smoke alarm goes off, I'm out of here."

"Yet," he corrected. "You haven't agreed *yet*."

Good God. The cocky bastard thought he'd get her to agree. And heaven help her if she did.

They walked down the hall together to the door of his apartment. The building's beautiful art deco style architecture had called out to her art-loving soul, demanding she look into its history. It had originally been planned as a high-end luxury boutique apartment building. The street-level floor originally planned as a lobby and gym among other things. Each floor of the three-story building had two large—especially by Harbor City standards—apartments separated by a wide hallway. For whatever reason, though, the project had fallen through before the renovations had been completed. The company that owned the building had gone through with the plan, except for the street level, which had been turned into a space perfect for her gallery. Too bad the landlord had recently hit her up with building maintenance and taxes that had her accountant calling for mercy. It was a typical triple net commercial lease, though she thought she'd be in business a bit longer before the nut came due. But that problem could wait for another day.

She expected Tyler's apartment to be a replica of hers. As soon as he opened the door, though, she realized how wrong she'd been. While her apartment was dominated by a huge living space filled with color and walls begging to be decorated with thought-provoking art, his was centered around a massive gourmet kitchen divided from the living room with an island big enough to seat eight. Other than the slate gray of the granite countertops, almost everything else in the apartment was done in tasteful and completely boring taupes, creams, and whites. There weren't any photos or art on the walls or the fireplace mantel. The place kind of looked like a professionally designed apartment for a luxury furniture store website. Of course, the photographer would have insisted on hiding the five boxes stacked one on top of the other near the sliding doors leading out to the balcony. She could think of only a single explanation for the boxes and the lack of a personal touch.

"Are you moving?" she asked as she did a full 360.

He snorted. "Don't sound so hopeful."

"I'll take that as a no," she said, doing her best to sound disappointed even though that wasn't *exactly* how she'd describe the feeling zinging through her, because she wasn't going to describe that feeling. Stubborn? Her? Never! "That's some kitchen."

"Yeah, it was exactly what I wanted." He wandered into the kitchen and pulled out a high-back chair from the island. "Take a load off and watch me make magic."

"I warned you about the puff of smoke," she said, only half joking as she slid into the seat.

Tyler shook his head as he rounded the island and headed toward the shiny pots hanging from a rack suspended above the counter opposite. "Don't give up your day job for the comedy."

It gave her the perfect opportunity to admire the way he filled out a pair of suit pants—well. Very, very well. He set the pot down on the counter, turned, and rolled up his shirtsleeves, revealing some premium-level arm-porn forearms thick with sinewy muscle and a smattering of dark hair. *Oh mama, that's not fair.* Arm porn was a weakness. Whatever he did when he wasn't on the job or being a pain in her ass was working— between the strong shoulders, highly smackable ass, and arms that made her bite her lip to stifle a groan, the man was an underwear model in suit pants and a button-down shirt.

Pull it back, Ribinski! The mental reminder stopped her from drooling on the island, but it had been close. "Didn't you know I have my own comedy YouTube channel?"

He strutted—yes, strutted—across the kitchen and filled up the pot with water. "Is it called Being Salty?"

She laughed out loud, caught off guard by the easy comeback. "That was pretty good for someone who went to a fancy prep school."

"On a scholarship." He pushed down the faucet lever and put the pot on the high-end gas range.

"What?" Oh, that didn't make any sense at all. Everything about Tyler, from the custom suits to the jaw-dropping wine selection in the built-in wine cooler next to the restaurant-grade refrigerator, screamed Daddy's money.

"You thought I was like the Carlyles?" he asked, something cautious in the response.

Shutting her mouth before she could utter, "Hell yeah," she considered the question as he started the gas flame under the pot of water and got a package of spaghetti from a cabinet. Okay, so she'd been a little overeager to paint him with the rich douchebag brush.

He was just so infuriating with his cocky confidence, swagger, and laissez-faire coin-flipping addiction that it short-circuited her brain and set her straight to flipping-off-the-world mode, blocking out the details she should have noticed.

"Not exactly like them," she said, articulating what she hadn't really put into words until now. "You *do* live in the same building as I do, which while being nice isn't exactly in the Carlyles' neighborhood. I figured you for a slightly less rich upper-crust Harbor City guy."

He grinned at her. "I'm from Waterbury."

Uh-uh, she wasn't falling for that. "No way."

"What?" he asked, his voice dropping into the unmistakable accent from the other side of the harbor. "You think ya the only one who changed zip codes?"

"No shit?" she asked, her brain playing catch-up. "But you don't sound like you're from there, and you sure have the cocky I-can-buy-you-and-sell-you Harbor City attitude down pat."

He shrugged and dumped the pasta into the boiling water. "Years of practice to talk correctly—we won't mention the voice coach I stupidly mentioned to you before—and the attitude I was born with, if not the money."

There were two kinds of people who made the transition from one side of the metaphorical tracks to the other. One, those who held onto their roots and attitude. Two, those who cut out almost every part of their old life like a skilled surgeon with a scalpel. She was more the first kind. Tyler? She'd have to put him in the second category, if only because he hid his roots so well.

"So how did all of that happen?" Nosy? Her? Hell yes.

He crossed to the wine fridge, pulled out a bottle

of white, and opened it up. "Mrs. Diaz, who taught sixth grade algebra and thought she saw something special in a kid she caught doing calculus on his own in the library."

She processed this tidbit as he got two glasses from the cabinet and brought them and the wine over to the island.

She could totally see a young Tyler elbows deep in boring math books. "That was you, huh?"

"Nah." He poured a glass of white wine and slid it across the island to her, then poured one for himself. "I was the guy beating him up."

Her jaw dropped, and he laughed hard enough that he nearly choked on the sip of wine he had just taken. After a short spluttering, he caught his breath and gave her a shit-eating grin.

Cocky bastard.

"Okay, you're right," he said with a hoarse chuckle. "I was the math nerd, and that led to a full scholarship to prep school."

The pieces clicked into place. "And that's how you met Sawyer and the Carlyles."

"Yeah, my family life was…interesting, and I ended up spending time over at Sawyer's house." He took a drink, something dark brewing in his eyes that made her think he didn't like all the memories bubbling to the surface. "By the time we graduated from college, the new doorman thought I was a cousin, and I'd promised myself that I was never going to be just another guy from Waterbury again. I was going to be more, and I was going to have it all."

It was a nice story, but it didn't make any sense. The guy had been a class-A dick to that same friend. "And you walked away from that because you had a disloyal bitch of a fiancée? That's pretty weak."

One of his eyebrows went up. "Don't take it easy on me or anything."

"I won't." Okay, maybe she was being a bitch, but she had the feeling that there just weren't that many people who called Tyler on his shit, and he needed to be. She took a sip of the wine—oh my God delicious, so crisp and fresh—and waited.

He held out but finally gave in with a sigh. "The truth is that what happened with Irena humiliated me." Tyler stared off in the distance, a scowl forming between his brows. "Do you know what Sawyer said after he'd told me what happened?"

He looked her square in the eyes now, and she shivered. There was so much pain swirling in his inky-blue depths, her heart ached for him.

"He said it's better I found out now she was just in it for the money. They'd all overheard her talking and knew she wasn't right for me. My best friend had known my fiancée was only with me for my money, and he'd never once said a word? That's not what I call friendship."

She blinked. "But what if he'd hoped he was wrong?"

"Would you let Kiki marry some guy you knew didn't really love her without telling her? Wouldn't you at least share your fears with her?"

Well, that cut to the heart of it. She tried to imagine Kiki with some creep and no, she wouldn't. The job of best friend wasn't always to tell them what they wanted to hear. Sometimes, you had to be the one to save them from themselves, too. Tyler was right. Sawyer hadn't been much of a friend if he'd known what kind of person Tyler's fiancée was and said nothing. And it sounded like even though they were closer again, they still hadn't talked about what really upset Tyler.

Because to hear Hudson tell it, well, the story was very different.

She reached and placed her hand over his. "No, I wouldn't."

The only sound in the kitchen was the boiling water on the range. The moment stretched, something unexplainable passing between their gazes that neither of them wanted to examine too closely. It almost felt like friendship.

The sizzling splash of water overflowing from the pot on the range startled both of them. Tyler rushed to it, grabbed an oven mitt that, not surprisingly, was one of many in a stack by the stove, and took the pot off the flame. Unable to sit by and watch, she hustled to his side and took the colander off the hanging rack, setting it in the sink. Tyler poured the pot's contents into it, and she turned on the cold water, rinsing the pasta so it would stop cooking. Not that it did much good. By the time he'd turned off the range and she'd finished draining the pasta, it was more than a little overcooked.

Standing next to her at the sink, Tyler poked at the twisted, soggy mass with a fork. "I blame you for distracting me."

"Uh-huh." She did a light hip check. "Keep telling yourself that. Where's the sauce?"

Tyler opened up a cabinet, clanked a few bottles together as he searched, and finally pulled out—a bottle of ketchup. "I don't think we can use this, but it's as close as I've got."

"God no." That was just nasty, so much so she couldn't help but laugh. "Butter?"

He put back the ketchup, pivoted, and opened the fridge, staring for a minute and turning back to her with a sheepish grin. "So in addition to not being a great cook, I kinda suck at grocery shopping."

Searching her memory banks for anything helpful, she finally hit on one last option. "Olive oil?"

Tyler opened another cabinet, peeked inside, and then shook his head. "Sorry," he half said, half laughed. "It's been nuts lately, and I've been eating out a lot."

The entire situation was ridiculous. It was pasta. How did you mess up boiling noodles? The cooking gods had cursed the man. She looked down at the mushy, kinda slimy spaghetti and started giggling. She clamped her mouth shut, trying to hold it in, but all it took was one look at Tyler, and the giggles were fighting to get out again. Tyler walked over to her side, snatched a wet noodle from the colander, and waved it at her with an evil wiggle of his eyebrows. It was too much. The laughter escaped.

Once they both had caught their breaths, she asked, "Alternatives?"

Tyler dropped the piece of spaghetti back into the colander and opened the cabinet next to the sink, bringing out two boxes of instant oatmeal. "Peaches and cream or apples and cinnamon?"

"Peach me up."

A few minutes later they were sitting around the island, each with a bowl of oatmeal and a glass of wine. The combination wasn't exactly high class, but she was willing to roll with it—especially since she was starving. The usual tension that surrounded them had abated, and they ate for a few minutes in comfortable silence. Everly had just gotten the first peek at the bottom of her bowl when Tyler shifted in the seat beside her, drawing her attention.

"Look, I know you have your reasons for thinking I'll screw over Alberto, but I won't." He used his spoon to push the little bit of oatmeal around in his bowl. "All I'm asking for is the opportunity to have a little face time. I won't even bring up business. I just need an in so I can finally get an appointment with him, that's all."

Maybe it was the sincerity in his voice. Maybe it was the fact that she realized now that they had something in common. Maybe it was the fact that the man was in such desperate need of a cooking class. Maybe it was because all he wanted to do was get his foot in the door, and she knew *exactly* how that felt. It was just an introduction. There was no guarantee Alberto would even meet with Tyler later. Whatever the reason for her second thoughts, she couldn't deny she was feeling a lot more open to the idea than before when she'd lost the coin flip in the gallery.

"Flip you for it?" she asked, not sure where in the hell that came from beyond her wanting—for once—to leave the final call up to fate.

"I've won the past two flips in a row. Doing it again doesn't seem fair," he said with a growly little tease in his voice. "Tell you what, how about you do this favor for me and I'll do one for you."

This should be good. She leaned forward, the move bringing her in closer to him. "What's that?"

"I'll get the landlord to cover your first triple net fees."

Her back stiffened. That scumbag landlord. The company wasn't supposed to share confidential information like that with other tenants. She was going to nail the sucker who leaked that information, just as soon as she dragged it out of Tyler. "How did you know about that?"

Gathering up the last of his oatmeal in his spoon, he kept his gaze lowered. "I own the building."

"What?" She sat up in shock. That lasted all of about thirty seconds before the embarrassment of being stupid enough to have a war of words with the man who controlled her fate took over. And BAM! The anger at Mr. 2B's lie of omission hit her smack between the eyes. "You insufferable ass. How could you keep that a secret?" In the midst of taking a breath to unleash a round of fury on his hot ass, one thing stood out. "If you can afford to own this building, what in the hell are you doing living in it?"

"It was my first one." He shrugged and ate the last spoonful of oatmeal. "It's got sentimental value."

"First one?" *First one???* "How many do you have?"

He almost looked embarrassed as he fiddled with his empty wineglass. "A few."

"Un-fucking-believable." This whole time, he'd been double fucking with her—as her pain-in-the-ass downstairs neighbor and as her greedy landlord—all without any orgasms.

"Look, I know it was wrong, but after our awful beginning, well, things didn't seem to ever improve." He ran his hand through his hair again. The poor man would be bald at this rate. He shrugged and offered, "Would you believe there just never was a right time that wouldn't make you uncomfortable?"

He seemed sincere, but her mama didn't raise no fool. "I'll concede you might be telling the truth, but I reserve judgment to bust your balls about this later."

"Fair enough." He nodded. "So what do you say? That'll give you more time to establish your gallery and firm your financial footing. I'll have the intro that I've been trying to get for months. We both walk away happy."

Damn it. She hated it when an asshole made sense. But he did, she couldn't deny it. And there was a lot more riding on her gallery's success than just her personally. Nunni had given her so much after her mom died when she was twelve and her dad flaked, refusing to take her in. What should have been her grandma's golden years became a second tour of parenthood duty. She had to do right by Nunni and ensure she was cared for properly. Not to mention if she was on more secure financial ground, she could finally start paying Kiki for her catering services instead of adding to her IOU tab.

All she had to do was spend the afternoon with a man who made her want to strangle him as much as he made her want to jump him. Surely her sense of self-preservation and self-control could make it through a few hours of playing nice with Tyler without promises of anything beyond an introduction. Then, they'd return here and things would go back to how they were with her stomping in stilettos and him stinking up her apartment with his failed cooking attempts. She could totally do this. She could—but she wasn't about to be dumb about it.

She pushed back her chair and stood up. "I want the triple net fees to be covered for at least a year, and I want it in writing."

His eyes went wide, and he practically jumped up from his stool. "Done."

Before she had a chance to realize what was going on, he'd encircled an arm around her waist and swung her in a celebratory circle. When the whirling had stopped, they were not even a half inch apart, with his butt against the island, their positions the opposite of how it had been in the parking garage when they'd ended up making out on the hood of her car. Her breath caught. Her pulse sped up. He shifted his stance, and there was no mistaking his hard length pressed against her stomach. Awareness ricocheted through her body like a pinball in a machine, touching every part of her. If they'd switched positions, that meant it was up to her to kiss him. The idea of it made her nipples pucker as she tugged her bottom lip between her teeth. The move snagged Tyler's attention, and he let out a soft groan. His hands went from around her waist to her hips. Teetering on the edge of temptation, she nearly fell over, but the last gasp of her survival instinct saved her.

She stepped back before she tumbled over. "I have to go."

"Running away?" he asked, shoving his hands in his pockets.

"I'm not running." Okay, she was *totally* running, but she wasn't about to admit that.

He chuckled. "Just walking really fast?"

Wasn't she the one doing *him* a favor? Yes, she was. And she was making a strategic retreat. There was nothing wrong with that. "You are so annoying," she said as she opened the door.

He waved from his spot at the island. "See you tomorrow, sugar."

Determined to disappear before she did something she'd regret, she hustled out the door, her feet moving as fast as her heart rate up the stairs to the third floor. What in the hell had she been thinking? A whole afternoon with Tyler Jacobson without kissing or killing him? She was going to have to put out a call to her nunni's friends to light a candle for her because she'd never make it through the afternoon without ending up in trouble for one or the other.

Chapter Seven

The follow-up phone call Saturday morning with Kiki went just about as expected. It was a tradition they'd had since Everly had opened the Black Heart Art Gallery and Kiki had been catering events for an IOU and a ton of referrals to the rich art lovers who needed someone for their cocktail parties. Usually it was the nitty-gritty debriefing of what happened and what could be done better next time, because Kiki not only ran an amazing catering service and gave the best unfiltered feedback, but her waitstaff always brought back the best unfiltered reactions from patrons about who liked what so Everly could follow up later in the week. However, this morning's call had gotten sidetracked when Everly had mentioned that she'd sorta accidentally kissed Tyler. Twice.

"What do you mean you accidentally kissed him?" Kiki asked, her voice coming through extra loud on the speaker of Everly's cell and bouncing around the sun-drenched walls of her practically barren kitchen. *"Twice!"*

"Settle," Everly said, trying her best to squash the laughter in her voice or she'd just encourage her outrageous bestie. "My coffee is still brewing and you just woke up a dog six buildings away."

"Oh yeah, like your first make-out session since you broke up with Dickless McGee wasn't going to get a reaction," Kiki said.

That had been eight months ago, and it sure hadn't been the love affair of her life — it had lasted all of two months—but she still felt the need to stick up for him, if only because things had gone so, so wrong in a nightmares-of-social-media kind of way.

"His name is Warren Stannic and he has a dick," she said as she watched the glorious black brew stream from the machine and into her cup like a modern-day miracle.

Kiki snorted. "Yeah, just not much of one."

She grabbed the French vanilla creamer out of the fridge and poured it into her cup, turning the liquid to a nice nut-brown color. "I never should have shown you that dick pic."

"You didn't exactly show me," Kiki shot back, her words coming in fast enough that if she wasn't already on her second Diet Coke of the day, she was about to pop it open at any second. "The moron sent it in a group text to you, me, and ten of our closest artsy-fartsy friends."

That had been bad. The art community in Harbor City wasn't tiny, but gossip sure spread like it was—add to that the fact that Warren was an art critic who had made plenty of enemies by royally roasting more than a few artists and galleries, and it was the kind of schadenfreude that a lot of people were going to revel in. She'd been about to break up with him when the picture went out, and then she'd felt so embarrassed for him that she'd waited another week before she'd ended things. Even with the delay, it had been awkward.

"Anyway, stop trying to distract me with sad cocks and explain what you mean by *accidentally* kissing your smoking-hot downstairs neighbor who also just happens to be loaded enough to own your building and a few others," Kiki said with a groan. "I swear to God, if I would have known those little tidbits last night while he was trying to eye fuck you, I would have shoved you to the side and hauled him away like I was a cavewoman and he was the first box of chocolate-covered cherries ever invented."

More power to her. It wasn't like Everly wanted the cocky bastard. "You can have him."

"Uh-huh." Kiki didn't bother disguising the sarcasm. "That sounded *totally* convincing. So about the *accidental* kisses, what did you do, trip in those obnoxious shoes of yours and land ever so conveniently with your tongue in his mouth?"

"It just happened. Once in the parking garage when I threatened to run him over and once last night in the gallery when we were standing too close and arguing. And then I thought it was going to happen again in his kitchen, but I got the hell out of there before anything could."

"Sounds like it's a little too late for that," Kiki said. "My vote is you jump him and ride what I really hope is a big cock all the way to Orgasmville."

Her girlie bits liked that idea—a lot. "That is not going to happen."

"Why not?"

Lots of reasons, chief among them the little voice in the back of her head that always reminded her exactly where she was from and that people like Tyler—who'd buried their working-class roots under six miles of voice lessons and money—wanted only one thing when they trolled for a Riverside girl. Temporary fun. She'd seen the results of that firsthand with what had happened with her mother. Hell, she *was* the result of it. She might not be looking for forever, but that didn't mean she was willing to be someone's version of slumming it. All of that was a little heavy before she was at least three cups of coffee into her day, though, so she went with the obvious reasons.

"He owns the building and he's Mr. 2B."

"Yeah," Kiki said. "Mr. To Be Your Train to Happy Town."

Everly almost spewed coffee across her rarely used stove. "I'm beginning to think you're the one who needs to get laid."

"That may be, but you're right there with me, sister."

That, unfortunately, was way truer than Everly wanted it to be, considering she was about to spend the afternoon with Mr. 2B—without going on any trips to Orgasmville, Happy Town, *or* Climaxopolis.

Chapter Eight

E verly was trying to kill Tyler. How did he know this? That dress. Seriously.

Traffic had been light, but he'd still been in a car with Everly for just over an hour. That was more than long enough to have the vanilla-and-musk scent of her perfume embed itself in his head. She'd worn a dress—black, of course—made out of some kind of sweater material that clung to her curves and snuck up to mid-thigh when she'd sat down in the passenger seat. It wasn't that he'd noticed. It was that he hadn't been able to *stop* noticing. Add to that the knee-high black boots with silver spikes for heels and the way she'd tucked her black hair into a knot-roll thing at the base of her skull, showing off her long, delicate neck, and it went a long way to explaining why he'd missed the turnoff to Ferranti's house on Skyview Lane even though the navigation system in his Mercedes had notified him in plenty of time.

"Second time's the charm," Everly teased as she flipped the visor down and popped the cap on her lipstick.

Watching her out of the corner of his eye as she opened her mouth into a perfect *O* and slid the silky red color across her lips almost sent him off-roading in Ferranti's yard.

Now wouldn't that make a great impression, dipshit. The guy wouldn't be able to stop himself from hiring you after you do donuts in his landscaped-to-the-gills front yard.

"There's nothing to be nervous about," Everly said,

capping her lipstick and dropping it into her purse. "Alberto's a sweetheart and Carlo is so laid-back he's like the Italian version of a surfer dude. I haven't met his fiancée yet, but I'm sure she's lovely."

Nervous? She thought he was nervous? His dick sure as hell wasn't nervous. His right hand just wasn't the companion either he or his cock was looking for. He needed to get laid. Then he'd stop thinking about his upstairs neighbor and her sexy fucking high heels and killer ass—not to mention he'd stop kissing her every time they spent more than ten minutes together. By the time he pulled into a parking spot near Ferranti's four-car garage, he was white-knuckling the steering wheel.

"Okay, this quiet no-talking thing is starting to freak me out," Everly said, twisting in her seat and pulling the soft material of her dress tighter across her tits. Not that he *knew* it was soft. He'd just spent a good portion of the drive imagining how it would feel, that's all. "Is this about last night? Nothing happened. Of course nothing happened. It wouldn't—couldn't—between us. Especially not now that I know you hold my apartment and gallery lease in your fiendishly strong hands. Shit. Fiendish hands. Not fiendishly strong. I don't know where that adverb came from. Must be the lack of sleep. Not that *you* caused my lack of sleep, it's just…I'm shutting up now."

Damn he was off his game—or too fixated on how being this close to her was wreaking havoc on him to consider he might be doing the same to her. The running commentary on everything from Picasso's blue period to modern sculpture on the drive here? It was because she was nervous. About the lunch or about him? Like always, he bet on himself. Was he an asshole if he admitted that pumped up his ego? He considered. Yeah, it did. That was okay. He could live with it—

especially since he needed an ego the size of Ferranti's six-bedroom beach house to make this deal happen.

Pivoting in his seat, he looked at the normally unflappable tough chick fidgeting beside him. "It's going to work out fine. We're friends and maybe a little more. It's the truth, so you don't have to be nervous."

"I'm not nervous. *You're* nervous." She toyed with her hair and tucked a loose strand behind her ear. "Anyway, saying we're friends is being pretty generous and saying we're maybe a little bit more is *totally* off-the-charts wrong."

Oh really? That was how she wanted to play this? Like the skin-sizzling need driving those kisses had only been on his end of things? He didn't think so. "My tongue has been in your mouth twice in the past week."

She wrinkled her nose. "That's just an ew way to put it."

"That's not how you react when it happens, though." He leaned toward her, draping his arm across the back of her seat. "You don't ew, you moan so fucking sweet." Needing to see her do just that—at least a little—he glided the tip of his finger up the creamy column of her neck to the pulse point below her earlobe. "And you kiss back like a woman who always gets what she wants."

Her chin went up, and she leveled a challenging look his way. "Ego much?"

He dipped his head lower, so close and yet so far away from her perfect red mouth. "It's not ego if it's true."

Fuck. This was crazy. It was all impulse and passion, two things he'd worked to get out of his life. But at this moment? There wasn't a damn thing he wanted more. He couldn't make the move, though. This needed to be on her. Miss 3B who wanted to pretend there wasn't anything more between them when a blind man an ocean away could see it. She fucking sizzled when she was near him, and he couldn't stay away from her.

"Maybe what we need, sugar, is to get each other out of our systems."

"Oh yeah?" she asked, her voice a breathy demand and her pupils blown. "You think I should just fuck you in front of Alberto's house?"

Yes. His dick liked that idea a lot. *Down, you horny fucker, it's not the time or the place for that.*

"I like your sense of adventure, but I plan on taking my time when I get you naked, so a quickie in the car doesn't really work for me." Even though it just about killed him, he retreated a few inches, dropping his hand to the outside of her thigh. He relished the feel of her smooth skin under his fingers. The little shiver that shook her shoulders was its own kind of reward even if he'd rather be tasting her lips. "However, you should kiss me."

"Me?" she asked, her dismissive tone betrayed by the way her pink tongue darted out to wet her bottom lip. "Kiss you? Your ego is humongous."

"That's not the only thing big about me." And getting uncomfortably larger by the millisecond.

She let out a shaky breath. "You're ridiculous."

"And you're delaying the inevitable because you are going to kiss me." All she had to do was lean a little forward. He'd meet her halfway. More than halfway. Shit, his willpower was nonexistent around Everly Ribinski.

She raised one haughty brow. "And why in the world would I do that?"

"If you don't," he said softly, his blue eyes glittering knowingly, "you'll spend the entire lunch wondering when I'm going to kiss *you.* Because, sugar, it's going to happen. The question is, do you want to control the where and when, or would you rather leave that up to me?"

She rolled her eyes. "You think I'm so hot for you, I can't make it through one meal without wanting to jump your bones?"

He smiled. "I think we can't make it through thirty minutes without fighting about something, and we both know how our arguments are ending lately, regardless of where we are."

And there it was. "If I do this now, will it shut you up?"

"Probably," he said, in for a kiss, in for so much more. "It's hard to talk when my tongue's busy doing other things."

Something flickered in her gaze, a decision that he doubted would end his way. "That is true and would be the only thing that would make kissing you worth it."

And just when he'd prepped himself for her to unsnap her seat belt and reach for the door handle, she surprised him again by closing the distance between them and kissing him. It wasn't sweet. It wasn't perfunctory. It was hot as hell on the sun. Her tongue was in his mouth, her hands gripping the front of his shirt as if she were afraid she'd fall off the earth if she let go. He knew the feeling. The planet was definitely off-kilter for him, too. Electricity went straight to his dick, and he gripped her thigh. Fuck. More. Just a little more.

He slid his hand up higher, and she widened her legs with a needy whimper. His thumb brushed the damp curls between her legs. God, she was commando. If he'd have known that during the drive, he would have steered them straight off the road while dirty fantasies played in his head. He stroked her curls, not hard enough to part them but enough to make Everly let out a sexy little gasp.

"You naughty girl," he said, desire thick in his voice. "Where are your panties?"

"Does it matter?" she asked, her breath hot against his neck.

No, it didn't, not when he was just outside of heaven's door—when the sound of another car managed to pierce the fog of lust clouding his better judgment. It was enough to remind him of exactly where they were and where his hand was and *exactly* where he wanted it to be.

It took almost inhuman strength but he pulled back, withdrawing his hand and sitting back against the driver's seat. Shit. This was an epic case of wrong place, wrong woman if he'd ever experienced one. Sneaking a peek at her out of the corner of his eye, he caught her in nearly the same position as him. Her cheeks were flushed, her lips swollen, and her eyes closed as she took in a deep breath. Insanity. That was the only explanation, because even knowing he shouldn't, all he wanted was to do it again.

A hard rap on his window made him jump in his seat and turn toward the noise.

Helene stood outside the car, wry amusement curling up one side of her mouth.

Hoping it didn't look like what it was, Tyler pressed the button to lower his window.

"If you two are quite done," Helene said, her tone carefully neutral, "I'd like to go see this fabulous art collection Alberto swears he has."

And that was that. Without a word to each other, he and Everly got out of the car and walked with Helene to the front door of Ferranti's house. He opened on the first knock.

"*Bellissima.*" Ferranti took Helene's hand, brushing a kiss across her knuckles. "I'm so glad you decided to join us."

For her part, the older woman glared at the Italian until his head was bent so he couldn't see her, and then a small little smile curled Helene's lips. It was enough of a thaw that Tyler opened his mouth to say something, but just at that moment Alberto stood up and the icy frost returned to Helene's face.

If Alberto noticed the change, he didn't show it.

Interesting. Tyler tucked away the little factoid about Alberto's interest in Helene. While there was probably some business use for the information—weak spots could always be exploited—he wouldn't go that way with it. The Carlyles may not be his family, but they were close, and he wouldn't pay their kindness back like that. Now if it had been anyone else, he would have taken the information and found a way to use it to further his aims. Great minds weren't lying when they said that knowledge was power.

Instead, he turned to Tyler and Everly with a huge, welcoming smile. "Please, let's go into the dining room. Carlo can't wait to introduce you to his soon-to-be bride, Everly."

The sun seemed to follow them as they walked from the foyer through a window-filled hall that looked out onto the ocean and into a dining room with gleaming floors, exposed beams, and—of course— massive windows that showed off the best feature of the house, the beach. As they crossed into the room, a tall man who looked like a younger, leaner version of Ferranti hurried over while a woman with a phone pressed to her ear and long dark hair tied in a high ponytail stood near the windows with her back to them. Thanks to the bright rays, he got more of an outline than a full picture of the woman, but something about her set off his warning sirens. It had to be the hair. Ever since he'd walked out of that church, he'd stayed away from any woman who reminded him even vaguely of his ex-fiancée—right up until he stopped being able to keep his lips to himself around Everly.

"It's been too long. I'm so glad you're here. I was afraid with my work schedule I wouldn't get to see you before the wedding," Carlo said, kissing Everly on both cheeks in a perfectly normal way that still made Tyler want to deliver a Waterbury-style hands-to-yourself message. "You must be Tyler. I'm so happy to meet you after all the good things Papà has said. Let me introduce you to my fiancée, Iren—"

Tyler didn't need to hear the rest of the name. The dark-haired woman near the windows turned. Her practiced smile cracked the moment she spotted him, but ever the actress, she recovered quickly. Tyler's palms turned clammy as the rest of him went ice-cold.

"Well, if it isn't Tyler from across the harbor," Irena said, her hips swaying as she strutted over from the window. "Why, last I'd heard you'd left Harbor City behind and gone back home. It's so nice to have you visit us so we can catch up."

A divot of confusion formed between Carlo's eyes. "You two know each other?"

"Yes." It was all he could get out from between his clenched teeth.

For a man who made his living out of seeing what was coming next, he'd never imagined crossing paths with Irena in Alberto Ferranti's beach house. And she was engaged to his son? Oh, this just got better and better.

There were two ways Irena could go in this situation: be her natural born shrewish self or play the sweetheart. Both had advantages. She could say that he'd done her wrong, which would give her a reason to be a bitch so she could jab the knife in as many times as possible and ruin any hope of Tyler making a deal with Alberto. The advantage for acting as if it had all been mutual and was water under the bridge is that she got to keep her true nature under wraps and keep playing whatever game she had going with Carlo, because there had to be one. He'd been fooled by Irena once, but he'd learned. She'd been born with every advantage money could offer, but a lifetime of being overindulged by her jet-setting parents had turned her selfish and mean early, and she had no interest in being any other way. The truth of it was, Irena liked being a bitch. It really was her happy place.

"Tyler and I were engaged about a million years ago," Irena said as she hooked her arm through Carlo's waist and drew in close to him, looking up at the other man as if he were her guardian angel instead of the meal ticket to the land of the rich for the poor heiress who'd burned through her trust in record time. "But don't get jealous. It was eons ago and it didn't work out, which was for the best because all that heartbreak led me to you."

Heartbreak? It took everything he had not to laugh out loud at that bit of theatricality. All she needed was some fake tears and Alberto's sucker of a son would wrap her up in his arms and carry her off. What a load of crap. Laying out all of Irena's dirty laundry was tempting, but that wasn't the Harbor City elite way. As much as he hated seeing the bitch, he couldn't let it show. That would only endanger the deal. He knew it. She knew it. Movement to his left caught his eye. Helene stood next to Everly looking as if butter wouldn't melt in her mouth. The grande dame of Harbor City high society hadn't ever steered him wrong before. He'd follow her example again—the deal with Alberto was worth more than the satisfaction of causing a scene. He may have grown up with parents who reveled in public spectacle, but he didn't cause scenes. He'd left that part of his history in Waterbury.

"*You're* the ex-fiancée?" Everly asked, stepping away from Helene and toward Irena, her accent thick with disgust and a look on her face that screamed, "You are dead meat."

Irena's dark eyes went wide. Obviously, her bitchy cat-fighting skills weren't up to getting a stomp-walk challenge from an Amazon from a neighborhood in Harbor City that made his blue-collar roots look like a shining beacon on a hill. Okay, there was a part of him that was dying to see what would happen next — maybe a bigger part than he wanted to admit — but it couldn't happen.

He intercepted Everly before she could make Irena pee in her pants, slipping his arm around her waist. "Everly Ribinski, may I introduce you to Irena Iverson."

Irena held out her hand, the left one with the gargantuan diamond solitaire on her ring finger. "Is that a Riverside accent? I just love it. Too bad it's so unusual for this area." The women shook hands like enemies on the battlefield. It was polite, but just. "Carlo has told me *so* much about you that I was a little worried, but I see that you're with Tyler and that's just perfect. I'm sure you two have so much more in common than Tyler and I ever did."

Yeah, things like not trying to sleep with your fiancée's best friend on your wedding night. God, he hoped Carlo didn't have friends who were richer than him — or then again, maybe he did. The idiot had the same made-stupid-by-love look Tyler had worn before he'd figured out what a deceitful hag Irena was. That's what happened to a person when emotion and passion mixed: temporary insanity, which was why keeping emotion out of it with the flip of a coin was the right move to make on the chessboard of life.

Everly must have sensed the tension locking his body tight because she softened her own stance, stretched to her tiptoes, and brushed a kiss across his cheek.

"We're like pasta and sauce; we go together," she said, her tone as light as the look she sent him was serious. Then she blinked, her face muscles relaxed into an easy grin, and she turned toward the others. "So I guess it was lucky that you two didn't work out because of…"

Tyler's heart stopped.

"Reasons," Everly finished after a pause that lasted a heartbeat longer than necessary.

Alberto may not know the reasons for that extra breath of Everly's, but he sure picked up on it. He stood next to Helene, his gaze going from Everly to Irena to him. It might take a little digging, but the older man would figure it out. He hadn't created a hotel empire by being dumb—or letting the rest of the world in on what he was thinking, it seemed, because the expression on his face went back to that of happy host.

"Come, everyone." He opened his arms and gestured toward the table, already laid out with food. "Let's sit. *Mangia, mangia.*"

Tyler made sure to sit directly across from Irena. As Michael Corleone put it, keep your friends close and your enemies closer. It made sense—just as long as he could keep his inner impulse to go all Waterbury tapped down and distract Everly from going into attack mode, then they'd make it through lunch without sinking the mission of connecting with Ferranti. It couldn't be easier. The devil on his shoulder laughed. *Yeah, and Everly isn't kissable at all.*

Chapter Nine

After lunch, when Alberto suggested a tour of the house to see his collection, Everly had to fight not to let out a sigh of relief. The meal had been awkward to put it mildly. Judging by the stilted conversation, everyone—with the exception of Carlo, who was on another business call—had noticed the negative undercurrent of what was supposed to be a fun, casual meal among friends and family. Never had baked ziti tasted so much like cardboard paper.

Of course, her relief had been short-lived.

"Oh, I'd love to join you," Irena said, her eyes sparkling with fake sincerity. "It's such a marvelous collection, and I'm dying to hear the stories behind your favorite pieces."

Next to her, Helene mumbled something that sounded a lot like, "That can be arranged," but Everly must have misunderstood. The older woman hadn't been anything but gracious, if a few degrees colder than normal, since they'd sat down, continually drawing Irena into conversation. Of course, that could have been just so the woman kept her claws sheathed. Everly gave Helene a covert once-over and caught the other woman's nearly silent groan of frustration. Yep, Helene hadn't been acting nice, she'd been acting as distractor-in-chief.

"Don't you want to spend more time with Carlo?" Alberto asked, obviously wanting to soften the edges building up around their little party and keep her with his son when he returned.

"We have the rest of our lives for that." Irena flashed a beauty-queen smile at her future father-in-law and stood up. "Shall we?"

A flash of annoyance tightened Alberto's features, but he recovered quickly and ushered everyone out of the dining room and through the house on a sort of art appreciation scavenger hunt before ending the tour in front of a Rembrandt in the sitting room. It was fantastic. Irena gazed up at the painting, everything about her screaming "art lover" except for the bored, slightly glazed look in her eyes. Alberto and Helene stood nearly shoulder to shoulder, discussing the painting, while Tyler stood a few feet away, thumbs flying as he texted on his phone. The rush of protective fury that had filled her when Irena unleashed her poisoned claws evaporated. How in the world could anyone be so close to something as amazing as this Rembrandt and *not* be in awe? Irritation pinched her nerves and a flush of frustration heated her cheeks. There was something seriously wrong with that man when he couldn't take even a few minutes to turn his attention from whatever plot for world domination he was hatching to a painting that had brought tears to people's eyes. Turning, she caught Alberto staring at her, an indulgent expression on his face.

"I know you disapprove of breaking up the collection," he said, standing with his hands clasped behind his back as he admired the painting. "But art is like love; you never really own it, you can only enjoy it with an open heart while you have it. Anyway, beauty should be shared with the world, not hoarded indefinitely."

It was hard to argue with his logic even if it broke her heart a little—the leftover nicks and scrapes of growing up watching everyone leave, no doubt. Getting maudlin about someone else's art collection wasn't going to patch up those hurts, and it sure wasn't going to end in a commission that helped to keep her gallery afloat.

"If your mind's made up, then I know several people who would be interested in this Rembrandt and the others you have," she said. "We could host an invite-only show or make it an exclusive one-on-one sale so you can find the right buyer for your paintings."

"All I ask is to find someone who will love them as much as I do, but I'll do what you think best," Alberto said. "However, I do have several more pieces that I'm not sure about parting with. Irena, I know you have wedding arrangements to make, but why don't the rest of us go down to my house in Key West next weekend, and you can argue with me to keep them."

"What makes you say I'd argue?" she asked with a chuckle.

He laughed. "Because I know you, *tesoro*."

She could argue about a lot of things, but not that. The Italian had her number.

"So I'll arrange for the jet to take all of us to Key West," he said.

Helene's eyes widened, but she recovered quickly. "I don't think my schedule will allow it."

"*Bellisima*," he said, beaming at Helene. "We both know you could will the world to your liking. Something like a calendar with activities penciled onto its pages can't stop you."

"You're a horrible flirt. It's most unbecoming," she responded, the beginning of a smile curling her lips. "But I'll see what I can move around."

Seemingly satisfied—for the moment—with her answer, Alberto turned his big brown puppy-dog eyes on her. Oh, that was so not fair. She traveled for clients on a regular basis to appraise or advise, but a trip to the Keys when winter was just starting to think about slamming into Harbor City seemed more fun than work. She rolled options in her head as Alberto watched her expectantly. Even Tyler had looked up from his phone and was watching her.

"Oh, say yes," Irena said, sauntering closer to the rest of them, an evil little glint in her eye. "I'm sure Alberto will cover everything so you don't have to worry about cost."

Everly didn't think of herself as a violent person. Argumentative? Okay, she'd cop to it. A pain in the ass? Sometimes. But actually fist-to-face violent? No way. Then she met Irena the bitch ex-fiancée who'd gotten her talons into totally too trusting Carlo, and Everly had a sudden urge to smack the other woman stupid—or, more correctly, stupider.

Oblivious to the risks she was taking with her life, Irena went on. "I remember, Tyler, how you used to worry about how much to spend on things. This one time we were at dinner and he saw the wine list and he had to ask…"

The rest of what the hag was saying faded into static as red ate away at Everly's vision. Oh, that was it. What a classist bitch. Pulling back from the hold-my-earrings edge, she strutted over to Tyler with an extra bit of aggression in the sway of her hips. The muscles in his jaw were getting a workout with the effort it was obviously taking him not to lash out at the future daughter of the man whose business he was so determined to land. Everly had been there, done that, and it sucked. She wasn't about to stand by and watch someone else get humiliated in the snide little rich bitch fashion.

"Alberto," she said, cutting off Irena's passive-aggressive verbal attack and taking Tyler's hand in hers. "Of course we'll come. And no need to worry about cost. Tyler's become incredibly successful since his days with his ex-fiancée."

One of Tyler's black eyebrows went up in question. "We will?"

"Wonderful," Alberto answered before Everly had a chance to respond. "So it's decided. Let's celebrate with a glass of champagne and then we can look at our schedules, Tyler, because I believe we have some ideas of yours to discuss about bringing my hotels to America."

Irena, Helene, and Alberto headed back into the dining room, but Everly lingered in front of the Rembrandt, trying to unravel what she'd just done. Spending time on a tropical island with Tyler was the last thing she wanted. The man was one of the most exasperating people she'd ever met, but her passion had gotten the better of her—something that seemed to happen all too frequently around him.

Tyler squeezed her hand, making her realize she was still holding his. A blush creeped up her chest, and she tried to unwind her fingers from his, but his strong grip held her close.

"You don't have to do this," he said, something that looked like a mix of confusion and gratitude swirling in his eyes. "Our agreement was just for the introduction. You did your part."

"I know," she said, her gaze falling to their hands again before she forced her attention back to his face. "I just couldn't help myself when she was acting like that. It was either say yes on your behalf or punch her in the face."

He didn't laugh, but one side of his mouth went up in a crooked smile that did funny things to her stomach.

"You are the epitome of restraint."

Hoping to cover the shakiness jumbling her insides because of the uncharacteristic easy camaraderie flowing between them, she laid her accent on thick. "Don't you fuckin' know it."

They laughed, just two people from the wrong side of the tracks, trying to make it in a foreign land. They might be unlikely allies, but for the moment that's exactly what they were—and it felt good…right. This wasn't the time to unpack what that might mean, though, so she started to walk toward the dining room where the others were waiting—or at least tried to. Tyler hadn't taken a step, and he hadn't let go of her hand.

She glanced back at him. He stood there, staring at her—the look on his face all but screaming that he was plotting all sorts of devious schemes that would leave her naked, sweaty, and satisfied. Her stomach did the flippity-flop thing again with the addition of her thighs going quivery and a rush of electricity going straight to her core. Fuck. What in the hell had she been thinking? She hadn't been. And *that* was the problem.

Tyler stepped closer, his eyes stormy with a predatory want that made her breath catch. Her lips parted of their own volition and her nipples puckered in anticipation. But all he did was look at her. Not that it mattered. She was still on the edge of falling over into pure unadulterated trouble of the naked kind.

"We'd better catch up," Tyler said as he tucked a hair behind her ear that had fallen from her French knot.

"Yeah," she said, her voice barely audible over the thundering in her chest.

Neither of them moved for a second as the world skittered to a stop around them. Anticipation thick as a cotton ball encased them, and her core clenched. Then, just when she was ready to kiss him or pass out, he shook his head, mumbled something under his breath that she couldn't catch, and let go of her hand.

The tightness was back in his jaw. "Come on, before they send a search party back for us."

Nodding her agreement, she fell into step beside him as they walked toward the dining room, passing the portrait of a woman in Regency garb looking out very judgmentally as if she couldn't believe Everly's life choices.

You and me both, sister.

The next day, guilt was messing with Everly's ability to down her regular pot of morning coffee. There was no way she could let Carlo marry Irena without letting him know about what the woman had done to Tyler. She didn't want to. Really, who wanted to have *that* conversation, but she and Carlo had been friends for too many years for her to wimp out on him because she had to spill information that was not going to go over well.

If she said nothing, she'd be no better than how Sawyer had treated his best friend. And she knew firsthand how that kind of betrayal could hurt someone far worse than the person in question.

After pouring one more cup of java for good luck, she picked up the phone and hit Carlo's name on her contact list.

"*Ciao*, Everly," he answered on the first ring.

Of course he couldn't have been underwater basket weaving or something else that made having his phone on him an impossibility. "Do you live with your phone attached to your ear?"

"Will you be mad if I say yes?" he asked, his accent giving the question a roguish charm.

What she wouldn't give to just play along, but she couldn't. Squeezing her eyes shut, she stood in the middle of her living room, the soft Ikea rug tickling her bare toes, and pressed forward. "You might be mad at me after this call."

There was a beat of silence in which every single horrible possibility of how this conversation could end played through her head.

"What's wrong?" Carlo asked.

"It's about Irena." *There you go. Suck it up, girl.*

"Is this about how she tried to sleep with Tyler's best friend the night she was supposed to marry Tyler?" Carlo asked with an easy chuckle.

Her eyes popped open in surprise. "You knew?"

"My father and I share more than just our genes. We have the same private investigator, too."

Needing to get out the stored-up adrenaline that built while she was giving herself a mental pep talk to make this call, she started pacing from one corner of the rug diagonally across the middle and back again. "And you're okay with all this?"

Carlo made a noncommittal sound. "Considering that this marriage is more of a business deal than anything else, yes, I'm okay with it."

Just when she thought it couldn't get weirder. "What are you talking about?"

"In Italy, things go smoother in the business world if you're married. It's old-fashioned but it's true."

"So you're doing it for work?" That sounded about as romantic as a handful of unsalted pistachios, but at least it helped explain why in the hell he'd asked Irena of all people to marry him. His chances of actually falling for the she-devil were next to nil. "That's crazy."

"It's the complete opposite of that. It's business. Speaking of which, I need your help with some family business. You remember my nonna?"

She nodded while she took a sip of coffee as if he could see her. "Of course."

"She is coming to the wedding," Carlo said, his voice warming while talking about his hilariously grouchy grandma. "Would you mind being with her during the ceremony to translate? Normally, my father or I would do it, but I've asked him to stand up with me during the ceremony as a...what's the word? Best man?"

"I'd be happy to sit with your nonna." The woman was hysterical, all whispered snide remarks in Italian helpfully muffled by the black lace handkerchief she often held up to her mouth.

"Fantastico!"

Despite Carlo's enthusiasm, she couldn't help but worry that he was thinking only with his head and ignoring his heart and his conscience. "Are you really sure you want to go through with this?"

He grunted in what had to be the Italian verbal equivalent of rolling his eyes. "Unlike a certain secret romantic I know, I'm not waiting for true love."

"Are you calling me a romantic?" That was so not her. She was a Riverside woman through and through. She grew up knowing that happily ever afters were bullshit.

He laughed. "If the high heel fits."

"Well this one most definitely does not."

And it didn't. Really.

Chapter Ten

The best thing Tyler could say about an unscheduled client hand-holding trip to Denver was the necessary space it gave him from Everly. Physical space, anyway. Mentally, she'd set up house in his head and was clomping around in her ridiculous shoes that showed off her sexy ass. His dick perked up at the image. *Damn.* He was beginning to worry about his sanity when it came to her.

Beginning?

Shut up, self.

What he needed to be doing was planning his next move with Ferranti. His secret sources had outlined the hotel locations Ferranti's team was considering and they were wrong—not all of them but enough that what could be a billion in profits was going to shrink to millions. Not that Tyler could present it that way in a proposal. People tended to react badly to being told they were idiots, but it had to be done. He just needed to figure out the right angle to take. What better time to do that than tonight while he was in one of Ferranti's future competitor's properties? Tyler forced his attention to focus on the upscale hotel room he was in tonight.

It was nothing like the house he'd grown up in. Plush carpet. Thick curtains. Pillows fluffy enough to skydive into. And he fucking hated it. It wasn't that it gave off the don't-touch-anything vibe of expensive places, but that the only thing he wanted to touch was across the country probably wearing four-inch heels

and giving someone tons of I-don't-give-a-shit attitude.
Or did she only do that with him? Probably. Which was
exactly why he shouldn't be relaxing back on the king-
size bed with its million thread count (or some stupid
high number) sheets in only his boxers and reaching
for his phone.

Too bad he was doing that anyway.

TYLER: *What u doing?*

EVERLY: *Who is this?*

TYLER: *Your fav amateur chef.*

Yeah, the one who happened to be grinning like
an asshole for the first time in two days since he left
Harbor City. Oh, and his dick was waving hello, too.
Thank God he was smart enough not to share that tidbit
of insider information with her.

EVERLY: *How did you get my number?*

TYLER: *It's on your lease agreement, Sherlock.*

EVERLY: *So you hide out in your apartment
and just text insults? Is this your new hobby?
Your smoke alarm hasn't gone off lately.*

TYLER: *I'm in Denver.*

EVERLY: *Vacay?*

TYLER: *Nervous client.*

EVERLY: *I take it you're bored.*

TYLER: *Why?*

EVERLY: *You're in Denver.*

TYLER: *I'll have you know the mountains are beautiful.*

They were and he was. Everything had unfolded as predictably as a five-cent plot with his client who was having second thoughts about an investment. A few conversations and a site visit had settled the man's nerves. For a guy who always rubbed a particular someone the wrong way, he was damn good at calming others and getting them to focus on exactly what he wanted. No doubt a shrink would say it was a survival skill learned from his chaotic upbringing, but he wasn't deep-diving into that—not when he had Ms. 3B in her favorite black nightie ready to sext it up. Okay, he had no idea what she was wearing and steamy hot texting wasn't what they were doing, but his cock had a powerful imagination and a very hard need.

EVERLY: *I'll take your word about Denver. I like my nature hanging on the wall.*

TYLER: *Ha… Got the email from AF about the trip to the Keys. You still good with this?*

The four of them for a long weekend on Ferranti's private island in Florida. It would be sand, sun, and Everly-induced hard-ons that wouldn't find relief. Well, at least for him when he wasn't on the job trying to land the old man's hotel account. He had to get some distance from her. It was too hard to think strategically around her when all his blood was draining from the big head to the little one and taking half his IQ points with it.

EVERLY: *I wouldn't have agreed if I didn't mean it. I don't do things half-assed.*

Ass. She had to say ass.

TYLER: *I believe it.*

EVERLY: *Have to head to bed. It's 2 a.m. here.*

Bed. God, he loved to picture her spread out on a bed, her long legs open for him. His cock twitched. *Fuck.* There was pre-come pooling on the head of his dick and leaving a spot on his boxers. All he wanted was— He shoved his fingers through his hair, pulling out a few in frustration. *Keep it clean, Jacobson. She's not for you.*

TYLER: *Night, sugar.*

There was a pause while the typing bubble did its thing. Whatever message she was sending, it took more letters than N.I.G.H.T. Finally, her message popped up.

EVERLY: *That's it? No questions about what I'm wearing?*

And just when he thought he couldn't get any harder, he did—achingly so, because she'd surprised him again. His super-fine upstairs neighbor who told him to fuck off just as often as she kissed him and who came to his defense from Irena after giving him the stink eye herself had just thrown down a challenge. He read her text again as he gave his cock a hard squeeze and stroke, needing to relieve some of the pressure before he came in his boxers from one six-word question: *No questions about what I'm wearing?* He let go of his dick and typed.

TYLER: *I already know.*

A pause that gave him hope for a picture, but all that came through were words.

EVERLY: *Oh yeah? What?*

TYLER: *Not a damn thing.*

A little fantasy on his part or his gut feeling? Did it matter? Not to his dick. Another long pause with the typing bubble on his screen.

EVERLY: *Night, T.*

His lips kicked up into a grin at the answer. Ms. 3B wasn't about to give it to him that easily; she never did.

TYLER: *What, no confirmation?*

He stared at his phone in one hand while shoving his boxers halfway down his thighs with the other and then wrapping it around the hardest part of him. There wasn't a typing bubble. He gave it a minute and when the little blue bubble never appeared, he set his phone down on the nightstand.

He was right. He knew he was. He'd pictured her often enough. Nothing but long limbs, soft curves, and full lips. His hand moved up his shaft, rounded the head slick with pre-come and back down again. And in that moment it wasn't his hand stroking him, it was hers. She wasn't interested in drawing this out. She was kneeling on the bed next to him, watching her fingers speed up and down his cock. And she was talking filthy, telling him how much she wanted to see him shoot and that as soon as he did she was going to take that pink tongue of hers and lick it off his abs until his stomach was as wet as her pussy. And that was all it took. Fifteen strokes — twenty tops — and he was coming all over his stomach in hot bursts.

But unlike the fantasy, there was no Everly here to clean him up. And if she were? There was no way he'd have ever gotten to the point of coming without burying himself between her thighs and feeling her squeeze him tight as she came all over him. And this was why he needed to stop thinking about her like this. She was his annoying and argumentative neighbor who happened to be his in with Ferranti, that was all. The sooner he could land the hotel magnate as a client, the sooner he and Everly could go back to their regularly scheduled war of stomping shoes and burning food, so he could focus on his next scheme instead of her.

She was messing with his orderly world, and they both knew a relationship could go nowhere. He was looking for old-money class when he finally settled down, and she wanted… Well, he actually had no idea what she wanted. He refused to acknowledge the burning in his chest at the thought that it was someone from a better upbringing than he'd had. *Touché, Ms. Ribinski.*

E verly woke up the next morning with hard nipples, a slickness between her legs, and the memory of a dream that had brought her right to the edge of coming before her alarm went off. She'd been sitting on the edge of Tyler's kitchen island with him in front of her, his strong fingers pressing against her inner thighs, holding her legs open as he licked and sucked her clit. Sure, it had been a dream, but he'd been so good that her body ached for relief. Refusing to open her eyes and acknowledge the day, she dipped her fingers between her legs and nearly arched off the bed when she brushed her clit. Circling the sensitive nub, she pulled back every wispy thread of the dream. The way the muscles in Tyler's shoulders undulated as he worked one finger and then two into her, rubbing against the bundle of nerves inside her entrance. In her bed, with the morning light trying to push its way through her eyelids, she followed Dream Tyler's lead as she heard his dirty whispers from the dream.

"Open those legs wider, I want to watch you take my fingers."

She did, letting them fall open under the covers, the top of her hand brushing against the sheet.

"So soft and wet."

And she was—so much so that her fingers slipped around, adding to the fantasy that it wasn't her touch, but his, as she rubbed her clit faster and harder.

"Come for me, sugar. Squeeze me."

And just like in the dream, she did with a hoarse cry, arching her back as the orgasm pulled her body tight.

It took a minute to come down, and when she did, the wrongs of the situation hit her. Tyler was the last man she should be thinking about when she touched herself. The man was an arrogant pain in her ass. The only reason she'd even had that dream was in response to the unexpected texting last night. What had ever possessed her to make a comment to him about what she'd been wearing? Obviously, the dream had just been working out her surprise when he'd said, "Nothing at all," like a cocky jerk. The fact that he'd been right had nothing to do with it. There was no way for him to know that. That he did had just burrowed its way into her subconscious. It wasn't that she wanted him.

Okay, she wanted him. But she couldn't have him.

He owned her building and held her gallery's financial future in his hands. When things went sideways—not *if* but *when*, because guys like him who were obsessed with climbing the Harbor City society ladder always would with someone like her—she couldn't afford to be at all-out war with her landlord. Nunni was depending on her, even if she didn't realize it and thought Everly was her mother most times she went to visit.

And that sad bit of life was enough to kill off any remnants of her post-orgasmic buzz. Refusing to wallow in the unfairness of what had happened to the vivacious and determined woman who'd raised her after her mom died, Everly threw the covers to the side and got out of bed. The gallery was closed on Wednesdays, which meant catching up on paperwork during the day and, after five, going out to visit Nunni and play bingo in her honor with the cutthroat gang of octogenarians who'd followed Nunni to the best assisted living center in the neighborhood. who'd been a part of Everly's life for as long as she could remember.

Eight hours later, her head was still buried in the paperwork that was spread out over her coffee table and on the couch beside her, because she couldn't stand another moment locked in her office, when the message notification flashed across the top of her screen.

KIKI: *So what's with u and the hottie in 2B?*

She shook her head. The fact that her bestie had managed to make it days without interrogating her about Tyler had been a world record.

EVERLY: *Nothing.*

KIKI: *Oh, I totally believe that.*

Of course she didn't. Just like Everly didn't believe—no matter how many times her bestie denied it—that Kiki's divorce from her cheating asswipe of a husband hadn't left her totally suspicious of the entire male population and questioning her own appeal. They'd been friends for too long to pretend about stuff like that—but they also didn't press each other on the sensitive spots any more than absolutely necessary. Being supportive didn't always mean calling someone on her shit.

EVERLY: May you be cursed with an annoying neighbor.

KIKI: Don't you put that evil on me, Ricky Bobby!

She laughed, the sound bouncing off the walls in her empty apartment. When was the last time she'd seen that movie? It was her favorite and it had been too long.

EVERLY: We need girls' movie night soon.

KIKI: Beers and Will Ferrell? I'm in.

EVERLY: You have the weirdest taste in men.

KIKI: I like 'em big and furry.

EVERLY: Dork.

KIKI: Wanna do it tonight?

EVERLY: Can't, it's bingo night.

She glanced at the digital clock display on her laptop. Shit. She needed to get moving. Hudson and Felicia were meeting her at the assisted living center tonight. Hudson was working on a new series of paintings of side-by-side portraits of people in their early twenties based on photos and in their eighties based on in-person sittings. When he'd told her about the idea, she'd introduced him to her nunni's bingo buddies, who ended up adopting him and by extension Felicia. Now Hudson and Felicia were regulars at bingo night, and Nunni's buddies were all planning to attend Hudson's show at her gallery in the spring.

KIKI: Say hi to Nunni for me.

If only her nunni had gotten to find out that Hudson—who had come home from college some weekends with Everly and inhaled an entire tray of cannoli—was actually the world-famous painter Hughston, she would have been thrilled. As it was, most days she still thought Everly was a toddler and new information didn't take hold in her mind. Dementia fucking sucked.

EVERLY: Will do.

KIKI: xoxo

*EVERLY: *mwah**

She logged off and gathered up the stack of bills that were nearly due, sales slips, and bank statements. Promising herself that she'd finish up tomorrow, she stuffed everything back in its respective manila envelopes and laid them on top of her kitchen counter. Then, she grabbed the bakery fresh coconut cream pie—its box still wrapped up in a pretty blue ribbon—her keys, and her purse before heading out the door.

Fiddling with her phone in one hand while she held

the pie in the other, she'd made it three steps before a flash of something in front of her forced her gaze up from her cell. Then she almost dropped everything.

Tyler stood in the middle of her hall in broken-in jeans that looked like they'd been made to hug his impressive thighs and a lightweight gray sweater that brought out the silver in his blue eyes. The look on his face as he watched her was as hungry as it had been in her dream followed by her solo sexting fantasy. Fuck. This was not what she needed.

Maybe, but you can't deny he's exactly what you want.

Straightening her shoulders, she shoved that super-annoying voice of self-awareness way back into the basement of her brain and added a little extra attitude to her strut.

"I didn't smell anythin' burnin'," she said, adding some extra Riverside to her words. "So I figured ya were still in Denver."

Chapter Eleven

If it hadn't been for that quick intake of breath followed by an appreciative slow perusal of him from head to toe as they both stood in the hall outside her apartment door, Tyler just might have believed Everly wasn't totally happy to see him. It was almost enough to hurt a normal man's ego. Good thing his was supercharged. What else had a little extra oomph today? His dick after seeing her for the first time in days—especially since she was in black heels, form-fitting jeans, and a long pink sweater that managed to cover her from shoulders to ass and yet highlight every single dip and swell of her body underneath.

"You're in pink," he said, proving once and for all that his IQ left the building whenever Everly Ribinski came within touching distance.

She shrugged, sending one side of the sweater's scoop neck sliding down her arm and revealing her shoulder. It shouldn't turn him on. It did.

"It's my nunni's favorite color."

He forced himself to look away from the woman and instead focus on what she was carrying. "You bringing her pie?"

She flinched just the slightest bit but more than enough for him to notice. "The coconut cream is for her bingo buddies; she's not so into pie right now."

Whatever he'd said wrong, it had taken some of the punch out of her body language and the piss and vinegar out of her tone. He didn't like it. It didn't seem right that something could suck the personality out of

Everly like that. He closed the distance between them in three strides, for once not with the goal of touching her but needing to comfort her.

Shit. He was screwed. So fucking screwed.

He stopped just out of arm's reach because this was new territory for him, and if there was a chance that curling his arms around her would make the moisture in her dark eyes spill over, he knew she'd never forgive him. "Is everything okay?"

Everly's chin trembled for a second before she inhaled a deep breath in through her nose and closed her eyes. When she opened them a moment later, there was resignation, stubbornness, and more than a little sadness reflected there. "She has dementia, and I go to visit her every week and then play bingo with the eighty-and-older set."

He had no fucking clue what the protocol was here. He spent 95 percent of his talking time around other guys. Did he acknowledge the hurt? Did he brush over it? He didn't think it was the latter. His friend Frankie, who he'd grown up next door to, had four sisters. They loved talking about their feelings. Okay, they loved shouting and laughing and crying and giggling about their feelings. He should ask her more, invite her to say what she wanted because she was obviously close to her grandma and dementia wasn't a kind disease.

After taking in a steadying breath, he opened his mouth and said, "I kill it at bingo."

Yeah, he'd totally chickened out.

Asshole, know thyself.

Her lips went from pressed hard together to curling upward. Looked like he'd assholed his way into saying the right thing.

Everly looked him up and down. This time, though, it was as if she were trying to decide if he was worthy of an important quest. "Are you angling for another invitation?"

He didn't mean to press his luck, but being around her fucked with his head. "Not if you're too scared to play with me."

His dick liked that idea. Liked it a lot. He hadn't totally meant the challenge to come out as a double entendre, but he had a dirty mind and judging by the way her dark-brown eyes turned nearly black and the pulse picked up in her neck, so did Ms. 3B. He'd been worked up after their conversation last night. Had she? The tip of her pink tongue snuck out and wet her bottom lip. Oh yeah, she had. He got dumb around her, but he didn't lose all his brains.

Taking some pity on them both as the air crackled around them, he pulled his wallet out of his jeans and took out his lucky quarter. "Loser has to drive."

"What makes you think I'm taking you to bingo?" she asked, her voice a little breathier than it had been before.

He took a step closer, near enough that he could smell the vanilla of her perfume and see the light-brown freckles he'd never noticed before on her exposed shoulder. "Because you missed me."

Her gaze never wavered from his; she wasn't ever the kind to give an inch. "You sure think a lot of yourself."

"And I know you've been thinking a lot about me." Otherwise she never would have thrown in that text last night about what she was wearing. She may not want to want him any more than he wanted to want her, but the reality was that his upstairs neighbor had the hots for him and he had it bad for her. What harm was there in a little meaningless flirting? It wasn't like it would ever go anywhere beyond wrinkled sheets and sweaty satisfaction.

Just when he thought she wasn't going to play along, she gave him a smirk before saying, "Heads."

Using the tip of his thumb, he flipped the quarter into the air. It went end over end several times before he caught it and slapped it down on the top of his hand. Tails.

"Well," he said, putting the quarter away in its special pocket. "It had to go your way one of these times."

She snorted and led the way down the stairs to the garage. He didn't mind—the view was amazing.

"If I weren't holding a pie, I'd beg for a ride on your Harley." She grinned as they passed the covered beast.

He was going to need to enroll in classes or something soon. As mad as she was that he'd kept from her the fact that he owned the building, he could only imagine the size of the doghouse buying a bike you couldn't even ride would cost him. He wasn't even 100 percent sure he knew how to start the damn thing.

The Lakeland Community Center didn't have a lake nearby, but it sat up on a hill and had an amazing view of the harbor. When the wind hadn't whipped off all the leaves from the trees lining the walk up to the front doors, it had to be a great place to sit at the outdoor tables dotting the lawn and play chess, have a coffee, or talk about the good old days when the dinosaurs roamed the earth and milk was fifty cents a gallon. He was kinda looking forward to doing the same when he hit his seventies.

Everly led the way inside through the double doors, past the attendant manning a desk by the door who knew her name, and into a room full of comfortable chairs and a wall of windows looking out at a massive garden that had to be pretty impressive in the spring. Most of the people in the room were either residents at the facility or about to be—except for one couple nearby in an overstuffed floral love seat.

"You know Hudson and Felicia," Everly said as she led him over toward the other couple.

That was putting it mildly. They each were a younger sibling of two of his closest friends and had fallen for each other. "Only for most of my life."

"Great," she said, her voice strained, and handed him the pie. "They'll get you squared away with bingo and introduce you to Mary, who'll get the pie ready for the refreshment break."

He didn't like the slight droop to her shoulders or the way she'd pressed her lips together. This wasn't the ball-busting woman who gave him grief on an almost daily basis. This was someone about to knowingly go ballroom dancing in a minefield. His hand was intertwined in hers, turning her toward him before he even realized it.

"Are you okay?" he asked, searching her guarded eyes for any clue of what he could or should do next.

Her step faltered, but she recovered and slipped free of his hold. "Of course. I'm just going to visit my grandma before the bingo starts. I'll see you inside. Save a spot for me."

And then she was gone down a hall painted a cheery yellow. The temptation to follow was a burn in his gut. But what could he do? Nothing. Her grandma had dementia. He didn't have the cure. He wasn't her boyfriend. They were…neighbors, with any luck soon-to-be fuck buddies. There was no strategic reason for him to go with her. Then again, there wasn't any reason for being here with her at bingo period.

So why are you here, numbnuts?

Because… Fuck. He didn't even know anymore. "Hey, wait up."

She turned around, obviously as confused as he was about why he'd called out. "Yeah?"

"Can I meet her?"

Her eyes rounded. "Nunni?"

"Yeah." In any other situation, this would totally be a move to gain her trust and confidence in order to have forward momentum on a scheme. But that wasn't the case here—and that was even weirder than his wanting to go along to bingo.

Her shoulders seemed to relax a few inches, and one side of her mouth curled up in an almost smile. "Okay, but don't freak out if she thinks I'm my mom."

"Is that pretty common?"

The line of her jaw tightened. "Often enough that I usually get warned at least three times each visit that she doesn't trust that man my mom was dating. Nunni wasn't wrong on that score."

He nodded and, after telling Hudson and Felicia that they'd catch up with them before bingo, they walked together down the hall past the doors with nameplates on the wall beside each one until they finally stopped at one marked PATRICE RIBINSKI.

After exhaling a deep breath, Everly turned up the wattage on her smile to blinding and opened the door. "Hey, Nunni, how are you tonight?"

An old woman sat in the recliner in front of a TV playing a game show from three decades ago, judging by the clothes. Her hair was snow-white and cut into tight curls that framed her face. With her tiny frame and unassuming posture, she couldn't have been more of Everly's opposite right up until she turned to look at them. There was no mistaking those no-nonsense eyes.

"You brought a man," Mrs. Ribinski said,

unabashedly eyeballing him up and down as if she could see every flaw he had or bad deed he'd ever committed. His skin suddenly felt too tight.

"I did." Everly nodded. "This is my neighbor Tyler Jacobson."

Neighbor? Okay, he could play the part of neighbor.

Mrs. Ribinski shot Everly a yeah-right look before turning back to him. "Are you a nice man?"

Now wasn't that the one-billion-dollar question. "Most of the time."

"Honest. I like it." The older woman smiled at him before returning her attention to Everly. That's when the happy look slid away, replaced by a seriousness that didn't allow for any doubt about what would come next. "Never trust a man who pretends to be what he isn't. Now, tell me about the gallery."

Tyler stood in the doorway holding the pie and watched Everly and her grandma talk, each gesturing with their hands and laughing. Not once but four times in the span of ten minutes, they finished each other's sentences. It was totally foreign from how he'd ever talked to a blood relative. The bond between the women was more like what he'd seen at the Hartigans' house than anything he'd ever experienced at home. The easy intimacy of what he was seeing made him realize he was an outsider here, who'd pushed his way into a moment that both women obviously cherished. He needed to go.

He cleared his throat and lifted the pie box. "I'm just going to take this out to the pie table."

Everly and her grandmother looked up at him and smiled.

"I'll be out in a few minutes," Everly said.

"Take your time. It was good to meet you, Mrs. Ribinski."

The old woman nodded. "You, too, Trevor."

Not wanting to point out the slip, he just nodded, eased out of the room, and walked down the hall back to where Felicia and Hudson were waiting.

"Did Everly finally brain you with one of her shoes?" Felicia asked, pushing up her glasses that always seemed to slide down on her nose. "What are you doing here?"

"I heard there was pie." Yeah, that seemed totally believable. Really. Solid answer. In another dimension, anyway.

Hudson reached over and lifted up a corner of the pie box's lid. "You do realize you're carrying a coconut cream?"

"It's Everly's," he said, pulling it away before Hudson could take a swipe of the cream top. "I'm supposed to give it to someone named Mary."

"Come on," Felicia said, taking pity on him. "She's right over here."

Next thing Tyler knew, the pie was on a table with about ten others and he had a red and a blue bingo marker as well as four bingo sheets in front of him. Hudson and Felicia were across the table with two sheets each. The empty seat next to him with four sheets and three markers was for Everly—the old guy manning the bingo supply table swore that was her usual bingo order. Steps lighter than they'd been before, Everly hustled across the room and slid into her seat just as the woman with the bullhorn called out the first letter and number combination.

He leaned over even as he pressed his marker onto B5. "Good visit?"

"Great visit," she said, her shit-eating grin back in place. "Now, let's see if you're all brag and no bingo."

• • •

Whenever Nunni made it through an entire visit without calling Everly by her mother's name, there was an undeniable lightness that filled Everly's chest and, for at least a little while, it was like having her nunni back with her again. Of course, the little nugget of knowledge in the pit of her stomach that Nunni wouldn't stay like that weighed heavy, but she refused to give in to the feeling of dread tonight. She'd take the visit as a win even though she was getting her clock cleaned at bingo.

In fact, Everly had never laughed so much during bingo night in her life, because it turned out that Tyler had no bingo game. None. The man could barely keep up with one bingo card let alone the four he had in front of him, and his attempts to do so were so hilariously inept that they were both laughing. Hudson and Felicia hadn't fared much better than Tyler, giving up the bingo for the pie table across the room halfway through the night. Tyler was obviously too stubborn for his own good, though, as he muddled through trying to keep up with Mary yelling out numbers at a quick clip. There were only two explanations that accounted for Tyler's predicament: the male ego and Bernie Henderson.

She leaned in close and dropped her voice to a whisper. "Bernie shamed you into getting more than one bingo card, didn't he?"

Tyler nodded, fumbling with the marker. "He said the money raised went to a good charity."

Money? Oh God, the old coot got Tyler good. She glanced over to her left where Bernie sat on the other side of the empty chair between them, his lips twitching. Oh, he might complain about his hearing aid never working, but he wasn't having any problems hearing right now. The resident confidence man didn't bother to look ashamed—in fact, he looked damn proud of himself at the moment. The giggles started up again as she pictured what had happened. Bernie, with his Coke-bottle-thick glasses and Santa beard, had probably given Tyler some sob story about three-legged dogs or homeless sea turtles. So much for the chess master's ability to read people. "Yeah, that charity is called the Bernie Needs Bus Fare to Go to the Movies Fund. There's no cost for the cards."

Tyler's blue eyes went wide. "You're kidding."

Mary called out G48.

"Nope," Everly said as she stamped her six cards with the marker in a clockwise motion her nunni had taught her. "You got scammed by an old man."

"I thought old people were supposed to be sweet and bake cookies," Tyler grumbled, missing the G48 on the bottom left of his bingo card collection.

"These are Riverside seniors," she said amid another fit of giggles as she marked the card for him. "You might be from Waterbury, but you look like an uptown Harbor City mark, and Bernie is one of the best."

She couldn't testify to it in court, but she was pretty sure she heard the sound of "damn right" off to her left before Mary called out O70.

Bringing Tyler here could have been a huge mistake. Inviting him to come meet Nunni? A total disaster. Instead, Nunni and her friends at the assisted living center had welcomed him even if they were shooting her questioning looks. Everyone wanted to know who he was to her, and she didn't have an answer for that. Just trying to think up a definition for them made her chest tight and her nerves jangly.

Tyler stamped the space on one of his cards and

turned to face her, totally missing the O70 on the card next to it. "You know some people are actually intimidated by me, right?"

"Oh yeah," she said, rolling her eyes as she searched her last card for O70. "The ones who've never been smoked out of their apartment by you."

He snorted, trying for offended, but the twitch to his lips gave him away. "That hasn't happened in days."

"You've been out of town, remember?" Not that his being half a country away had stopped her from thinking about him.

"How could I forget after your text?" His lips curled into a sly smirk that did things to the panties she was wearing for once, and he pivoted in his seat, their knees brushing.

Even that mere touch was like a match to a can of hairspray, setting every nerve in her body ablaze. Mary called out I19, but Everly didn't bother with her marker, since she was white-knuckling it as the fantasy she'd had earlier that morning about him played out in her mind. Were his hands really that talented? His tongue that sure? His cock that fucking hard? She clenched her thighs together, needing some sort of relief. Damn. She had to get him out of her system because this was nuts. She didn't fuck around with men like Tyler Jacobson. He might be from the wrong neighborhood, but he was all upscale Harbor City now. And while the whole across-the-tracks thing may work in the movies, it sure didn't in real life as her own family's history attested. So why did her pulse tick up the second his gaze dipped down to her mouth?

"Are ya two going to kiss already or keep up ya yammerin'?" Bernie asked, his voice pulling her away from the fall that had too often ended up with her mouth planted on Tyler's. "I have my hearing aid turned up all the way, and I can still barely hear Mary call out the numbers over the sound of ya hormones."

Embarrassment slapped her cheeks, but she knew better than to duck her head or show any hint of weakness. "Seems that finicky hearing aid of yours is working well enough tonight."

The old man just grinned at her. "I'm still waiting for an answer."

Oh, she had an answer, and as soon as she could clear her brain a little, she'd get it out.

Tyler didn't seem to suffer from the same problem. He threw his arm across the back of her chair and trailed a finger along the column of her neck, scattering the few basic words she'd strung together in her head.

"Don't worry," Tyler said to the older man. "I'm going to kiss her."

Jana Milbank, who'd taught her the tricks of buying groceries on a budget from the corner store, looked up from her bingo card, squinting in their direction because she'd forgotten to take her glasses from their perch on top of her head, and put them on. "Who's he kissing?"

"That cute fella is gonna kiss Patrice's granddaughter," Catherine responded, never looking up from her bingo cards, as focused on them as she'd been on teaching Everly the basics of a well-placed elbow to the sternum or the heel of her palm to the nose before she'd gone out on her first date.

More than a little flustered, Everly fought to keep her cool as her nunni's friends continued to chatter about something that so was not going to happen— again. "I am *not* kissing him."

"Well not now she's not," Tyler said, playing up to the crowd. "But she has before and she will again."

"I don't blame her. If I were thirty years younger,

I'd be kissing him, too," Jana announced.

"Thirty? Try fifty, Jana," Catherine shot back.

Oh. My. God. This was just… There weren't even words for it because while one part of her was counseling her to resist, the other part was setting up a cheer routine rooting for her to get in the game and go all the way. She knew which way the crowd of seniors at the table would vote as they watched Tyler and her as if they were characters on the screen during movie night.

"Bingo!" a woman cried out from two tables over.

Everyone at their table groaned their disappointment—except for Tyler and her. He leaned in close and dipped his head so his lips almost touched the shell of her ear. Pulse jackhammering loud enough that she just knew he had to be able to hear it, she held her breath, anticipation stringing her whole body tight. But he didn't turn and kiss her. Didn't whisper a teasing word. Instead, she felt the vibrations of his soft chuckle against her skin before he sat back in his chair, a satisfied expression on his too-handsome-for-his-own-good face and picked up his bingo marker right as Mary called out the first number in the next round.

And, for once, she had to scramble to mark all her cards before Mary drew the next number. Tyler Jacobson would pay for this.

Chapter Twelve

Everly wasn't any more settled a few hours later when she pulled her car into the spot at the back of the garage. She turned off the engine, and Tyler unbuckled but didn't move from the passenger seat. There wasn't another person in the garage.

He leaned over, pivoting in his seat to look around her to the cement wall on the other side of her door, the move bringing him in closer. "You're a little near the wall there."

"Yeah," she said, shooting him what she hoped was a cool glare, considering how hot she'd grown sitting next to him on the drive home. "My neighbor's a real ass who talked me into flipping for the better parking spot and left me this P.O.S. parallel parking job."

He shrugged and settled back against the leather seat, not the least bit regretful. "Sounds fair to me."

"Of course it does; you won the coin toss."

"Now, don't be a sore loser," he teased as he got out and walked around to her side.

"It's not too late for me to run you over," she grumbled as she looked up, way up, at him.

He held out his hand. "Come on, we have a truce tonight."

"Says who?" she asked as she ignored his hand— because that way lay danger—and got out.

"Said Bernie when he was egging us on to kiss."

Tyler didn't move, which left her standing, thankfully, but trapped between the open car door and his six-foot-two-inch frame. They were close, too close. She could smell the fresh, clean scent of his soap and see the five o'clock shadow on his jaw. *All that rough would feel so good against my inner thighs.* The mental image that accompanied that thought came fast, hard, and unbidden, leaving her body tingling with anticipation. As if that wasn't enough, she made the mistake of looking the devil directly in the eyes. The bright almost aqua color of his irises had turned to a deep ocean blue and desire had dilated his pupils. Standing this close to him in the parking lot where they'd had their first kiss that had left her hot and needy for days, it tripped something inside her so that what she knew was a very bad idea started to seem like the best one ever. Really it made a kind of twisted sense. There was no way he could be as good as the fantasy, men so rarely were, so all she had to do was demonstrate that fact and poof! The itch would be scratched and everything would go back to normal.

"That man is a menace," she said, hoping he could hear her because the words were barely audible to her over the thunder of her pulse.

His hot gaze dipped to her mouth. "Doesn't make him wrong."

No. It didn't. So she didn't think, she acted—kissing him the way she'd been wanting to do all night. It wasn't nice and soft. It was hot and demanding, and she gave him everything she had and he returned it, teasing and tempting her until there wasn't anything in the world but them. Everything that had been building between them exploded in a wave of desire that obliterated her better judgment. She wanted—needed—to touch him everywhere, to strip him naked, taste him, feel him, ride him until she could rid herself of this overpowering craving for him.

Ending the kiss with a hard shove to his chest, she

sent him stumbling away a few steps until he was even with the back end of the car, and then she reached behind her to close the car's passenger door without ever taking her eyes off him. He was fucking magnificent with his broad shoulders and heaving muscular chest stretching the limits of the lightweight sweater he was wearing. His blue eyes had a wild look to them, telling of just how close to the edge he was. If she had to bet, she'd guess his toes were dangling over the cliff just like hers were. Her gaze traveled downward, pausing at the visible bulge in his jeans—impressive enough to make her mouth water. *That* she wanted to see so badly her core clenched. Of all the men in Harbor City, it had to be him who did this to her. And they said the fates had no sense of humor.

Stalking forward, she closed the distance between them, desperate to feel his skin beneath her fingers, his tongue everywhere. "You drive me nuts."

"Really," he said, not backing down an inch as his Waterbury accent came out in his passion, wiping away the veneer of Harbor City elite that he clung to so fucking hard. "Never woulda guessed."

She stopped in front of him, just out of reach, and, instead of touching him, she grabbed the hem of her pink tunic sweater and yanked it over her head and dropped it on Helga's trunk. "I should try to be less subtle."

Faster than she thought possible, his hands were on her hips, lifting her up and setting her down on the BMW's small trunk. His mouth was on the column of her throat, then on the upper swell of her breasts before traveling back up to claim her mouth. His fingers slid in between her legs, cupping her through the denim of her jeans, adding enough pressure to make her beg for more. And she did, pulling her mouth away from his to do so.

"Is that what you want, sugar?" he asked, his voice a growl against her skin. "You want me to touch you there?"

She rocked her hips forward against him, fighting to find relief for the need building up inside her.

"Tell me."

Decision made, the words flew from her lips sure and true. "I want you to strip off my jeans and fuck me right here."

She didn't have to ask twice. He had her jeans hanging from one ankle on the next breath.

"Fuckin' A," he groaned. "Pink."

Momentarily thrown out of the moment, she glanced down at her panties, one of the few pairs she owned. "They came with the bra."

"Just soft girlie pink underneath it all, aren't ya?" He traced a finger across the top band and then glided it down the middle, damp with her desire. "So wet already for me. Maybe I should slow down." He teased the tip of his finger over her. "Take my time. Make you beg some more. You sound so hot when you do."

She curled her fingers around his wrist. "You do and you'll live to regret it."

"Impatient, sugar?" He had the balls to grin down at her.

She should have run over him when she had the chance. She knew a challenge when it was issued. Slowly, she released his wrist, but instead of letting her hand fall back to grip the trunk, she brought it to the strip of silk between her legs, pulling it to one side. The hungry look on his face as he watched her slide one finger over her swollen flesh was almost better than an orgasm. Almost.

"Oh, I can be patient." She let her finger circle her engorged clit. "But don't get mad if I get there without you."

Letting out a low curse, he grabbed his wallet from his back pocket and yanked out a condom. "You better fucking not. I've spent too much time thinking about you squeezing my dick while you came for that."

"Then I don't need these." She hooked a thumb in the waistband of her panties, ready to rid herself of the barrier.

"Don't you dare," he said, his voice rough and demanding. "I'm gonna fuck you in those pink panties until you come all over me and beg me for seconds."

"You seem awfully cocky for a man with his jeans still on."

"It's not ego," he said, undoing his jeans and shoving them down along with his boxers, "if it's true."

Tyler was a sexy man—beautiful to look at on most days—but with the wild look in his eyes as he rolled the condom over his hard, thick cock, he was the kind of man a woman didn't forget. Ever. Not that she got to look all she wanted. The second he had the condom secured, he spread her legs wide and looped a finger around the center of her panties, tugging them to the side.

"Later, I'm gonna take my time with you." He glided the tip of his cock over her sensitive clit, dragging it across her folds, letting her know just how slow he planned to go. "But when you asked so prettily for me to fuck you, how could I deny you?"

It was a good thing his question was rhetorical because he chose that moment to sink into her, filling her in one fluid motion that left her breathless. It felt good—he felt good, right. She hooked her legs around his hips, the weight of the jeans hanging off one ankle dragging that leg down a bit. It was a minor annoyance she forgot about as soon as he began to move, plunging in and out of her. The back of his knuckle holding her panties aside rubbed against her clit. Already the tension built inside her, strengthened by the weeks of fighting as foreplay that had primed her for this moment. For him. Her hard nipples strained against the fabric.

He leaned down, pulling one bra cup down and lashing her nipple with his tongue before sucking it into his mouth. Her back arched as sensation flooded her. It was almost too much, the pleasure of his mouth on her breast, his cock buried inside her, and the pressure against her clit, but he didn't stop, gave her no quarter. She threaded her fingers through his hair, pulling it tight as she moaned and surrendered to it all. She was already climbing higher and higher when he released her breast and stood tall, changing the angle so he hit the bundle of nerves inside her with each thrust.

"So close, please," she mewled, the building sensations too strong to care she was following his prediction and begging again.

His pace increased, the strain of holding back clear in his body's tightness. "Yeah, sugar, what do you need to get there? Tell me."

"My clit."

He brought his knuckle more firmly against it. "What about it?"

"More." It wasn't a direction, but it was all she could offer as she climbed higher and higher.

"Is this what you want?" He circled his knuckle around the sensitive spot before bringing the pad of his thumb against her and pressing in a varying rhythm. "Or that."

The vibrations started in her thighs as she met each of his thrusts, her palms flat on the car's trunk. "All of it."

And he gave it to her, taking her closer and closer until there was only Tyler and the pleasure he gave, the kind she didn't realize she'd been missing, the kind she could get used to. The vibrations built until there was nowhere else they could go and exploded in an orgasm that had her calling out her appreciation. She wasn't alone. Her orgasm had just begun to abate when he thrust inside her with more force, once, twice, three times and then orgasmed as he drove into her.

Eyes closed, legs still wrapped around his waist, their bodies still connected as their heavy breathing bounced off the concrete walls of the parking garage, Everly slowly came back to herself. Her jeans were way more off than on, her shirt was underneath her nearly naked ass, her panties were off-kilter, and one boob hung free from her bra. Tyler meanwhile still had his clothes on, only his jeans and underwear had been shoved down. Just as soon as her brain returned from its trip to Lustopia, the realization that she'd just fucked her landlord and quasi-nemesis on the trunk of her car practically in public view—well, at least the view of any of her handful of neighbors who might wander down—hit with the force of a Mack truck sliding on a sheet of ice and slamming into a wall made out of marshmallows.

Hair tousled and a lazy smile on his face, Tyler pulled back. While she scrambled to get her clothes on, he got rid of the condom and pulled his jeans back up.

"I'd offer to flip you for whose apartment we spend the night in, but mine's closer and I want to get you fully naked and take my time," he said, all traces of an accent washed away, replaced by that almost-but-not-quite Harbor City accent.

No matter how good that sounded—maybe *because* it sounded so damn good—she couldn't do that. This was just to get him out of her system because Nunni's warnings about men like Tyler were screaming in her head. He ran his hands through his hair, and the black strands settled back into place. Despite the satisfied set to his shoulders, he looked like the kind of man he wanted to be—one of the Harbor City elite. It was just that he'd gotten his rocks off with a woman who'd never fit into that crowd even if she wanted to get rid of every trace of Riverside that clung to her.

"I gotta go," she said, her voice muffled by her tunic as she pulled it over her head.

He flinched. "But I thought—"

"Look, we're both adults; it was just a good time." She was already walking toward the door to the stairwell, clutching her car keys hard enough that they dug into her palm. "Scratching an itch. That's all. It was what it was, and it can't happen again."

He caught up to her but didn't try to stop her. "Why not?"

"Because." She couldn't repeat her mother's mistakes. She knew what happened when a Riverside girl fell for a boy with blinders on to be part of the rich Harbor City set. This had disaster written all over it for her heart.

"That's all the explanation I get?" he asked, his voice loud enough that the question echoed in the stillness of the garage.

Her gut twisted. "Good night, Tyler."

His silence followed her to the door and up the stairs, but he didn't. And that was for the best. Life wasn't like the movies. No one knew that more than her.

Chapter Thirteen

Sitting at his desk, Tyler stared out at the other high-rises from the window of his corner office in one of Harbor City's most exclusive business towers. He shared the eightieth floor with two other companies, a high-end independent realtor and an attorney whose boutique firm's client roster was long with bold names. He could afford the entire floor, but he didn't need it, and not all lessons from his childhood were negative—like the one extolling the virtues of waste not, want not.

With the exception of his assistant, Jason, Tyler was usually alone in the office, preferring to meet clients on their territory in order to get a better sense of who they were and what motivated them. Today, however, was the exception. It wasn't a client lounging on his leather couch with his size-sixteen work boots on the glass coffee table, it was one of the few men who could get away with it—his best friend since his family had moved in next door to the wild Hartigan clan, Frankie Hartigan.

Frankie was in the middle of a story about the firehouse groupie he'd met up with at the Barnaby Pub, a neighborhood dive and local hangout for firefighters and cops alike, when a notification popped up on Tyler's laptop screen letting him know that he had less than two weeks to put the finishing touches on the hotel proposal or risk losing out to the other sharks circling the Italian. Too bad he hadn't been able to spend more than twenty minutes focusing on it today instead of the woman who'd fucked him dumb and then strutted away like it hadn't been the best sex of their lives. He let out a groan and hit snooze on the reminder with a little more force than normal.

"Why are you so damn growly?" Frankie asked, dropping his feet to the ground with a *thunk* and leaning forward, propping his elbows on his knees.

Whether it was the Irish in Frankie, the fact that he'd grown up in a hive of neighborhood talk, or the fact that firefighters gossiped like old women on wine and paint night, the fact was the giant ginger could smell good dirt from five miles away.

"Because I finally got an in with Alberto Ferranti, and I need to get my presentation together but my concentration has been for shit."

"And who is Albert Ferranti?"

"Alberto," he corrected gruffly.

Frankie rolled his eyes. "I heard ya the first time; I'm just busting chops, man."

Fuck, he knew that. Anyone else and the name swap would have been accidental, but with Frankie and his near photographic memory, it was just another attempt—just like his outrageous story of banging the firehouse groupie in Barnaby's bathroom—to get Tyler to loosen up and relax. They didn't have a touchy-feely friendship, thank God, but it was a real one, and friends helped where and how they could. Going over to the Hartigans' house where nine people shared three bathrooms had been chaos, but of the good kind, not the simmering ugly at his house next door.

"Shit, I'm sorry." He rammed his fingers through his hair. "I'm a little on edge, that's all."

"Really? I never woulda guessed." He chuckled, the sound deep and booming. "What you need is a guys' night. Come on home. We'll go out to Barnaby's, have a few beers, and make nice with the ladies."

The beer sounded good, but the mention of ladies only made him think of the one woman he couldn't get out of his head. "No time."

"There's always time to get laid," Frankie said, ever the man for subtlety. "And that's exactly what you need. Trust me. I'm related to Ford, and if there's one thing that actually gets the stick out of my baby brother's cop ass, it's finding heaven between a pair of long, smooth legs."

"Trust me, that's not my problem." No. It was the fact that he'd found it and lost it without a clue as to why.

Frankie leaned farther forward. "Details, man."

Shit. Why in the hell had he said that? "None of your business."

"She blew you off, didn't she?" Frankie relaxed back against the couch, a smug look on his face. "Damn, she did." He laughed, one giant hand slapping his knee. "You have got to tell me this woman's name because I'm already in love with her."

That wasn't going to happen. "You don't know her."

"It's true," he said with a shrug. "But there are a *few* women in the Harbor City metro area whom I've yet to charm the panties off."

Now that was about as close to the truth as it got. One of these days, though, that fact was going to kick Frankie right in the teeth. "You need professional help."

"That's what the department said when I told them there was no way I was taking time off just because I had a shit-ton of leave accrued."

Play hard, work hard. That was the Frankie Hartigan way.

"What did your lieutenant say?" Tyler asked.

"Oh, she huffed and puffed, but as long as we're shorthanded at the house, then I'm golden."

"You know most people *want* to take a vacation."

"Really, and when was the last time you had one?" Frankie asked, nailing him with a don't-even-bother-to-try-to-lie glare.

"I'm going to Key West this weekend." While it wasn't technically a vacation, it sure would be a definite side benefit. All he had to do to make it worthwhile was keep his blood supply going to his brain instead of his dick—something that was bound to be a challenge around Everly.

"With the mystery babe?" Frankie asked, ever the optimist.

"Sort of."

Frankie lifted one ginger eyebrow in a nonverbal order to continue.

And this was the problem with being friends with someone for as long as they'd been friends—you couldn't lie. It fucking sucked.

"We're going down to stay with Alberto on his private island."

"'We're,' huh?" He let out a low whistle. "So it's just a work thing with this chick?"

How to answer that? By not answering it. "Not exactly."

"Devil's in the details, my man."

"No," Tyler said, pointing a finger at his friend. "The devil's in a six-foot-six redhead who won't leave my office so I can get to work."

"Touchy today, aren't you?" Frankie asked with a laugh. "Trust me, get your panties out of a twist, spend some more time with your secret hottie, and you'll be right as rain."

"She doesn't want to." Fuck. Since hitting the rewind button on life wasn't an option, Tyler just braced for the good-natured shit about to rain down on him.

"Ouch." Frankie slapped his hand over his cold black heart in mock horror as he stood up. "I'd give you some advice on how to deal with the one who got away, but the ladies *always* want to spend time with me."

"Your day will come." Now *he* was sounding like the touchy-feely one, which just went to show how much Everly had fucked him in the head.

Frankie shrugged. "And I'll probably lose my hair someday, too, but I'm not worrying about it now."

"This explains why you run into burning buildings for a living."

"Pure awesomeness?"

"No." Tyler shook his head because it was an argument they'd been having since almost the first day they'd met. "A lack of planning."

"I leave the schemes up to you." Frankie headed for the door. "See you at poker night next week?"

Guilt stuck a knife right in his spleen with a sharp jab that made him flinch. "I don't know."

"You've skipped out on the last three. Don't make me come back into the city just to haul your ass home to Waterbury."

And there it was, the fact he could never get away from. Waterbury wasn't home, hadn't been for years, and yet that was all anyone saw when they looked at him. For Frankie and the rest of the Hartigans, it wasn't a bad thing. For a lot of his current and potential clients, it was a reason for hesitation. After all, what could a scrapper from the wrong side of the tracks know about big business? The degrees, the experience, the reputation, none of it seemed to matter as much as his working-class roots. And that's why he'd stayed away. Judging by the tension in Frankie's shoulders as if he was bracing himself for another brush-off, Tyler had said no too often. He should say it again, but he didn't want to. Being around Everly had reminded him of how much of a relief it was to not worry about what everyone else was thinking and just be—and that wasn't good.

"I'll be there."

"Good." Frankie grinned. "It's Fallon's turn to bring the beer, so keep your delicate beer-snob tendencies on the rich side of the harbor."

Tyler flipped off his best friend as the other man walked out of the office, laughing at his own insult, and for the first time since he'd watched Everly strut away from him last night, Tyler felt like the whole world wasn't a total shit pit. Settling down behind his desk, he opened up the proposal template he'd started for Alberto's hotel expansion into the United States.

Tyler knew what the other consultants would be offering: safety, snobbery, and a massive budget. That wasn't what would be going into his proposal. There was a huge opening for quirky and unique properties at the high end of the boutique hotel market. That's where Alberto and his board needed to focus for their American expansion. Let the Ritz be the Ritz, but let the Ferranti Hotels be themselves—that was the road to success. All he had to do was secure an appointment to present his vision to Alberto and the board, which he would find a way to do in Key West—no matter how tempting it was to focus on his pain-in-the-ass upstairs neighbor who'd left him sated and slack-jawed with surprise. Definitely not something most people could accomplish.

Everly was in pink again and walking through the clinical-smelling hallways of the Lakeland Community Center's dementia wing. There were cries of help coming from Mrs. Gover's room, but when Everly peeked in she saw the older woman staring at the bare wall opposite her bed as her daughter, Shelby, wrung her hands nearby and tried not to cry. Everly's heart twisted inside her chest, but she kept walking. She'd been in Shelby's place before and other than giving the woman a hug when her visit was over, there wasn't anything she could do. Some days, this was the reality.

Dementia was a horrible disease, robbing once thriving people of their own selves and locking them behind an impenetrable door in a place and time where no one could reach them. And—for better or worse— sometimes the door cracked open just enough for the person to realize momentarily where and when they were before it smacked shut again. Was that heaven or hell? It was both at the same time, for everyone.

Pausing outside the door labeled PATRICE RIBINSKI, Everly took a deep breath. There was no knowing which Nunni she'd find on the other side. Smoothing her hair, she took a deep breath, raised her chin, pasted on a smile she hoped passed for authentic, and then she opened the door and walked inside.

The Nunni of her childhood had been small but bold as bar brass with a quick comment and an iron will. Now, the unbreakable woman from Everly's memories just looked fragile. Her ebony hair had turned to the color of steel. Her skin had become soft and papery. Her smile—always a little wicked—had gone hazy around the edges. The sound of the opening door had caught her attention, though, and she looked over and smiled.

"Hey, Nunni."

"If it isn't my little Evie," she said, her eyes lighting up. "Come give me a hug."

Breathing a sigh of relief she didn't realize she'd been holding, she crossed the room and gave her grandma a careful hug as the older woman sat in the chair next to the window decorated with hanging plastic suncatchers that made the windows look like they'd been made from stained glass. Then, she sat in one of the overstuffed chairs next to Nunni that was motorized to lift the person sitting into a standing position to help those residents in the community who needed some assistance getting up. Photos filled nearly every available flat surface—pictures of Everly as a gap-toothed grade-schooler, her mom laughing in the kitchen, all three of them together, looking ready to take over the world, and so many more.

Nunni patted Everly's hand. "I swear, you're looking more and more like your mother every day."

"Thank you." Maybe it was because she wanted it so badly, but she always saw her mother when she looked in the mirror, and it was something that had felt like a hug from the beyond in those early days after her mother died. "So I saw your friend Bernie the other night when I came over and played bingo after seeing you."

"Did you win?"

Win? With Tyler there, she'd been lucky to find half her numbers. "Not even close."

"That's the way life works." Nunni gave her a wink. "You'll get 'em next time, Evie, you always do."

"Are they treating you okay here?" she asked, looking around for any signs that they weren't. The room was spotless, though, and Nunni's hair had been recently done, which lessened her anxiety and guilt for coming to visit only a few times a week.

"I can't complain," Nunni said. "There're movie nights on Tuesday and bingo. Did you know they have a weekly bingo game here?"

The slip was a gut punch, but Everly couldn't let it show. "I had heard that."

"I wish I could go but the numbers get confusing for me…" Nunni said, her voice trailing off as her gaze dulled and her attention went once more to the window. They sat in silence for a few minutes before her grandma turned back, her attention focused. "I hope you're not still seeing that man, Melanie."

Everly dug her fingernails into the palm of her hand to keep from reacting. Melanie had been her mom's name. Nunni was again behind that door stuck in a time before Everly was born, revisiting again and again the conversation she'd had with her daughter about Everly's father. This was her loop, the one she always seemed to return to at an ever-greater frequency. It used to happen only occasionally. Now, more times than not, Nunni looked at Everly and saw only Melanie. Everly losing her mother in one quick instant had been horrible. Letting go of Nunni one millimeter at a time was devastating. However, calling attention to Nunni's confusion or trying to correct her never had a positive impact, so Everly kept her mouth shut—especially since the parallels between what had happened decades ago and what was happening in her life now were too spot-on to ignore.

"Men like that may play in Riverside, but they fall in love and marry on the other side of town," Nunni went on, her fingers picking away at the frayed edge of the blanket draped over one arm of the chair. "A man who only cares about making his mark on the world never cares who he hurts in the process."

The air in the room changed around them as Nunni became more obviously frustrated, her hands moving quickly and her gaze darting around the room as if she knew something wasn't right but couldn't figure out what.

Everly covered Nunni's hands with her own and looked her grandma in the eye. "Don't worry, I'm not seeing him."

"You're not?" Nunni asked, desperation thick in her tone. "Promise me."

"I'm not seeing him." Everly's entire body ached with the effort not to give in to the urge to cry or scream out the truth that it was too late because Melanie did keep seeing that man and Everly was the result. And Nunni had been right all along, and he'd abandoned them. "I promise."

"Good." Nunni relaxed against the chair. "I'd hate to see you hurt, Melanie. I love you too much for that."

She squeezed her grandma's hand. "I love you, too."

No matter what—no matter if in the end Nunni never saw her again but only her mother—because love was loyalty and always being there for the other person. A light tap on the door drew their attention. One of the nurses stood there with a paper cup of pills.

"I'm sorry to interrupt, but it's time for your stories, Patrice. Would you like me to turn on the television?"

"Oh yes," Nunni said. "I can't miss what's going to happen next."

What was going to happen was the same storyline that had happened years ago before her nunni's favorite soap opera had been canceled, but her grandma never realized. She just watched the DVDs Everly had found. The show was one of the few things that calmed her down when she became agitated, and even though she seemed calmer now, Everly knew the longer she stayed, the more likely Nunni was to warn her away from that man. So as the nurse turned on the TV, Everly got up and gave her nunni a hug.

"I'll see you in a few days."

"Always joking, Melanie." Nunni patted her cheek. "You know I'll see you tonight for dinner."

Then, her grandma turned her attention to the TV, accepting the pills from the nurse without complaint, and got lost in her stories.

Gulping past the emotion, Everly turned and walked out of the room, blinking away tears.

Chapter Fourteen

Helene was sure that none of her acquaintances let alone friends would ever spot her at Grounded Coffee. The trendy Harbor City chain was popular with the younger set, not people her age, and definitely not Alberto's age. He had to be pushing sixty-five if he was a day, and men who were as exuberant as the Italian didn't age well—or so her mother had always said. He was far too old for her. She was, after all, only in her late fifties. Not that she was looking for a companion. She still wore Michael's ring for a reason. She'd already had the love of her life, and now that part of her life was over. Still, she'd agreed to this meeting, so she smoothed her newly platinum hair back and walked into the coffee shop.

The patrons looked like a great unwashed mass—really, when did it become acceptable to go out in public in what had to be pajama pants and a sweatshirt—but the place smelled like heaven, the sugary, buttery kind she'd denied herself for decades. Her mouth remembered, though, watering at the sight of an untouched flaky croissant baked to the perfect golden brown on a man's plate. The customer in question looked up. Alberto. Of course he would indulge in something so without nutritional value just because it tasted delicious.

"*Bellisima*, it's so wonderful to see you." He stood up and pulled out a chair, somehow managing to not look like a man who ate croissants with abandon. The fact that men's metabolisms worked as fast as they did would forever be an annoyance to her. "Please sit down."

She did, balancing her weight on the balls of her feet so it wasn't fully on the chair as he pushed it in. The musky scent of his cologne wafted around her, not enough to overwhelm but enough to inspire her curiosity. Not that she wondered about this man. She was here only to discuss Everly and Tyler, after all, a point she'd made clear to Alberto in her emailed response to his invitation that had arrived via a stunning bouquet of orchids.

"Thank you." She didn't relax against her chair, not even when he released it and strode back to his side of the small table. Something about the man made her not jumpy exactly, but she couldn't deny the zing of expectation, and she didn't particularly like it. "So you want to discuss Everly and Tyler?"

"Yes." He cut the croissant in two, picking up one half and leaving the other on the plate that he pushed over to her. "I want to know more about this Tyler Jacobson."

The temptation of the croissant was potent, a hint of the forbidden followed by the promise of exquisite pleasure. Still, she resisted, turning her attention to the man who failed to freeze when she leveled a frosty glare his way. It was most frustrating.

"Tyler is smart, savvy, and is always looking for new opportunities."

"No," Alberto said with a flourish of hand gestures. "I mean is he good enough for Everly? I might not see as well as I used to, but I can definitely see a spark between them, and I am worried because Irena didn't have the nicest things to say about Tyler after he left."

Helene just bet she didn't. "I'd recommend considering your source for that information."

"What do you mean?" he asked, tearing off the end of his croissant half and popping it in his mouth.

Helene had spent a lifetime gathering information about her so-called peers, not necessarily sharing it. Gossip wasn't usually part of her repertoire, but this was more of a warning than rumor or innuendo. Considering her options, she gave Alberto a hard look. He might seem like a man who resembled a former model who'd aged out of the profession, with his shock of silver hair that set off his tan skin and made his brown eyes sparkle, but he didn't waver under her cold stare, and the slightest nugget of respect started to form. Okay, maybe he wasn't just a flirt. Maybe there was more to Alberto than she'd first noticed.

"Has Irena bothered to tell Carlo why she and Tyler didn't get married?" she asked, toying with the crusty point of the croissant.

Alberto shrugged. "She just said they were young and weren't ready."

"That's one way to put it." A completely fabricated one. "She tried to sleep her way up the bank balance line and tried to slip into bed with my son Sawyer—who'd been friends with Tyler for years. Sawyer turned her down. Tyler called off the wedding. She went on an extended cruise with a pair of Middle Eastern princes."

He crushed the piece of croissant in his hand to dust. "I have to tell Carlo."

"If he's like my sons, he won't listen." There must be something about that Y chromosome that made men unable to take valuable advice the first time it was offered. Lord knows they didn't get it from her. Okay, maybe they did a little. Still, if she didn't love her boys so much, she would have knocked their heads together. "They always have to figure things out on their own."

"If this is the kind of person Irena is, I can't let

him marry her." Alberto reached across the table, pressing her hand between the two of his, sending an unexpected thrill of awareness through her. "You're so knowledgeable on this, could you help me with Carlo and also Everly?"

The question shocked her into stillness, and she allowed her hand to remain in his. "You want the two of them together?"

"Oh no, her heart is already interested in someone else; she's just being too stubborn to see it. Women, always so set in their ways." He leaned forward across the table and brought her hand up to his mouth, brushing a light kiss across her knuckles that made her chest tighten.

"Someone else?" she asked, mentally fighting to suppress the zing of anticipation speeding up her pulse. "You mean Tyler."

"*Sì*," he said, lowering her hand but not letting go. "*If* he's good enough for my Everly."

Offended on Tyler's behalf, Helene pulled her hand free, ignoring the way her fingers felt too cool without his welcome heat. "Oh, he is."

"How can you be sure?" he asked, watching her with wary eyes as if she were the one who needed to prove herself.

As if that could ever be possible. She was Helene Carlyle, and she hadn't cornered the market on scaring the salt out of Harbor City's elite when necessary by lacking self confidence—or at least the appearance of it.

"A woman knows these things," she said, matching the fire she felt inside with ice chips in her tone. "Which is exactly why you'll need me to have this matchmaking mission go well."

Where had that come from? Needing something to do when Alberto's eyes widened with shock and then glee, she reached for the croissant and picked it up, taking a bite before she even realized what she was doing. The flaky, buttery goodness practically melted on her tongue as the carbs rushed through her system, making her jittery. At least that's what she attributed her reaction to—it definitely was not because of the way Alberto's brown eyes had turned the color of dark hot chocolate as his gaze traveled over her. She was a married woman. Okay, a widowed woman, but that didn't matter. She wouldn't be disloyal to Michael's memory like that.

"I will gladly accept your help," he said, his broad smile lighting up his face and making her wonder just how he must have looked as a young man because even knocking on retirement's door, he had a certain something about him that made her breath catch. "And I have just the plan for our trip to the island."

Island? She'd nearly forgotten about it. There was no way she could be alone—well, practically alone— with this man and keep her sanity. Just sitting with him in a coffee shop had her eating a croissant and openly agreeing to matchmake, what would being on his island be like? Nothing good, she was sure.

"About the trip," she said, placing her hands in her lap to stop from taking another bite. "I don't think I'll be able to make it."

He shook his head and muttered something in Italian that she didn't quite catch. "But without you, the plan will fail."

Wait. He'd approached this as if it was all new to him. She wasn't some fresh-faced girl who didn't realize when she'd been hustled. Still, she couldn't stop the logical question before it popped out. "What plan?"

"I will tell Everly that I am trying to seduce you and ask her to leave on an earlier flight for Key West than you and I so I can get you alone and charm you."

After making that announcement as if he'd just told her the weather report, he sat back in his chair and demolished the rest of his croissant half.

Seduce her. Of all the ridiculous things to say. "I'll have you know that I'm a widowed woman and have no interest in seduction," she said, putting every ounce of haughtiness she'd learned in finishing school into it. "Anyway, no one would ever believe that."

He scoffed. "Why wouldn't they?" he asked as he picked up the espresso cup that looked especially tiny in his large hand. "It's the truth."

Alberto may have been the one getting a shot of concentrated caffeine, but it was her heart that was racing.

Chapter Fifteen

The Saturday sun was high, but it wasn't anywhere close to being Florida warm out on the tarmac at the private Paisley Airfield. Everly couldn't wait to get down there and peel off the sweater she'd tugged on this morning to fight the blast of frigid air announcing winter was near. She was a woman made for the tropics—at least according to her heating bill, which had arrived today and told her by adding in one too many numbers in front of the decimal point that she needed to learn to love wooly socks and blankets more than turning up her thermostat.

Tyler stood by Alberto's jet. He wore a long-sleeve gray Henley, jeans, and a scowl as if he were impervious to the cold. He probably was. The fact that she hadn't seen him since she'd lost her sanity in the parking garage had her discombobulated. It wasn't a feeling she was used to but was all too common around Mr. 2B. Not that she really thought of him like that anymore. No, she spent way too much time over the past few days imagining him naked for that.

He must have felt the heft of her gaze because he turned and stared at her. Suddenly, it wasn't so cold out on the tarmac anymore. Heat curled in her stomach and places lower—exactly what she didn't need. Her visit to Nunni had brought back all the memories of nights spent hoping that somehow, someday she'd be good enough for her dad to want her in his life. He never had, and she'd promised herself that she'd never pin her hopes on a man looking to climb the social ladder instead of finding what he needed in the people he already had. Tyler may not be exactly that kind of man, but there was no denying his determination to be a part of the world she could only ever be on the periphery of. The fact that the realization had hit at the very inopportune time of being right after one of the best orgasms of her life stung almost as much as the frigid blast of wind that blew back her hair.

"*Tesoro*," Alberto said as he stopped beside her near the nose of the jet. "There's been a slight change in plans."

That was the story of her life lately.

"Do we need to reschedule? It's no problem." Probably it was for the best. Maybe by then she'd have time to get this attraction to Tyler under control.

"Oh, there's no need for anything that drastic. I just need a favor."

She looked at Alberto in his wool sweater with his silver hair dancing in the wind. He didn't seem to be enjoying the early arctic blast any more than she was.

"Of course, anything." And she meant it. He'd done so much to help her career after they'd met in Italy, how could she not? But it was more than that. Alberto had become family, the kind a girl like her tended to adopt and keep close out of loyalty and love.

"There was a scheduling mishap and I need you to go ahead to Key West with Tyler. The house is all ready for you and you can start on your valuations right away." His gaze drifted over to where Helene stood in her cream full-length coat, the wind not daring to move even a strand of her perfectly coiffed hair. "Helene and I will meet you there later."

Her and Tyler? Alone? On an island? Her pulse sped up, whether because of panic or excitement didn't matter. Either way, Alberto's plan did not sound like the way to clear her head—and her body—of whatever was drawing her to him.

"We should wait until we can all go together."

"You misunderstand, *tesoro*, this mishap was, how do they say it, accidentally on purpose." Alberto ran his fingers through his mussed hair and gave her a sheepish grin. "Helene and I would like a chance to get to know each other a little better when it's just us."

"Oh," she said, understanding dawning.

Alberto had been running his A flirting game with Helene, and while the other woman hadn't been returning the attention at the same level, she hadn't been shutting him down like she was known to do without a second thought. While Everly's love life, or lack of one, was for the best, she wasn't about to ruin the start of something between two people who would in a weird way be perfect for each other. For as outgoing and enthusiastic as Alberto was, he had a solid, dependable core and was loyal down to his custom-made Italian loafers. And Helene? She'd had a rough time of it since her husband had died and maybe it was time for her to remember how to enjoy life for herself again. If helping them get there meant spending a little alone time with the man she thought of way more than was good for her sanity? Well, she could do that. It was all part of being there for those you love.

"Tyler and I will be able to manage on our own for sure."

He took her by the shoulders and planted a kiss on each cheek. "Grazie, *tesoro*."

Alberto hurried off to Tyler, no doubt to explain the change in plans, and she followed a few steps behind, giving herself a pep talk with each foot forward that she could do this. She could keep her hands— and her lips—to herself. It was the smart thing to do because she wasn't about to make the same mistakes her mother had.

Tyler stepped off the plane into the slap-you-in-the-face heat of South Florida. The flight to Key West was as silent as it was uneventful. Everly had read a book on some Flemish artist on one side of the aisle while Tyler had pretended to play solitaire on the table in front of his seat while in reality he spent the four-hour flight watching her. The way she twisted a lock of hair around her finger as she read. The way her body had tensed when the jet went through turbulence. The way she ignored the hell out of him as if he wasn't even there.

After bingo night, he'd thought they'd gotten past the push and pull, one step forward and two steps back of their what…friendship? That wasn't what he wanted from her. What did he want after that mind-blowing bout of fucking? Hell if he knew, he just wanted more whenever he was around her. Calling it distracting was an understatement. It was like sitting too close to the fireplace while wearing a parka but not being able to move away.

The cab was waiting for them just outside the airport with the WELCOME TO THE CONCH REPUBLIC sign meeting its arrivals. Without any bags beyond their carry-ons, they went straight to it. Still not speaking. This quiet wasn't like Everly, and it was starting to drive him nuts.

She'd no more than closed the door on her side of the cab when he turned to her. "Is the silent treatment your game plan for the entire weekend?"

She stiffened but turned to face him, the smile on her face the one she used for clients at her gallery, not the real one she'd been wearing during bingo. He fucking hated that smile.

"I wasn't aware I was being too quiet for your tastes," she said, her voice even. "What would you like to discuss?"

"How about what happened the other night?" The quiet words popped out before he could stuff them back into the do-not-talk-about-even-under-extreme-duress box in a dark corner of his brain. Shit. He might as well turn in his man card. What was next, asking her intentions?

Her chin went up a few degrees, but she didn't fluster. "That's best forgotten."

"Look, folks," the cabbie said, turning around in the front seat to eyeball them both. "While whatever happened the other night, I'm sure, was a doozy, why don't you tell me where you need to be going before I remember all eight thousand and forty-two reasons why I divorced my wife and moved here?"

Frustration marching through him like ants on their way to a picnic, Tyler took a deep breath and forced his voice to sound calm. "The Hemingway Marina."

"All righty, then," the cabbie said. "Now you two can go back to your fighting."

"We aren't fighting," they both grumbled at the same time.

The cabbie scoffed. "That's what my wife always used to say, too."

The cab pulled out of the airport, driving along a single-lane highway that gave a breathtaking view of the ocean. The muscles in his shoulders ached from tension, his palms were clammy, and the urge to keep pushing Everly, to make her say what she wanted, continued to build inside him. This wasn't how he should react to this situation. He'd always been excellent at stilling his emotions—a useful skill to have in a volatile house growing up—but it was one that always seemed to disappear around her. He became rash. Their little war over the parking spot, the kisses, stripping her down and fucking her until they were both senseless in the parking garage, were all symptoms of a far worse disease—that of falling into his parents' bad habits. Maybe, in this instance, silence really was the better part of valor.

And that's how he kept his mouth shut despite every instinct in his body being ready for a verbal throw down as the cab puttered its way through the tourist-lined streets to the marina where the private charter was waiting for them just as Alberto had promised.

Captain Hank was in board shorts, a bright yellow T-shirt with STAY WEIRD printed onto it, and a captain's hat that covered his suntanned-to-a-nice-level-of-leather bald head. Tyler offered to take Everly's bag aboard, but she declined with as few words as possible. He was half-tempted to kiss a few extra ones out of her, but even in his current condition he knew she'd be more likely to impale him with her stiletto in a very strong but vulnerable place than open her mouth and let him in. So he gave her her space during the short boat ride to Treble Key, which, according to the information he'd gotten out of Alberto, was a six-acre island, two of which were submerged, with a large solar-powered house sitting right in the middle. A four-wheeler would be waiting for them at the dock, and they'd use that to trek two miles inward to the house. It couldn't be any easier, and the amount of cold coming off Everly would negate any need for air-conditioning during the trip.

When the captain pulled up to the dock, though, there wasn't a four-wheeler waiting. There wasn't even much of a dock. It was more like a set of weather-worn boards haphazardly put together and held in place by gravity and a prayer.

"This can't be right," Everly said, the dread in her tone matching his.

Captain Hank took off his hat and wiped his head with a red handkerchief bleached to a light rose by the sun. "Oh, sorry, forgot to tell you about the change. The other dock was a no-go, so I have to let you off here."

Tyler took another look at the dilapidated dock. For a guy who hadn't been outside of the Harbor City metro area until he was in college, this was way out of his comfort zone. Like at least three time zones out of it. Everly stepped closer to him, her fingers gripping the boat's railing tight as she looked down at the sorry excuse for a dock.

"Will it even hold us?" she asked, looking up at the captain on her other side.

"Of course it will. Anyway, you can swim, right?" He winked at Everly and handed over an envelope to Tyler.

EVERLY AND TYLER,

SO SORRY FOR THE INCONVENIENCE, BUT YOU'LL JUST NEED TO WALK DOWN THE PATH TO THE HOUSE. DON'T WORRY ABOUT ALFRED. HE'S CURIOUS BUT HARMLESS. JUST DON'T FEED HIM OR PET HIM. HE HASN'T BITTEN ANYONE YET, BUT I'D HATE FOR ONE OF YOU TO BE THE FIRST.

CIAO,
ALBERTO

There was nothing about this that sounded good.

Tyler hated surprises; growing up where there were emotional bombshells that usually exploded and sent shrapnel everywhere on a daily basis, he had a good reason for it. He handed the note to Everly, who read it with lightning speed.

She turned to the captain, who was off-loading their bags onto the dock. "Who's Alfred?"

"Better question is *what's* Alfred," Tyler corrected, not sure he wanted to know the answer.

Captain Hank got back on board the boat, one hand on the rope tethering it to the dock.

"He's a Florida Keys raccoon and a complete mooch, so if you've got any food in your bags, you should probably leave it on the boat." He jerked his head toward the dock. "Now, stick to the path right there among the mangroves and you'll be at the house in a jiff. You can't miss it."

A few minutes later and Tyler was standing next to Everly on the dock, watching Captain Hank head back toward Key West.

"Well, let's get this over with," Everly said as she turned and picked her way across the dock, choosing each step with care in her high heels.

There was no way she was making it two miles in those shoes even if she wasn't hauling a carry-on roller bag. Correction. She could make it, probably powered on pure Riverside attitude alone.

"Here," he said, catching up with her and putting one hand on her suitcase handle. "Let me."

Her grip tightened. "I appreciate the offer, but I can do it myself."

She could and she would, but she didn't have to. Telling her that was the very last thing he should do, however.

"I don't doubt it. In fact, you could carry both the

entire two miles in those ridiculous shoes when it's a million degrees out in the shade." He reached back and pulled out his wallet, withdrawing his lucky quarter. "How about we flip for it? Whoever loses has to take both bags."

Her eyes narrowed. "I'm not carrying your bag."

"Not if you win." There, now if that wasn't enough of a challenge for her to react to, he didn't know what was.

"Fine," she huffed and set her suitcase on the ground. "Flip your grubby coin."

"It's not grubby. It's well loved." Now that didn't sound lame at all. "Heads or tails?" Not that it mattered. It was going to land on her side regardless, as much as he could add a little spin in her favor.

She crossed her arms, the move accentuating the perfect fit of the black tank dress she'd been wearing under the sweater she'd stuffed in her oversize purse when Alberto's jet had touched down. "Tails."

He adjusted the angle of his thumb and flicked the quarter in the air, caught it, and flipped it over on the back of his hand. Tails. Imagine that.

"Well, someone finally got lucky." He held out his hand. "Looks like I'll be carrying that."

She didn't seem happy at winning. In fact, the suspicion in her eyes had to be visible from the space shuttle. "I'm gonna figure out how you do that."

He shrugged. "It's just flipping a coin."

"And it always seems to go your way."

"My way?" he asked, picking up both bags by the handle because there was no way the little wheels would last on the dirt path to the house. "I'm hauling both bags."

"Which you totally didn't mean to have happen." She raised one eyebrow suspiciously.

He set his bag down and held up three fingers close together. "Scout's honor."

She shook her head, but her smile was back—the real one. "Like you were ever a Boy Scout."

"Most popcorn sold three years running." It had been his first taste of business, a chance to use his ability to read people and the situation for something other than staying the hell out of the way when tempers were short.

Everly threw back her head and laughed. "Now that doesn't surprise me at all."

The tension seeped out of his shoulders, and they headed inland together.

Chapter Sixteen

Key West wasn't what Helene expected. One, she could get an amazing Chardonnay. Two, whatever a conch was, it was delicious in a stew at the waterside restaurant they were in near Mallory Square. Three, the heat must be doing things to her head because she hadn't been so at ease in years. Perhaps that was due to being away from Harbor City for the first time since Michael died. Perhaps it was because of the company. The more time she spent around Alberto, the harder it was to maintain the crusty exterior she'd held onto out of habit, and it felt…rather good. Not that she'd admit it out loud.

"Do you think they're okay?" she asked as she looked out over the water in the general direction of Treble Key that Alberto had pointed to when they'd sat down for drinks and appetizers.

Alberto gave her an indulgent smile and poured her another glass of wine. "The captain said he dropped them off in the designated spot and everything was fine. Now we just have to wait and hope the beauty of the island works its magic."

"I'm not sure it will be that easy."

"It will. Have faith, *bellissima*."

"I hope you're right about that."

Alberto sat back in his chair, the warm breeze ruffling his hair and his aviator sunglasses giving him a rakish look. "I'm right about almost everything. For instance, I was correct in knowing that you would be the perfect partner for this endeavor."

He couldn't have really known that. The man was a hopeless flirt. Still, she found herself playing along. "And why, exactly, is that?"

"Because you like to meddle in everyone's business."

Only years of training kept her jaw from dropping. "I do not."

He waved his hands around as if he could brush her denial out of the air. "But of course you do, but you do it out of love…and boredom."

"I am never bored."

"You wouldn't be if you let me seduce you as I am trying so very hard to do."

"You're very forward."

"I'm Italian. It's in our blood." He took a sip from his wine, the movement drawing her attention to his very kissable mouth. "Plus, there's no other way for me to be when I'm around beautiful women, let alone the most beautiful woman."

"That ship sailed years ago." Sure, she'd kept herself up; she had an image to uphold. "I've aged into being regal, if one is generous."

Alberto leaned forward, propping his surprisingly toned forearms on the table. "I know this will shock you, *bellissima*, but you are wrong."

Wrong? Her? Almost never. She wasn't foolish enough to say absolutely never. Any sign of weakness, though, wasn't acceptable. A woman didn't get to her rung on the Harbor City high-society ladder by allowing for personal vulnerabilities. Time to end this little talk.

"I won't have this discussion with you."

"Why?" He drew off his sunglasses and gave her an assessing look. "Because of your Michael?"

Just the mention of his name was enough to make

her chest clench. Three years and it hadn't gotten any easier. Every room she walked through in the home they'd made together echoed with his absence. Every fund-raising event she attended was a battle of self-control not to give in to the melancholy. Every night alone only served to highlight the emptiness of their bed.

"I love..." She paused, taking a deep breath to slow her heart rate before correcting herself. "Loved... my husband."

"No one would argue that. It is as obvious as the feistiness of your nature. But was he the type of man who would want you to live out your days alone?"

Is that what she was doing? No, she wouldn't accept that. "I'm *not* alone. I have my children."

"That is not the same, *bellissima*, as you very well know."

It wasn't, but it was her life, and she wasn't about to allow some overgrown man-child with his handsome face and flirtatious ways to know that. It wasn't the Harbor City way. She played things close to the vest. Always had. Always would.

Setting down her wineglass, she pulled her most impervious mask into place and let her voice drop the temperature out on their waterside veranda. "It is enough."

"For a woman like you?" he asked, not taking her hint to drop the subject. "No."

Of all the— "And who are you to tell me what I need?"

"A man who has been in your very spot." He reached out across the table, taking her cold hands in his warm ones. "Losing my Sophia so many years ago...I thought the hurt would never go away, but it did, leaving behind an empty place in my soul. For many years, I thought it would consume me."

"Until you filled it with much younger women and wine, I suppose." Just like a man. She'd been appalled by the number of men who so casually dated around after losing a spouse. She'd never dishonor Michael's memory that way.

"No." He gently squeezed her hand, holding it firm in his as his gaze pierced her with an empathetic sincerity she hadn't expected from a man who seemed to flirt as easily as he breathed. "That place, Sophia's place, in my heart never closed up, but it changed from one of cold emptiness to a warm place filled with all the laughter and love we shared—and it happened when I let myself stop focusing on the fact that she was gone and instead began to remember how we lived."

Helene had never cried in public a day in her life. Not as a child. Definitely not as a full-grown woman. Even at Michael's funeral she'd maintained a stalwart appearance for the sake of her boys. But Alberto's heartfelt advice—though not asked for— shifted something inside her and the tears slid down her cheeks. It wasn't a waterfall, but it was enough. Slipping her hand free, she patted at her cheeks with a napkin and took several steadying breaths. When she had herself back under control, she looked at the man who understood, knowing he deserved more than a cold brush-off. He deserved the truth.

"I'm not sure I can do that," she said, her voice a little shaky. "I know it's been more than three years, but even considering moving on still feels like betrayal."

"I understand, but I hope that will change and when it does you will reach out to the bold Italian who would like nothing better than to sweep you off your feet." His face broke into a broad smile, and there was a little something extra twinkling in his eyes. "Just make sure not to wait too long; we're not getting any younger."

Despite the emotions swirling around inside her, Helene couldn't help but laugh at his audaciousness, more than a little grateful that he didn't press for more confessions. His flirting she could deal with. His quiet understanding she could not, not without losing her composure again. "No, we're not."

Alberto lifted his wine, the sunlight piercing the glass, turning it into a prism and making a rainbow on the white tablecloth. "To the tomorrows we've yet to see—may they be as wonderful as your smile and as exciting as a first kiss."

She clinked the tip of her glass against his, a weight she hadn't realized she'd been carrying lifted from her shoulders. And as they sipped their wine, both watching the ocean, she couldn't help but think that the man next to her might be onto something and that it just may be time to stop mourning in her heart and celebrate what she and Michael had had instead.

Chapter Seventeen

Everly's pinkie toes were staging a rebellion. Who'd have thought a well maintained but still dirt path on an island ninety miles off Cuba would finally be the thing to make her curse her addiction to high heels? Okay, any non-crazy person would have known that, but she hadn't been dressing for sanity this morning. She'd been putting on armor—because of the man currently walking next to her, hauling her suitcase and his as if they didn't weigh an ounce when she knew damn well hers, at least, weighed close to forty pounds.

She took another step forward, and her right heel sank into the ground and stayed there, making her lose her balance. Desperate to stay upright, she flung her arms out and clamped down on a very firm biceps. One she still hadn't seen, despite the fact that he'd been buried inside her with another part of his anatomy. The whole situation made her pissed off at herself again, but it didn't stop her body from reacting to him with a stomach flutter and a hello-there-hottie clench in her core. This was fucking ridiculous.

"You okay?"

"Fine." Holding onto him, she yanked her foot and the corresponding shoe heel out of the dirt.

"I have a pair of tennis shoes in my bag. We'd need to stuff some socks in the toes, but it might make the last mile easier."

"I said I'm fine."

She sounded like a petulant bitch. She knew this. She had to.

"What in the hell is your problem? You've been a pain in my ass since the parking garage."

"You mean since we fucked on my car?"

"Yeah. Tell me, do you have some weird disease where orgasms make you mean instead of relaxing you?"

"That's totally it, so you'd better stay away."

Of course, the skies took that cue to do one of the Florida-midday-sudden-rainstorm things. One instant it was hotter than hell, more humid than a sauna, and sunny. The next it was pouring gigantic droplets of rain, was still hotter than hell, and—weirdly enough—sunny. It made no sense.

"Come on." He swapped a bag so he was holding one under his arm and the other in his hand, then looped an arm around her waist and half walked her, half propelled her under the protection of one of the few palm trees dotting the path.

Since getting soaked to the bone wasn't on her agenda for the day, she went with it. Okay, the fact that her body had reacted with the "Hallelujah Chorus" when he'd touched her and short-circuited her brain probably helped make that happen. He set their suitcases down and shoved his fingers through his wet hair. His now partially see-through white button-down shirt clung to his chest. He'd rolled up the sleeves earlier, and she'd been tormented with some solid forearm porn during the flight. This was worse because all she wanted to do was look and touch and taste what had stayed covered the other night.

He threw open his suitcase and rummaged around in the distractingly organized interior, then pulled out a pair of Nikes and some gym socks. After flipping the lid shut again and zipping it closed, he stuffed the toes of the shoes and only then did he look back up at her. The combination of now wet black hair, determined blue eyes, and hideous footwear made her catch her breath.

He pointed to a stump next to the palm tree's trunk. "Sit."

"You don't get to order me around," she said, falling back on the one thing she could always count on, her attitude.

"Sit or I'll make you." He took a step toward her, frustration coming off him in waves, practically sizzling the rain that had the balls to land on him. "There's no way in hell you're wearing those shoes for the rest of the walk. I can actually hear your feet crying out in agony. 'Please save us, Tyler. You're our only hope.' That's what they're saying."

The Star Wars reference was what made her sit down on the uncomfortable stump that was still better than standing in her demon heels. It was funny. It surely wasn't the buzz of anticipation vibrating along every inch of her skin. "It's just the toes."

She expected him to hand her his shoes. Instead, he squatted down in front of her, wrapped his strong fingers around her left ankle, and lifted it. The gesture was intimate, more than she could handle at the moment, and she stiffened.

He let out a deep sigh but went to work on unbuckling the strap around her ankle. "I have no clue what I did to piss you off so much, but whatever it was, I'm sorry."

"I'm not mad at you."

"Really?" He undid the strap and slid off her heel. "Coulda fooled me."

The Waterbury he tried so hard to hide slipped into his speech, letting her know just how much of a bitch she was being and how unfair it was to him. "I'm not mad at *you*. I'm mad at myself."

He kept his gaze on her foot as he slid his size-twelve tennis shoe on it and began to lace it up. "Why?"

"Because…I confused fighting with foreplay. We both know nothing more could ever happen between us."

He didn't disagree. That hurt. It wasn't that she'd been expecting him to but, yeah, a little protest would have been nice. Instead, he went to work on the strap of her other shoe.

"I don't know what to say to that," he said, pulling it off and sliding on his tennis shoe.

"Then let's not." She brushed away his hand, needed desperately to regain a semblance of control, and tied the shoe herself. "I'll stop being a hag and we'll move on as if the parking garage never happened."

"The incident that will not be spoken of." The seriousness of his tone was totally ruined by the twitch of his lips as he tried not to smile.

"Now a butchered Potter reference?" She accepted his outstretched hand and stood up, her fingers tingling. "You really were a library nerd."

"I'll break out the Tolkien later," he said, not bothering to stop the smile now. "I can tell you all about the one ring and do it in Elvish."

"Oh my God." She laughed. "Please don't."

He slapped a hand over his heart. "Direct hit."

"I'm pretty sure you'll live."

He peeked out at the sky, which was a beautiful blue without any hint of its weather split personality. "You ready to do this?"

Looking down at his shoes on her feet, she wiggled her toes. It felt like heaven. "Always."

"Once more into the breach." He grabbed both bags and headed back onto the path.

Taking a few tentative steps, she followed him. It was weird to have her feet flat on the ground, and she felt way shorter than she was used to being but lighter, too. Maybe she and Tyler could find a way to go from being warring parties to one-time lovers to actual friends. In the moment, it totally sounded plausible. Of course, that was if she ignored the fact that she was walking behind him just to watch that glorious ass of his as he trudged forward.

Girl, you're officially a hot mess.

Tyler spent the last mile tormenting Everly with Elvish—or at least what she thought was Elvish. Since ninth grade had been a long time ago, he'd improvised. She didn't seem to notice, judging by her fits of giggles. Now that was something he hadn't expected. His hard-ass Riverside girl was a giggler.

Your Riverside girl? That was so wrong on so many levels. One, she most definitely wasn't a girl. She had the brains and body of a full-grown woman, a fact that hadn't gone unnoticed by his dick giving him the uncomfortable knowledge of what it felt like to walk a mile with a semi. Two, she wasn't his. As she'd so kindly pointed out, there wasn't anywhere for the intense attraction between them to go. Not that he was looking for a Mrs. Jacobson just yet, but he'd worked too hard to shake off the last vestiges of Waterbury to have her bring it all back. And she did a little more each time they hung out, not just the speech but the overwhelming urge to haul her up and fuck her hard against the nearest available flat surface. Or horizontal. Or just about anywhere. That had never happened with any of the Harbor City women he'd dated, which was for the best. It let him focus on what was really important—solidifying his position.

"Oh wow," Everly said in an excited whisper,

coming to a stop in front of the gate leading to Alberto's island home.

He couldn't have put it better. Shaped like the Pentagon, the two-story house had solar panels on the roof, warm soft-brown wood, and windows everywhere. There was a kidney-shaped pool next to it, a luxurious fire pit, and a hammock big enough for two. It almost made him want to chuck it all and move.

"It's gorgeous." She swung open the gate and walked inside.

He followed, and they strolled across the stamped concrete patio to the French doors leading into the house. He punched in the security code provided at the bottom of Alberto's note and they walked inside. It was cool but not frigid—a miracle in South Florida with how everyone blasted the AC—and the interior matched the exterior, making the whole thing look like a rich person's version of Swiss Family Robinson.

Setting down the suitcases on the bamboo floor, a little cloud of dust floated upward.

She glanced at her dirty suitcase. "We should clean up. I don't want to wreck the place before Alberto and Helene even get here tomorrow."

Of course, the first image to appear in his head was of her naked and soapy in the shower. "That's a great idea."

It would be better if he was in the shower with her, but that wasn't going to happen. They were going to do this whole pretend-it-didn't-happen thing instead. That sounded about as much fun as experiencing the Red Wedding firsthand.

They headed up to the second floor. She took the first bedroom. He took the next. He was shucking off his shoes when he heard the shower go on. Hello, insta-boner.

His imagination didn't have to do a lot of work to picture her in there with the warm water trailing over her skin. He hadn't gotten to look as long as he wanted the other night, and God knew he hadn't gotten to touch or taste her enough, but that didn't matter in the moment. His horny brain filled in all the missing pieces. The part that almost killed him was the image of big white soap bubbles sliding across her pretty peach nipples. They'd gotten so hard the other night, and her moans of pleasure were so hot that—

Stop acting like a fourteen-year-old perv, Jacobson.

He stomped into his room's private bathroom, stripped down, and turned the water on full blast. Then, for good measure, he turned the knob all the way to cold. If a little hypothermia didn't make things better, then he wasn't sure what would. Twenty shivery minutes later and he was in a T-shirt and board shorts, convinced he could spend a night alone with Everly and not have another parking-garage moment. Why? Because she'd been right, and sex would only complicate the truce they'd been able to make.

That certainty lasted right up until he walked into the kitchen to find her in a flowy white sundress that covered her completely down to the ankles except when she stepped in front of one of the large windows overlooking the pool and the sun outlined exactly what she was hiding underneath the miles of cotton. Yep. Mr. Semi was back. Needing very badly not to be looking at her right now, he hustled over to the fridge and opened it.

"I know it's early, but I'm starving." He spotted eggs, cheese, milk, and green onions. "How do you feel about omelets for dinner?"

"You're *not* thinking of cooking."

He stood up and looked at her over the fridge

door. She was still in front of the window basking in the island sun, and he was still getting a very good look—unknown to her—at what he could never again touch. It wasn't a gut punch, but his dick wasn't too happy about it. "Why not?"

She crossed her arms and one eyebrow went up. "You do remember the pasta the other night?"

That had been a six on a ten-point scale of epic kitchen disasters, barely a blip, so it hadn't fazed him. Now the time he'd forgotten the bacon in the oven until it had turned into charcoal briquettes? That had put him off bacon for a good month.

"This is eggs," he said. "Totally different."

"Oh yeah, I'm well aware of your"—she made air quotes—"talent with eggs."

Okay, so he'd overcooked some scrambled eggs to the point that the smell had taken over the apartment and lingered for a week.

"So does that mean you're cooking?"

She snorted and started toward him. "Not likely. How about sandwiches?"

He checked out the contents of the fridge. "You good with ham and cheese on rye?"

"Sounds perfect."

He gathered up the ingredients and laid them out on the island, and from there they fell into sandwich assembly. She sliced the romaine while he assembled the sandwiches. It was mellow, relaxed even as they laughed about the walk to the house, and he didn't set off a single fire alarm. Afterward, he gathered up the sandwich plates while she grabbed a couple of beers and they headed over to the sliding glass doors leading out to the pool and the fire pit.

Everly jerked to a stop in front of him. "Tyler, what in the hell is that?"

Since he'd been distracted by watching her ass as she moved, he had no idea what she was talking about. "What?"

"There, pacing in front of the sliding doors."

It was a raccoon, but way smaller than the thirty-pound bruisers that roamed Central Square Park. Leaner and narrower than the raccoons he was used to, this guy couldn't weigh more than an average house cat, and its fur was a light grayish-brown color. And he was standing on his back paws with his five-fingered paws pressed against the glass. He wasn't looking at them, though; this guy's eyes were trained on their sandwiches.

"My guess is Alfred."

Her face lost some of its color. "So we eat inside?"

He walked toward the sliding door, and Alfred took a few steps back but stayed standing on his hind legs. "Don't tell me you're afraid of something the size of a cat."

"It could be rabid." Everly took a few cautious steps toward the door, her attention glued to the hungry bandit on the other side.

He jiggled the door handle before sliding it open a few inches. The raccoon scurried back to the underbrush on the other side of the pool, disappearing from sight. Tyler stepped outside, the island's Florida heat more caressing than beating this time. Everly didn't follow, but she did poke her head out, looking each way as if a band of rabid zombie raccoons was just waiting for the perfect moment to pounce.

"Alberto promised he was harmless," Tyler said with a laugh and sat down in one of the nearby patio chairs, setting the sandwich plates on the small table between it and another chair.

"Uh-huh." She didn't take a step forward. "I'm sure

someone said that about every serial killer at some point before he started offing everyone."

Was it wrong to be enjoying this new, unexpected side to Everly? Because he was. The woman had an amazing capacity to surprise him—something he was beginning to enjoy far more than a chess player like him should.

"Come on, I'll protect you, Ms. 3B—and anyway, the sandwiches are out here, and if you don't come out, you can't eat."

Her stomach let out an audible growl. Victory was his.

"You know there's more food inside the house, Mr. 2B."

"Come on, live a little," he teased.

She took another suspicious look to her left and then her right before finally stepping outside into the sunshine. The breeze played with the hem of her skirt, lifting one corner of it around her calves—the ones he'd felt on his back as he'd fucked her against the trunk of her car. Shit. This was going to be a long, hard lunch.

"I'm warning you now," she said as she sat down, obviously oblivious to the path his thoughts had gone down. "If Alfred comes back with his murderous buddies, I'll take you out at the knees to get inside first."

Tyler laughed and accepted the beer she held out to him. "I would expect nothing less."

Because when it came to Everly, the best bet was to accept he never knew what to expect.

Chapter Eighteen

As Everly popped the last bite of one half of her sandwich into her mouth, her gaze still scanning the periphery for movement, she relaxed back against her seat and lifted her feet to rest them on the stool in front of her chair. The early evening sun warming her skin as she listened to the sound of the ocean breeze fluttering the palm tree leaves and the occasional chirp and call of birds somewhere out on the island. The combination mellowed the worry about Alfred right out of her.

"You could forget the rest of the world even existed out here," she said, giving in to the vibe and closing her eyes.

"It's like the Garden of Eden," Tyler said.

The absence of sight only accentuated the sexiness of his voice. The cultured tones hiding—almost completely—the rough and tumble accent underneath. The conflicting combination did dangerous things to her, the kind that led to banging him in the parking garage.

Before that memory could take over, she jerked her focus back to the here and now. "Just with a raccoon instead of a snake."

"Poor Alfred, hated before he's even had a chance to introduce himself."

The temptation to open her eyes and read Tyler's face was strong, but there was an intimacy to having a chat with your eyes closed that she didn't want to give up. "You have a lot of sympathy for that fur ball."

"I know how it feels to be prejudged."

There was a lot of weight behind those words, but their tentative truce wasn't made for seeking greater understanding. They were both just trying to get through the weekend.

"So you're saying I should give him a chance, huh?" she asked, and reached over to the small table between them for the other half of her sandwich, but instead of bread and meat, she encountered something fuzzy.

The scream was out of her mouth before she could even open her eyes and jump out of her chair, adrenaline pumping through her veins like a runaway train. In the next inhale, her feet were on the ground, her eyes open, and she spotted Alfred stuffing as much of her sandwich into his mouth while staring at her like she was the one invading *his* space. And this was why city people shouldn't leave their home environment. Nature was a beast. Her exhale started out as another holler, but before she could gain steam, Tyler scooped her up into his arms and marched her into the house, all the while laughing his stupid head off. After using his foot to slide the door closed behind them, he set her down on the island but kept his strong hands on her hips and stood between her legs.

"It's not nice to laugh at people," she said, needing to say something—anything—because the need for fight or flight was quickly morphing into an F need of a different kind.

"I can't help it," he said, his gaze dropping to her mouth, then the pulse point going crazy in her neck, then dropping down to the fast rise and fall of her chest before coming back up to her eyes. "The ferocious Ms. 3B is afraid of a raccoon."

"They can be vicious," she said, anticipation making her mouth move faster than her brain. "Anyway, it's not like there aren't things that scare you."

"Needles." It was just one word, but it came out low and husky.

"So no tats, huh? I thought they were required of anyone who rode a Harley." If only she'd gotten him naked in the garage, she wouldn't have to ask.

He shook his head, his desire-darkened gaze locked on her. "Not one."

"So you've never been tempted to have a woman's name written above your heart?" Ramble? Her? Oh yeah.

"That would be a big negative for a lot of reasons."

"I promise to keep your secret, if you keep mine." She made an *X* with her finger over her heart.

His gaze dropped to where her finger touched the upper swell of her breast. Her heart was slamming against her ribs, and there was no way he could miss seeing her hard nipples pressed against the soft cotton of her dress, especially since she'd skipped her bra along with her panties. She didn't need Freud to understand what that meant.

His grip tightened on her hips and he jerked her closer, bringing her flush against his hardness and holding her there. "Now that's a deal."

The contact was like flipping a switch, and her body was suddenly *on*. Her breasts grew heavy, her lungs tightened, her lips ached to make contact. Desire, hot and needy, slid through her, making her core clench, and she unconsciously arched against him, needing the friction to ease the ache already beginning to build. His tortured groan only emboldened her, and she did it again, this time on purpose, loving how he felt against her and the way lust darkened his blue eyes and made his jaw tight. He was holding back. The urge to make him let go guided her fingers to the waistband of his board shorts where she let them linger, torturing both of them.

"You better not tell anyone I'm scared of raccoons." The words spilled out of her mouth because her brain had shut down. There was too much going on in her body right now for actual thinking.

"Talking to other people about raccoons is not what's on my mind right now." His palms slid down the outside of her thighs to the edge of her dress, and he started pushing it up, not stopping until everything was exposed from her ankles to her upper thighs.

"Oh yeah?" There was a hopeful breathiness to her voice, one she normally wouldn't let anyone hear, but she was too turned on to care. "What is?"

"How you're going to look bent over this island with your dress pulled up to your waist while I slide my cock into your wet pussy." His hands glided under her scrunched-up skirt, thumb so close to where she needed him to touch that she could feel the heat from him, but he stopped short. "And it is wet for me, isn't it?"

The *yes* nearly popped out of her mouth before she managed to seal her lips shut. She shouldn't. Together she and Tyler were nothing but trouble. Still…she was alone on a tropical island paradise with a devastatingly hot man who knew just how to use his mouth, hands, and that glorious cock of his. Maybe just this once…

"Why don't you find out for yourself how wet it is?"

Something sparked in his blue eyes, an acknowledgment of the challenge of the fight between them. It might be friendly but it was still there, that push and pull of want and need and knowing that it was the last thing either of them should give in to. They were oil and water together, but it didn't matter because they were both burning right now.

"Because you're gonna show me," he said, his voice

dropping an octave and his accent coming on as if he couldn't control that and his body at the same time.

"And what are you gonna show *me*?" She dipped her fingertips into the waistband of his board shorts, pushing them down far enough that the backs of her fingers brushed the tight curls above his cock but, like him, she avoided brushing the good stuff—and there was lots of long, hard, good stuff straining for her touch.

"Whatever you wanna see." His hands stayed put on her inner thighs but his mouth got busy, trailing a line of hot kisses down her neck.

"Strip." Because that's what she'd missed out on last time, and if this was going to happen again—and get real, it was—she wasn't going to miss out on seeing him naked twice. The kiss-nip-kiss pattern halted, and she could actually feel him smile against her skin. Cocky bastard. "Now."

He withdrew his hands from her legs, leaving her wet and wanting, and took a half step back. The protective inch of air between them should have been a relief, but it only served to emphasize how badly she wanted this man. He reached back and grabbed the neck of his T-shirt behind his head and yanked it over, letting it fall to the floor. Her breath caught but her gaze kept moving, going from his broad shoulders, to his muscular chest, to the smattering of black hair that started right below his belly button and disappeared beneath his shorts. She wanted to hop down and trace that happy trail with her fingers and tongue until she got to the prize at the end. She wanted to lick and nip and kiss her way around his sinewy chest. She wanted to make him hers.

As if reading her mind, he stepped closer, bringing them back so they fit together perfectly even if there were way too many clothes still in the way. "Wait, there's something I gotta do first." His hands cupped her face and his mouth crashed down onto hers in a kiss that wasn't about satisfaction for either of them but desperation on both their parts.

His hands moved from her face to her breasts, cupping them through the cotton of her dress. It wasn't enough. It never was with him, though, because she always wanted more. What could she say? When it was this good, she got greedy. Tyler broke the kiss, and his mouth followed the path his hand had taken. He lifted up her breast, his thumb circling her nipple over the dress until it formed a hard peak and then he sucked it into his mouth, letting his teeth graze the sensitive spot all the while his talented fingers worked her other breast. When he switched from one to the other, leaving the wet material clinging to her pebbled nipple, the shock of his warm mouth on one and the quickly cooling damp sensation of the other had her reaching for him, needing to anchor herself to him as he tormented her in the most delicious of ways.

"Yes," she managed to get out in a moan as she threaded her fingers through his thick hair.

Pain in the ass that he was, he pulled away. "You like that, huh?"

"God, yes." And she'd like more.

"What else do you like?" His hands dropped to her bare thighs and he shoved her skirt up to her waist, leaving her exposed to his hot gaze. Then he spread her thighs wide as she sat on the island, watching as if the image of her like this was the best thing he'd ever seen.

She expected more teasing, more talk. Instead he jerked her ass so it was barely on the island at the same time as he lowered himself down so he was on the same level as her wet folds. When he lowered his mouth, licking and sucking her intimately, it was all she could do not to fall off the side of the world. She was so turned on, so ready for him that even the softest lash of his tongue had her on edge. When he sucked her clit into his mouth while working her entrance with his fingers, she just gave in and let herself tumble over into space.

"Fuck, I love how you hold tight to my fingers." He curled them inside her, rubbing the bundle of nerves there in a soft-soft-hard pattern that had her panting. "I can't wait to taste you when you come, and then I'm going to do what I promised and fuck you over this island."

Then he went back to tonguing her, sucking her, finger fucking her until she was right on the edge of the abyss. It was blissful torture that she couldn't get enough of as the vibrations built inside her, turning her entire body electric. So close. So fucking close.

"Don't stop," she cried as she tightened her grip on his hair and arched her back just enough to change the angle the slightest bit and everything went white for half a second before her orgasm hit, exploding her world into neon.

Watching Everly come down from that high was as amazing as it was agonizing, because as sweet as it was to see her shatter, Tyler was desperate to bury himself inside her and feel her come again right before he went over the edge himself. By the time her breath had steadied, his board shorts were on the ground and he was rolling on the condom he'd grabbed from his wallet.

"I might never move again," Everly said, her voice husky.

She still wasn't naked, and he wanted that. Needed

it. Having her mostly naked in the parking garage had been one of the hottest things he'd ever seen in his life, but he wanted to see and touch every inch of her. The plan had been to just flip up her skirt—there was just something sexy about Everly in disarray that turned him on—but that wasn't gonna happen. He picked her up off the island and lifted the dress over her head, leaving her naked and proud before him.

"You like what you see?" she asked, but she wasn't fishing for compliments. She knew he did. She just wanted to push him. They both knew it.

He traced a finger over the upper swell of her tits, entranced by the way her nipples tightened into hard pebbles without his even touching them. "You bet I do."

"Good, because I like what I see." She stepped out of his reach and circled him, making a *tsk-tsk* sound when he started to turn to face her. "Oh no. I missed out on this before; I want to see the entire package."

On the next breath, her lips were on him. His back. His shoulders. Part of his neck that he'd never given two thoughts to before. Then, when his dick was in a mixed state of misery at not being touched and ecstasy because of the anticipation, she brought her body flush against his back, reached around, and encircled his dick with her hand. With one hand stroking his cock and the other roaming his body, touching and teasing him, he was skating on the brink and there was no way he was coming without being deep inside her.

"Enough." It came out more as a growl than a word, but she got his message.

And when he whirled around and spun her so they traded places and she stood between him and the island, she looked at him with lust-filled eyes and tugged her bottom lip between her teeth.

"You know what I want," he said.

"You're so demanding."

"You have no fucking idea. Turn around."

She did—slowly, degree by degree—and then lifted herself up on her tiptoes, her legs spread wide, and bent over the island. Jesus. It was almost enough to make him come on the spot. She looked fucking beautiful. She *was* beautiful and confident and so willing to play the games that he loved because she loved them, too. That little upstairs neighbor/downstairs neighbor war of theirs *had* been foreplay that had led them to the other night in the parking garage and today.

"Don't make me wait, 2B."

Smart-ass. He smacked her on the butt. "Patience, sugar."

But he wasn't patient anymore, either. He lined himself up with her wet welcome and slid in without preamble, going at her as steadily as he could, considering every instinct in him was screaming for him to fuck her hard and fast, make her his. God, she was tight. Not giving in to the urge to drive forward was killing him, but he wanted to savor the curve of her spine, the lift of her hips as she rose to meet him, and the soft sigh of a moan when he finally sank balls-deep into her.

If he was a better man, he would have stayed there longer, drawn it out, but she did this figure-eight thing with her hips and he was lost. Keeping one hand clamped onto her hip, he reached forward with the other and rolled her hard nipple between two fingers, pulling the peak just enough to make her gasp with pleasure. Releasing her nipple, he grabbed her chin and quickly turned her face to the side so he could capture her lips. He plunged his tongue inside her sweet mouth, tasting her like that while he was buried inside her, his cock aching for release. Letting her go, he reached between them, brushing his fingers across her swollen clit. She bucked in response, her walls tightening around him.

"Yeah, that's it, sugar." He circled her clit with his middle finger, adding just enough pressure to make her cry out in pleasure. "You're gonna come again."

Plunging inside her and withdrawing, he kept his pace steady while increasing the speed and pressure of his finger until she cried out and her spine bowed as she came with his name on her lips. She squeezed him, milked him, and it was too much. There was no holding back now. Grabbing onto her hips, he yanked her back and forth against him in time with each thrust and retreat. It was intense and fast and borderline rough—but she gave it back just as hard. In and out, he thrust deep inside her, each stroke taking him higher and higher until the pleasure bordered on pain it was so intense. It was so damn good.

"Everly," he managed to get out right as his climax crashed into him, and he buried himself balls-deep in her and let go.

When he could open his eyes again, he realized he was practically squashing her against the island. Withdrawing, he apologized before slipping off the used condom and tossing it into the garbage.

He watched her carefully as she grabbed her dress from the ground and slipped it on. She wasn't talking. He didn't like that. Everly always had a lot to say. It was quiet Everly who was dangerous.

"Everything okay?" he asked, floundering around for something better to say.

"Don't worry, I'm not freaking out," she said, turning to look him up and down. "Just trying to figure out if this should happen again."

"I vote yes." A million times yes.

She laughed. "I'm so surprised."

"How about this?" He grabbed his wallet from the kitchen floor and took out his lucky quarter. "How about we flip for it? Heads we keep going like this for just as long as it's fun. Tails, we walk away, no harm no foul."

"Only as long as it's fun?" she asked, strutting over to him.

"Exactly." Now this was the kind of deal he excelled at. Everyone walked away a winner.

She thought it over for a second and nodded. "Flip."

He did and just as the coin started to make its downward turn, Everly reached up and snatched it out of the air.

"Heads," she said without even looking at it.

"That wasn't a complete coin toss."

Her only answer was a slight shrug of her shoulders as she turned and walked to the stairs, stopping just long enough to take off her dress again. Finally using that high IQ of his for good, he kept his mouth shut and followed her lead by leaving his shorts and T-shirt on the kitchen floor.

Chapter Nineteen

The sun bouncing off the ocean snuck in through the narrow opening between the hotel room curtains and tried its best to burrow into Helene Carlyle's brain. A morning person she was not and never had been. She turned away from the window only to encounter a broad back and a head of silver hair snuggled into the pillow next to hers.

The pieces came together in thrilling detail. The wine followed by a walk through the downtown area. Then there was dinner filled with more laughter than she'd experienced in a while as Alberto regaled her with stories about the trials and tribulations of working in a hotel. He'd started off as a bellboy and had spent his life working hard to get to the point where he could not only buy the company but expand it into seven countries. It was so much different than her life. She'd been born into privilege and bred to adhere to the Harbor City elite code. Then there had been a ghost tour, then more drinks, and a stop at a clothing-optional rooftop bar. She hadn't taken anything off, but it was definitely eye-opening. Finally, he walked her back to her hotel room. She'd invited him in for a nightcap and…now she was waking up with a naked man in her bed.

She should feel guilty—she was still wearing her wedding ring after all—but she didn't. She felt…as if she'd crossed into new territory and it was exhilarating. That annoyed her. What if her boys found out? What would Michael say? Okay, that was a dumb question because he'd been gone for more than three years, but it still landed with an ice-cold *kerplop* in the middle of her chest because so much of what she did now centered around how she thought Michael would react. It was enough of a wake-up call to clear out any of the cobwebs and propel her into action.

Sitting up and taking the sheet with her, holding it close to her bare chest, she poked a finger into Alberto's shoulder. "You have to go now."

He rolled over, looking mussed and more than a little devastating. He gave her a sleepy grin but didn't make a move to get out of bed. "Good morning, *bellissima*."

"Go on." She poked him again. "Scoot."

Instead of getting out of bed, he sat up, letting the sheet pool around his waist, and took her hand, then landed a kiss in the center of her palm. "Such fire first thing in the morning. I love it. Are you nervous? You weren't last night."

Electricity zinged out from the center of her palm and up her arm, making her nipples pebble under the sheet. "I'm never nervous."

His gaze dropped to her breasts, desire darkening his chocolate-brown eyes, before his attention traveled back up to her face, her mouth in particular. "You know it's all right."

Flustered by the unexplainable rise in temperature in the room, she tried to maintain as much dignity as possible while naked in bed with the first man she'd slept with since Michael died who *insisted* on thinking she wanted him to flirt with her—which she most definitely did not. She gave him the haughtiest look she could muster in her condition. "What is?"

"That we made love." He trailed the back of his hand down her arm, the tip of one finger nearly brushing her puckered nipple.

"I know that." Heat flamed in her cheeks while desire slid like warm honey through her. "I'm not an idiot."

He shrugged and settled back against the pillows. "But you are a worrier, and right now you are worried about what others would think if they knew."

The fact that he could read her so easily annoyed her. "You're wrong."

"Yes?" He leaned over and kissed her, his lips strong and demanding. "Then come to the Great Openings Gala with me when we return to Harbor City."

A date? Her? At one of the events she always used to go to with Michael? The fact that it was as much of a temptation as it was worried her. Damn it. She hated that Alberto had pegged her so perfectly. It brought out the stubbornness she usually laid at Michael's feet when it was Sawyer or Hudson displaying it.

"I already have a date."

"One of your sons?" He scoffed. "That doesn't count as a date."

She knew that. She'd told Hudson that specifically before he'd met Felicia, when he'd insisted on dragging his mother to events. At the time, she'd been trying to continue her mourning period well beyond when most people thought she should have been back to her normal self. She hadn't been, but the public outings had brought back some of the joy she thought she'd lost forever. Was she ready for another boundary crossing like that? Was she ready for a date? If someone had asked her before last night, she would have told them no. After last night? She wasn't so sure. And *that* really worried her.

Not sure what to do with the unfamiliar sensation

of her own indecision, she fell back on what she knew best—ordering people around. "You can go now."

If he was offended, Alberto didn't show it. In fact, he seemed to see right through her brusque manner for what it really was, a set of defenses. Giving her a knowing smile, he got out of bed, completely at ease with strutting around her hotel room naked, his back and butt a testament to his workout regime, and strolled through the room picking up his clothes where they'd dropped last night. Once he was dressed, he returned to the bed, placing a hand on the mattress next to her hip and leaning down.

"*Bellissima*," he said, his breath warm and sweet against her skin. "We'll make arrangements when we return home."

Anticipation skittered across her skin. "I didn't say yes."

"But you will." He kissed her, strong and sure.

Alberto was too sure of himself by half, but—in this instant—he had no reason to be. Because she couldn't say yes, and what would happen after that? She couldn't even begin to guess.

Chapter Twenty

After Key West, the pre-winter chill hit a little bit harder when they returned a few days later to Harbor City with the art to be sold categorized and Alberto having stated his interest in hearing more about Tyler's hotel expansion ideas and passing them along to the hotel board. Heading down Delancey Street with a bag full of groceries, Everly hunched her shoulders against the blast of wind cold enough to send the urban rats scurrying for shelter. The quicker she could get into her building, the sooner she could dig her wooly socks out from her dresser's bottom drawer and defrost her toes. Of course, that wasn't the only way she was hoping to warm up. There was a certain man in 2B who got her hot without even trying. Her Spidey sense tingled to life half a second before a deep, masculine voice hit her like a blast of the tropics. Forget wooly socks, she needed to go put on shorts and a tank top.

"I'll carry that right up to my place," Tyler said as his long legs brought him even with her.

"These are *my* groceries," she shot back, relishing the easy teasing between them after another rough visit with her nunni.

He reached over and plucked the paper bag out of her arms, giving her a wink that would have decimated her panties if she'd been wearing any. "It's easier for me to cook for you if there's food in my apartment."

"Oh no." She'd let him carry the bag the final block and up the three flights of stairs, but he wasn't gonna end her that way. "You're not cooking for me. I have a lot to live for."

His booming laugh warmed her as they stopped in front of their building and she punched in the entry code. For the first time since she walked out of the Lakeland Community Center with Nunni's warning to her — well, to her mom, really — to watch out for the wrong kind of man, some of the tension leaked out of her shoulders. Tyler completely fit Nunni's description of the wrong kind of man. He was a schemer, a plotter, a man intent on turning himself into the perfect Harbor City Richie Rich. Of course none of that mattered in their situation because it wasn't like her mother's. No one was falling in love and no one was going to get hurt. It was just some fun, nothing more.

"Does it make a difference if we won't be alone?" he asked as they headed up the stairs.

"You're moving on to cooking-related murderer with a partner?"

He flipped her off with a laugh. "No, I hired a cooking instructor."

She slammed to a stop on the second-floor landing. "No way."

"Yes way," he said. "And I need a taster."

Everly had no clue what Tyler was up to, but he was definitely up to something. The man never did anything without a plan. "What made you decide on this?"

"This horrible upstairs neighbor of mine keeps complaining," he said as he carried her groceries down the hall on a direct path for his apartment.

Yeah, that sounded about right. She had complained — a lot — to the building's owner, who had just happened to turn out to be her can't-cook-a-thing downstairs nemesis. Funny how life turned out sometimes. Her gaze dropped to his ass as he turned to unlock his door. Good Lord. One of these days she was going to snag that lucky quarter of his and just bounce it off his buns. Now *that* was a coin flip she would enjoy whether she won or lost.

Determined to play along with their little game rather than give in to the urge to jump him in the hallway, neighbors be damned, Everly said, "What a bitch your neighbor must be."

He unlocked his door, turned, and looked at her. "She has her positives."

"Oh yeah, like what?" Fishing for compliments? Her? Okay, totally.

Tyler stepped closer. The paper bag crinkled, and there was enough heat in his gaze that the grocery bag being crushed between them should have caught fire. "This thing she does with her tongue."

That thing? Oh yeah, it had made his eyes roll back in his head, so of course she'd done it again. And again. And again. Key West had been fun, that was for sure.

Everly dropped her voice to a conspiratorial whisper. "She only does that in Florida, from what I hear."

He *tsk-tsk*ed. "Saddest news I've heard all day."

The sound of someone singing off-key about having friends in low places filtered out from his apartment, snagging her attention. "Did you really hire a cooking coach?"

He took a step back and pushed open the door, and the most delicious scents in the world came wafting out of his apartment. "Come on in and find out."

The tomatoey, garlicky aroma was the smell equivalent of when someone cancels plans when all she wanted to do was stay home anyway. In other words, it smelled like heaven. The man in the WHAT'S COOKIN'? T-shirt and khaki shorts despite the blustery weather outside was instantly recognizable to anyone with a stomach in Harbor City and probably outside of it, too. Heath Hostile was a bad-boy chef who started out as a short-order cook at a diner and ended up running one of the most successful trio of restaurants on the East Coast, one of which—Wheat & Rye—was in Harbor City. He had his own TV show where he went and rescued failing restaurants.

A little starstruck, she turned to Tyler, who was still holding her groceries. "Why is the guy from *Hostile Takeover* in your kitchen?"

Tyler shrugged and put the grocery bag on the island. "I'm a silent partner in his restaurants."

"And *I'm* the only one who can stomach your cooking." Heath gave her a wave before returning to the simmering pot on the stove.

Okay, this was a secret she needed to learn. "How in the world do you manage to do that?"

"Iron stomach." Heath patted his flat stomach. "And you must be the mystery woman Frankie was talking about."

She turned to Tyler and raised one eyebrow. "Mystery woman?"

"Ignore him," he said, shooting a glare Heath's way. "He's an idiot about everything but food."

"Speaking of which, tell me there's pasta in that bag," Heath said. "It's almost time to put the pasta on now that your sauce has been simmering for four hours."

Tyler dug around in her grocery bag and pulled out the spaghetti, holding it up like a trophy.

"You made the sauce?" Everly asked, too shocked to think much about the proprietary way he had rooted through her groceries. "No way. He had to have helped."

"Only if you count yelling as helping."

"Welcome to my world, buddy," Heath said. "If you

can't take a little heat, get out of the kitchen."

And for the next two hours, they didn't. The three of them laughed and told bullshit stories and watched as Tyler finally boiled the perfect pasta—on his fourth try—before eating the best dinner she'd ever had in her life. By the time Heath left, they were down two bottles of red and she was more than ready to work off some of those delicious carbs in the best way possible.

She set her half-empty wineglass down on the island and started on the buttons of her black blouse. Tyler didn't say a word, his wineglass in a holding pattern halfway to his lips as he watched her fingers with rapt attention. Good. That was just how she wanted him—enthralled.

"That is the kind of meal that deserves a thank-you."

He set his glass down with a *thunk* on the island. "Any way in particular that you're thinking of?"

Forearms pressed against the island countertop, she leaned forward enough that her blouse gaped open, giving him an excellent view of her lace-covered breasts. "I've got this thing I can do with my tongue."

Now that jerked his gaze up to her face.

"God yes." It came out like a slow prayer, but he moved fast.

His mouth came down on hers, both of their clothes magically disappeared, and a few hours, days, weeks— who in the hell knew—later they both had pasta sauce splattered on places it normally would never touch and were too sated and exhausted to care.

She swiped her finger through a line of red sauce smeared on his shoulder and sucked it off. "I'll never look at pasta the same again."

"Makes two of us, sugar." Tyler stood up and tossed her over his shoulder like a caveman claiming his woman and headed down the hallway leading to his bedroom. "Now let me soap you off before I drag you to bed with me for round two."

"Whatever the chef wants," she responded, and smacked him on his perfect, round ass, laughing all the way to the shower.

Tyler hadn't ever brought anyone—let alone a woman—to Frankie Hartigan's poker night. Then again, he'd never had someone like Everly to bring. The other women he dated would have taken one look at the one-story bungalow across the harbor from their penthouses and asked to go back home. Everly had made herself at home the second Frankie's twin brother, Finian, had opened the door and asked her to marry him. She'd told the hulking firefighter that she'd had a wedding dress in cold storage for years just waiting for him. He'd immediately broken out into a cold sweat, which was the only thing that kept Tyler from coldcocking one of his oldest friends. Sure, he would have felt bad afterward, but even the idea of the other guy touching Everly had his Waterbury up.

"You're not really here with this idiot, are you?" Finian asked, busting Tyler's balls as usual.

"It's totally a pity date," Everly said with a wink.

The other man threw back his head and laughed, curled an arm around Everly, and pulled her into the house he shared with Frankie, calling out to everyone assembled that Tyler had finally found himself a keeper.

He hadn't, but the idea didn't scare him nearly as much as it should have. They'd agreed on the island that they were just keeping it casual. They knew exactly where they stood—a little fun, some good times, and no strings attached. That was all it could be, and they both knew it.

So why is the fact that Finian is touching her getting your hackles up?

Tyler shoved the unnerving thought to the back of his brain and put on his game face. Poker night with the Hartigans was a serious affair. They didn't play for money. Nope. It was all pride and bragging rights.

"Everyone, this is Everly Ribinski," Finian said, addressing the assembled bunch of Hartigans. "That big carrottop is my twin and fellow firefighter, Frankie; obviously we're not identical because I'm so much prettier. That card shark over there is Fallon. She's an emergency room nurse, but don't let the Florence Nightingale thing fool ya, she's been known to bluff on a total bust of a hand. And over in the corner on his phone as if he were saving the world instead of ordering six pizzas is our baby brother, Ford. He's a cop, but we try not to hold the fact that he didn't grow up to be a firefighter against him."

Ford flipped off his brother.

Fallon rolled her eyes. "Oh my God, Finian, don't scare the girl."

"I'm not scaring her," Finian said. "I'm welcoming her to the crazy."

"Well, if she came with Tyler, she's already used to that," Fallon said with a laugh. "You wanna beer? You're gonna need it to deal with all the testosterone."

Everly smiled. "I'd love one, thanks."

And just like that, the Hartigans welcomed her into the monthly cutthroat family poker night. After she'd won the third hand in the row, they were asking him if he'd brought a hustler. She took the ribbing in stride. That was the thing with Everly—she always did. The woman did not get fazed. She had a comeback for every teasing insult and a laugh for every joke. If he wasn't already fucking her every chance he got, he'd be damn jealous as hell of the guy who got to.

That was probably why he'd folded on a full house and again on a flush. His attention sidetracked every time she twirled a silky strand of dark hair around her finger and he got mesmerized by her mouth every time she took a sip of beer. He'd never wanted to be a beer bottle in his life, but the was before he'd seen her drink from one.

"Holy hell, T," Frankie said a few hours later in the kitchen when they were grabbing another round of beers. "Where did you find her and does she have a sister? Or better yet, has she figured out that she can do better than you yet?"

Tyler twisted off the cap on one of the beers with a little more force than necessary. "If she has, she sure wouldn't be going for you."

"And this is the one who's been driving you nuts?"

"The very one." Only now she was driving him to distraction.

"So how did all of this happen?"

Tyler took a long drink, taking the time to remind himself that Frankie loved nothing more than giving him shit just like Tyler did to him. "This?"

"Getting serious with Everly."

"We're not. We're just having some fun."

The look Frankie gave him was as close to pitying as the man could do. "Uh-huh."

"What's that supposed to mean?" he asked, as if he didn't know the answer.

"I guess I just missed all the other times when you brought a woman you were just having some fun with to poker night."

"Very funny." Yeah, the redheaded giant was a fucking comedian.

"I'm a riot." Frankie grinned. "That's why the ladies all love me."

"Right up until they want to nut punch you."

"Pretty much." He grabbed four of the beers, two in each hand, and gave Tyler a serious look. "You sure it's nothing serious between you and Everly?"

He nodded and forced his voice to remain neutral. "Completely."

"So you wouldn't care if I asked her out?"

The rush of *oh hell no* burned Tyler up from the inside out, and he took a step forward before it had even registered what he was doing. "Don't you fucking dare."

"Just having some fun, huh?" Frankie asked with a laugh and strolled back out into the other room.

Tyler grabbed the other two beers but stood in the kitchen sucking in some deep breaths and telling himself to get his shit under control. The competition of poker night must have been what had brought that reaction out in him. It had to be. He and Everly really were just having fun. That's all it could be, and he was good with that. More than good. He was fucking thrilled.

The next cooking class happened at Wheat & Rye's restaurant kitchen Saturday morning before it opened. Everly sat at the special VIP table in the corner watching Tyler's third attempt at pasta. The man was hopeless, but he wasn't giving up. That was more than a little sexy—just like the rest of him. Finally, he set down a plate of pasta with vodka sauce and two forks on the table in front of her.

"Feeling brave?" he asked.

She took a deep inhale of the mouth-watering scent

wafting up from the plate. "Always."

"I believe it."

They shared a grin and dove into what turned out to be one of the best dishes of pasta she'd ever had. Heath joined them, and they had a fun lunch of restaurant gossip and laughter. By the time they left the restaurant, slipping her hand into his as they walked down the street seemed natural. This was trouble. She knew it, but it felt too good to pretend it didn't. God, she was going to regret this at some point, but for now she was going to enjoy it just like they'd agreed. Even the sun was out and the wind had died down. It was like Mother Nature was smiling at them as they walked the ten long city blocks from Wheat & Rye to their building.

However, right as they turned the corner onto Eighth Avenue, a storm cloud in the form of Irena strode straight toward them.

The other woman stopped directly in front of them, forcing the couple walking behind her to swerve at the last second or slam into her. "Imagine running into you two."

"Hello, Irena," Tyler said, tension tightening his voice.

"I hear the island was productive," she said with a smile as fake as the watches the street dealers sold to the tourists. "Alberto said he just can't wait to talk to you about your ideas for the hotel expansion. I warned him that you brought some baggage with you, but he said he couldn't back out of the meeting, since it had already been set up."

"Baggage?" Everly asked, as if the woman in front of her didn't have the entire discounted luggage section at Dylan's department store hanging around her neck.

"Hasn't he told you, honey?" Irena asked in mock sincerity. "He's not all that he seems. The bank account might be bigger, but you can't ever take the Waterbury out of the boy or the history of familial violence. Is your dad out yet or is he still spending time behind bars?"

Everly's brain stuttered as she tried to process that. Tyler's dad was in prison? Domestic violence? He'd never said a word. It wasn't like they were actually boyfriend and girlfriend, but that was some pretty heavy shit to leave out of things.

The vein in Tyler's temple pulsed. "He's out."

"How lovely," Irena said. "Did you have a nice family reunion?"

Tyler didn't flinch, but he'd need some serious dental work soon if he didn't stop grinding his teeth like that.

Everly wasn't good with a dental drill, but she'd learned a lot about putting punk-ass bitches in their place while growing up. And if Irena needed anything, it was to learn she didn't get to treat people like that — especially not the ones Everly cared about.

Puffing out her chest, she took a step forward, using the extra inches from her high heels to look down her nose at the ex-fiancée from hell.

"You need to shut your mouth."

Irena didn't even blink. "How's the next line in this movie go? Or you'll shut it for me?"

"Something like that." Okay, she'd never actually hit another person in her life, but this woman didn't know that, and she obviously loved to stereotype everyone who didn't come from her elite little world.

"Oh, honey." Irena slathered on the fake pity. "This isn't Hollywood, it's Harbor City. And the gutter rats don't get to take over the city. You may be just fine on the fringes, but neither of you will ever really be a part of it." She turned her attention back to Tyler, cruelly erasing any bit of beauty the woman had. "Alberto might be humoring you now, but he won't accept your offer, Tyler. Face it—you're just not good enough. You never have been and you never will be." She let out a mean chuckle. "You think I went looking for something better on the night before our wedding because I was horny? Even you aren't that clueless. I did it because I knew I was worth more than anything you could offer and I was done playing with a Waterbury loser."

"Why you snobby piece of shit—" Everly's fingers were curled into a fist before she knew it, but Tyler clamped his hand down on her forearm.

"Good night, Irena," he said, the gravel in his voice more of a warning than Everly's posturing.

Then, he began walking past Irena, taking Everly with him. It didn't make sense, but she went with it. She knew it wasn't her fight. He wasn't one of her people, after all. But standing up for Tyler came as natural as breathing. Shit. She really was going to be in trouble soon.

Chapter Twenty-One

Everything inside Tyler was cold enough to give his internal organs freezer burn—just as it should be. Meanwhile, Everly was a fucking wildfire, stewing in silent fury the entire rest of the way home. The side of him that was always observing, always prepping for disaster, took note. A loud, passionate Everly was dangerous, but a silent Everly was deadly—at least for the poor asshole she was pissed off at.

"What in the hell was that?" Everly asked, pacing from one end of bookshelves lining a large wall in his apartment to the other. "How in the world did you not just let loose on her?"

He didn't break his stride as he headed straight for the fridge and the cold beer inside it. "Because I know where that leads."

She threw her hands up in frustration. "To putting someone in their place?"

He grabbed two bottles and headed over to where she'd wear a groove into his hardwood floor if she didn't stop. After twisting off the cap on each beer, he handed her one. She took a sip, looking at him expectantly, and continued pacing. Everly wouldn't let this go. That wasn't the type of woman she was.

However, explaining his upbringing was not something he ever did. Not to Sawyer. Not to Frankie or his family. Not to any of the helpful teachers who asked about the dark circles under his eyes—the only marks they could see. By the time he was old enough to realize that he could go for help, the worst of the physical stuff was in the past. He'd gotten bigger and smarter and knew when to keep his fucking mouth shut and plot his future. The fact that he towered over both his parents by the time he was fourteen hadn't hurt. The two assholes who'd made him hadn't taught him much, but they imparted one crucial lesson—don't let anything stand between you and where you want to be.

"Not to putting someone in their place," he said. "To becoming like my parents."

Her feet jerked to a stop and she whipped around, the righteous indignation lighting her up from the inside like an avenging angel tempered by concern. "What do you mean?"

"My dad is everything Irena said he was—a worthless asshole who wasn't above backhanding my mom when he thought she deserved it. In return, it all flowed downhill." And he had been at the bottom. "I can't tell you the number of times my mom swung that wooden spoon of hers and swore that I'd grow up to be just like him—just another Waterbury asshole who couldn't keep his emotions in check."

So when he'd gotten that scholarship to prep school in Harbor City, he'd promised himself that he'd be more than he was, that he'd leave that combustible house behind him and never look back. And he hadn't. Ever.

Everly set her beer down in front of his collector's edition of *The Lord of the Rings* and crossed over to him, winding her long arms around and snuggling her head into the pocket of his shoulder. "I'm so sorry, but she's wrong; that's not you."

"That's only because I won't let it be." He'd gotten rid of the accent. Changed his wardrobe. Limited connections to his working-class roots. He'd become a new man.

"Is that why this deal with Alberto is so important

to you?"

His first instinct was to lie, to shut down this conversation he'd never had with anyone, but the truth came out anyway. "Partly."

"Tell me." She broke away from him, going back and picking up her beer off the shelf.

How in the world she knew that he needed space for his confession, he had no idea, but she did. That fact should have given him pause, but he was in too deep for that. That was a problem. A big one. Everly was the one woman who had the ability to tie him right back to the one thing he'd spent most of his life running away from, and if he wasn't careful he'd go with her, smiling like a happy idiot. Forget it being a problem. It was a fucking disaster.

"I want to prove them wrong. All of them." If he closed his eyes, he could picture each one, from his parents to Irena to the society assholes who still called him "Scholarship Boy" when they thought he was out of earshot. "I want to show them that where I came from doesn't define who I am." God, he sounded pathetic. Weak. This wasn't the image he projected. He was success personified, not some kid whining about his rough childhood. "Nothing like screwing with a guy with parental issues to really make you rethink your dating decisions, huh?"

A wry laugh escaped her lips, and she shook her head. "You don't have the market cornered there."

Heat rushed up from the pit of his belly. "Tell me." So he could track down the people who wronged her and make them pay.

The pacing started again, but this time it was slower, more deliberate, almost like a hiker lost in the woods afraid that if she stopped moving she'd lose the last bit of hope she had left.

"My dad was an asshole, too, just a different kind."
She took a swig from her beer, turning at the end of
the bookshelf and heading back toward Tyler. "He was
a bigwig in the financial district. He and my mom met
when she worked for him as his secretary. She fell in
love. He thought she was the kind of girl you fucked
but certainly never married." She took another drink
and set the half-filled bottle on the bookshelf, this time
in front of *Great Expectations*. "When she got pregnant
with me, she thought everything would change between
them, and it did, but not the way she thought. He fired
her. Promised to pay child support without fighting
her if—and only if—she promised to go quietly. So she
did—and it broke her."

"What do you mean 'broke her'?"

Her bottom lip trembled, and in that moment
there was no one in the world Tyler hated more than
Everly's dick of a dad. No wonder she'd been so hard on
him in the beginning. He couldn't discount there were
some similarities between them—especially when he'd
started things off by suggesting she lose her blue-collar
accent. He wanted to kick his own ass again for that
ridiculous comment.

She bit her lip like she was struggling not to share
too much. He just waited patiently, hoping she felt
comfortable enough to open up to him more.

She took a deep breath. "Nunni used to tell me
that my mom wasn't always sad all the time and that
she'd come back from it, but she didn't. When she died,
I went to live with Nunni."

Probably the right choice, but it wasn't the one a
lot of courts would sanction if there'd been a custody
fight. "Not your dad?"

"I'd have to really concentrate to even pick that
man out of a lineup." She shrugged, but it was only a

shadow of her normal attitude. "I only saw him a few times before my mom died."

There were some people who deserved a little Waterbury justice. That asshole was definitely one of them. "Who is he?"

She shook her head, her long black strands giving her a temporary curtain. "It doesn't matter."

Needing to do something—anything—and since tracking down her dad and exacting revenge was a fight for another day, Tyler strode over to her and enveloped her, pulling her against him and holding her tight. "Our parents were real gems."

As their bodies melded together, a dam seemed to break in Everly. Her shoulders shook as he stroked her back, trying to offer comfort.

"My mom was all right," Everly said, her voice a little shaky as she still clung to him. "She just couldn't handle the hand she'd been dealt. I realized how true that was when I walked into our apartment after school one day and found her hanging in the bathroom linen closet."

The image stopped him cold.

He forgot how to breathe, his mind grappling with the thought of a little girl with long black hair and big, watery eyes staring up at her dead mother. She must have felt so alone. And abandoned by both parents now. His chest grew uncomfortably tight and he squeezed her closer.

"Jesus." No wonder Everly held so tight to that badass shell of hers. He didn't know what to say, so he said the only thing he could. "I'm sorry."

"It's okay," she said, sounding like it was anything but. They stood there for, hell, he didn't know how long, while Everly worked to regain her composure. Eventually, a stillness invaded her body, of acceptance or relief he couldn't tell, and she let out a soft sigh. "The whole situation with my parents taught me a lot about life and the importance of fighting for those you love, caring for them, making sure that no matter what I'd be there for them."

"That's why you do so much for your grandmother." He'd seen her financials, the visits, the cost of care; it all had her right on the border between making it and bouncing her rent check.

"As much as I can. If it hadn't been for her, I would have ended up in the system, because my dad sure as hell wasn't going to take in a little girl he couldn't acknowledge to his country club cronies."

That bastard deserved to have his clock cleaned with a tire wrench. "He didn't deserve you."

"But I still wanted him to want me," she said with a sniffle. "What can I say, the relationship between girls and their daddies, it matters."

What could he say to that? He had nothing to offer. He'd run from his family as soon as he could. So he just held her and they stayed like that, hanging onto each other for dear life before Everly took a step back, brushing away the few tears that had dared to fall. With a deep breath, she reset her shoulders and her nothing-bothers-me mask fell back into place. He could call her on it, but he understood the necessity of that barrier some days.

"No more sad stories that explain why we don't believe in happy endings." She cocked her head to the side and leaned for him, this time her fingers going to the buttons of his shirt, which she flicked open with determined speed. "This is supposed to be just for fun, remember?"

Just for fun? For her that was it, but for him it was starting to feel like more than that, which meant he had to end it before the stakes got any higher—but not tonight. For once, he didn't want to have to be the emotionally cold schemer. He wanted to melt in Everly's heat. Not giving himself time to plan or plot, he crashed his mouth down on hers, claiming her for tonight because soon everything would have to change.

Everly didn't tell that story. Ever. Her friends had either been with her at the time—like Nunni and Kiki—or they didn't know it. She slipped one of his buttons free. And she'd told it to the one man from whom she was desperately trying to keep her emotional distance. She unbuttoned his shirt a little more. That wasn't going to work, though, at least not tonight. By the time she got to the third button, she'd made up her mind to pretend—not to him but to herself—that tonight was just sex, that he was just a man, and that none of this mattered, because the truth was that it really had begun to matter more than just a little.

There wasn't any talk between them. Not yet. The air around them was too heavy, the need too great. When she slid her tongue into his mouth, it wasn't to challenge or tease, it was to get lost in him. She parted his shirt and slid her fingers underneath, gliding them over the hard planes of his chest as she trailed her mouth from his lips to his jaw prickly with a five o'clock shadow, then down his neck. He was hard, solid, totally there with her as if he'd never go anywhere, and it ripped something open in her, a place she normally kept closed up tight. And for once, she was just going to go with it, consequences be damned.

Grabbing ahold of his shirt, she lifted her head and looked him in those blue eyes of his that were six shades darker than normal and hooded with lust. Then, she yanked his shirt apart, snapping off the few buttons that had been holding the shirt closed and sending them flying across the room. The pings of them hitting this or that barely registered over the desire roaring in her ears.

"Is that how this is gonna go, sugar?" Tyler asked, one side of his mouth kicking up into a sexy half grin.

She whipped his belt through the buckle without ever breaking eye contact. "You gotta problem with that?"

"Fuck no." He watched her flick open the button of his pants and inch his zipper lower with a gleam in his eyes. "Are you going to suck me deep, take me all the way in that pretty mouth of yours?"

Lowering herself to her knees, she shoved his pants and boxers down to the floor. "If you have to ask, then I'm not very good at signaling my intentions."

He opened his mouth to say something, but she wrapped her fingers around the hot, hard length of him at the same time, and the words went unsaid. She liked the power of being able to make him stop thinking six moves ahead and to drown in the now. Leaning forward, she circled the head of his cock with her tongue, slow and exacting. His hands were on each side of her head, tangled in her hair, and when she opened her mouth and sucked him in, they tightened in time with the deep groan he let out. As she took him in deep, sliding her hands up the back of his thighs to his tight bare ass, she pushed him forward until there was no farther they could go.

"Everly," he said, gravel in his voice.

"Yes, Tyler?" she asked between long licks along the sensitive underside of his dick, taking time to swirl her tongue around his swollen head.

"Do that again."

He didn't have to ask twice. His ass flexed under her touch as she pushed him forward and sucked in the length of him until he hit the back of her throat. There went the tightening of his fingers in her hair, just enough pressure to make her want more. So she took as much of him as she could and retreated again and again while he stood, legs planted shoulder-width apart, his head tossed back. Only his hands on her head sending electric shocks of want through her, his groans of pleasure, and the strain of his muscles acted as her guide to know how much was too much and just how close to going over he was. Their positions were switched from the night in the parking garage. Now he was the one mostly naked while she was mostly dressed, but he didn't seem powerless; their power seemed to be growing from each other, and it was a huge turn on.

Pulling back, she licked the tip of his cock one last time as she stroked her hand up and down the length of him, her fingers barely touching. "I need to get naked."

He looked down at her with enough heat to melt her panties if she'd been wearing any. "Hell yes."

By the time she stood up, walked over to the bedroom door, and had her dress unzipped, he'd flipped off his shoes and shucked off his pants and underwear.

"You're too slow," he grumbled, stalking toward her. "Good thing I have the solution for that."

Grabbing her hips, he spun her around so she was facing the wall. He unzipped her dress with the speed of an Olympic luge team and shoved the material down her arms and over her hips until gravity took it to the floor where it pooled around her spike heels.

"Have I told you lately how much I love your aversion to underwear?" he asked, his breath hot and teasing on the back of her neck.

She would have answered if she could've, but as

the question came out of his mouth, he slid the back of his knuckles down her spine from the spot between her shoulder blades to her ass, all the speed gone from his movements stealing away her ability to form thoughts.

"Palms on the wall."

There was no questioning. No asking. It was an order plain and simple, and it made her core clench. Pressing her hands to the wall, she lifted the back of her foot out of her shoe. A quick smack on her ass stopped her.

"They stay on."

"So demanding," she managed to get out, barely recognizing the husky tone to her own voice.

"When I know what I want, you bet your ass." He rubbed his palm over her ass cheek, removing some of the sting. "Now kick that dress away, spread your legs, and don't turn around."

The thrill that went through her body made her nipples pebble into hungry hard peaks. She liked this Tyler. Scratch that. She loved this Tyler, the one who wasn't concerned with anything but the two of them. So she did what he said. And waited, anticipation making her body thrum. But he didn't touch her.

"Tyler?" she asked, the temptation to turn around and track what he was doing tugging at her.

"You might be the art expert, but seeing you like this—wet and waiting for me—is the most beautiful thing I've ever seen." He trailed a finger, and only one finger, across her back, ending the journey at the crack of her ass before closing in so his hard cock pressed against the small of her back. "I'm going to fuck you just like this, up against this wall, and the whole time you'll know it's me even if you can't see me because there's no one else who can make you feel like I can."

He wasn't wrong, but she wasn't going to tell him it

was too late. She already knew that and had since that first kiss when he'd made her forget the rest of the world except for him. She heard the sound of the condom wrapper being ripped open coming from somewhere behind her. Damn. She hated missing him roll it on. There was something so sexy about watching him take his cock in his hand and stroke it before putting on a condom.

"No looking or I'll make you wait to come." Tyler's command stopped her in mid-motion.

"It's not fair," she complained, her voice breathy.

"It'll be worth it." His hands were on her again, gliding up her front and cupping her breasts, rolling her aching nipples. "I promise."

She moaned, arching her back so she pushed into his hands. He responded just the way she loved, by pulling her nipples with just enough pressure to make her thighs quake. Giving in to the moment, she let her forehead fall to the wall, its coolness in stark contrast to the heat surrounding her, threatening to burn her up from the inside out.

"That's it." He kissed the sensitive spot where her shoulder met her neck. "Let me hear how much you want me. How good it feels. Tell me what you want."

"Your dick," she panted, her core pulsing with the need to be filled. "I want you inside me."

He chuckled against her overheated skin as he kissed his way up the back of her neck and tormented her nipples in the best fucking way possible. "Are you sure? Don't you want me to play a little longer?"

If he did, she'd implode. "Fuck. Me. Now."

He released one of her breasts, and she wanted to cry in disappointment, but the next second his hand slipped between her legs from the front and he spread her wet folds, sending waves of sensation through her.

On the next breath he surged inside her, filling her the way only he did.

He stopped halfway. "Is this what you want?"

"More," she whimpered. "More."

"Whatever you want, sugar," he said, and slammed into her. "So tight. So good."

The gravel in his tone let her know that he was just as on the edge as she was. It wasn't going to take long for either of them. Then, he started circling her clit with his fingers in concert with his thrusts, timing it so there was no moment where she wasn't feeling him, no retreat of his cock without an answering swirl of his fingers. She was so wet she could hear the sound of him fucking her over their breathing, over her racing pulse that roared like thunder in her ears.

"That's it, sugar," he said, and nipped her shoulder. "Take me deep until you squeeze my cock as you come all over it."

The combination of his fingers, his cock, and his words was too much to hold back any longer. Her orgasm slammed into her, blocking everything but the two of them as she cried his name.

"Everly," he let out in a throaty growl before plunging into her quickly once, twice, three times and coming with her name still on his lips.

Her skin damp with sweat and her own desire, she tried to catch her breath as they both came down. Jesus. The things this man did to her. It scared her as much as it thrilled her. She was still floating down to earth when he withdrew and tossed the condom in a nearby trashcan.

"You sure do know how to show a girl a good time," she said as she turned, glad for the wall at her back to support her because her legs sure as hell couldn't do the job on their own.

"Oh," he said with a wicked grin, "I'm not done showing you yet."

As Tyler picked her up and strode toward his bedroom, Everly had a moment of crystal-clear panic. It was all fun for him. It was supposed to be all fun for her. However, she didn't know how much fun she could take before her heart forgot the temporary parameters of this game, especially when she was pretty sure it was already too late.

Chapter Twenty-Two

A few nights later, the gallery was packed. The show from a multimedia artist, Celeste, had brought out everyone from art critics to avant-garde collectors to Harbor City trophy wives who were caught up in the rush of the rebellion in each piece. And when the critic from the *Gazette* pulled Everly aside to congratulate her on finding the previously unknown artist and helping to nurture her along, Everly could have passed out from the adrenaline rush. Well, that was if she wasn't already half-asleep on her feet as it was. Tyler might have developed into a passable cook, but he was so good at a million other things—most of which required being naked or damn close to it—that she wasn't getting much sleep lately.

"You look like a woman about to conquer the world," Helene said, handing her a glass of the house white she always served at the gallery shows.

"I feel like I already have." She took a sip, the middling wine tasting like champagne. Being giddy had that effect on her. It was weird.

Helene held up her glass in a toast. "To conquering heroes."

Even Helene took a sip after that, which was saying something, since she often compared the gallery's house wine to swill or worse. They watched the crowd move through the gallery, couples and small groups stopping here and there in front of Celeste's neon pieces. The artist herself was a natural at working a crowd and had a small gaggle of people around her as she told them a story, the retelling of which involved sweeping hand gestures and—Everly cocked her head to the side and listened closely—bird calls. *Okay, then.*

Of course, that meant she had a minute to pump Helene for information before she had to start mingling again. "So you and Alberto seem to be getting along well."

A hint of pink bloomed on the older woman's cheeks. "He wants to take me to the gala this week. Of course, I told him no."

"Why? You two seemed to get along so well on the island." And by "well" she meant like teenagers with their first crush.

"Probably because of that," Helene said with a firm, sure nod that wasn't reflected in the tone of her voice. "I'm not interested in anything like that back here in the real world."

To paraphrase the bard, the lady was protesting too much. Not that she could just go and say that to Helene. The woman could verbally take her out at the knees without blinking.

"Why do you say that?"

Helene took a sip of the wine, her face remaining neutral except for the disgusted twitch of her nose. "Because I've already had love, and I'm not interested in being greedy. Anyway, I couldn't do that to the boys and my husband's memory."

She shouldn't interfere. It really wasn't her place, but...Helene and Alberto so obviously went well together that she couldn't help but give a little push.

"It's too bad you feel that way, because Alberto is quite a guy. He loves art, is loyal, and can make a frittata that will bring tears to your eyes it's so good." Linking her arm in Helene's, she pulled the woman off to the side just enough that they could have some privacy to talk while still keeping an eye on how things were going with the show. "I know he seems like he's nothing more than a horrible flirt, but there's more to him than that. Has he told you the story of how his wife died?"

Helene shook her head, her eyes darkening with concern. "No."

It wasn't a story that Alberto often told, much preferring to let people think he was just a happy-go-lucky guy all the time, but there was something about seeing the two of them together that made Everly sure this was a story Helene needed to hear.

"It was ovarian cancer. She was thirty-two and Carlo was only four. Alberto saw her through it all, right up to holding her hand as she lay in their bed at home taking her last breaths." He'd told her the story years ago after a mutual dark night of the soul and too many bottles of Chianti. He meant the tale to be a story of hope. It had been. "Losing her nearly broke him, just like losing Michael almost broke you."

Helene's sharp gaze narrowed. "Is this your not-so-subtle way of telling me I should have said yes?"

Busted.

"Like I'd ever tell you what to do. You're Helene Carlyle, queen of the upper crust and despiser of the gallery house wine."

The other woman sniffed disdainfully at the wine. "It really is horrible."

She leaned in and dropped her voice to a whisper. "It's supposed to be, so people pay attention to the art instead of getting drunk on the wine."

"I should have known you'd thought about it." Helene chuckled and lifted her glass in a toast. "You consider all the angles almost as much as someone else we know."

"Is that how you segue into asking me about

Tyler?" She'd been expecting it ever since Key West. Helene wasn't exactly known for keeping her opinions to herself. "We're just having fun. It's not serious."

"Why not?"

Her muscles stiffened and she took a bracing drink of the house wine. Okay, this whole turnabout-is-fair-play thing wasn't exactly enjoyable. "Because that's not how things work out in the real world."

"And how does it work out?"

The uncharacteristic soft sympathy in Helene's voice was almost enough to undo her. A heavy sigh escaped, sinking her shoulders and taking her down from the high she'd been on for the past few days.

"With disappointment." She knew it, and not only because of her nunni's reminders.

"That's too bad," Helene said. "I think you two bring out the best in each other."

Only temporarily, though. That was their agreement—just as long as it was fun. Dwelling on that wasn't going to do her any good, especially not in the middle of a show. So after excusing herself from Helene, she made her rounds among the regulars and the newcomers. The feedback about Celeste's work was fantastic. By the time the last few stragglers were on their way out, she'd placed discreet sold stickers on a third of the descriptor cards hanging next to each piece. Really, the night deserved a celebratory toast with a better wine than their house white.

Right on cue, the door opened and in walked Tyler with a bottle of something that was probably both expensive and delicious. He was spoiling her, and she was getting far too used to it. She was getting too used to him, too. Still, the happy buzz of butterflies riding roller coasters in her stomach didn't abate even as she reminded herself of that fact.

Girl, you are in trouble. And what was worse, she didn't even care.

S itting at his desk, Tyler was starting to go numbers blind when a notification flashed across his screen from his assistant.

J. WEIR: *There's an Alberto Ferranti to see you.*

Tyler double-checked that the door between his office and Jason's desk on the other side was closed, then he did a fist pump. He'd been planting the seeds with Alberto, and it was all finally going to come to fruition. Not today, but soon. He'd bet money on it. All he had to do was keep things going in this direction and he'd make the deal. God, he loved it when a plan came together—especially one he hadn't been paying as close attention to as he should have been thanks to his sexy upstairs neighbor, who managed to distract him more now than she ever had before, since she'd stopped hating his guts. Dangerous territory, that.

T. JACOBSON: *Send him in.*

Alberto strode in like a man who never had a day that didn't go his way. "Tyler, I hope you don't mind my breaking in on you like this."

"Not at all." Tyler got up and rounded his desk. "It's good to see you."

He led Alberto to the small sitting area next to the windows, taking one of the wing chairs. Alberto eyeballed the matching chair for half a second then opted for the tan leather love seat—which not only looked more comfortable, it actually was.

"You had a good time on the island?" Alberto asked.

"It's so gorgeous that it would be hard to have a bad time." That would have been Tyler's answer no matter what, but in this case it was the truth. Of course, the fact that he'd spent a good portion of it naked with Everly hadn't hurt.

Focus, Jacobson. You can't afford to get distracted.

"Very true," Alberto said with a chuckle before brushing his hands together like a blackjack dealer at the end of a shift. "And now we must speak business. You have ideas for the hotel expansion?"

Thank God he was always prepared for any outcome, since he still hadn't been able to nail down Alberto on a date to present his ideas to the hotelier and the board. He bounded up from his chair, heading straight for his laptop with his presentation.

"Let me tell Jason to hold my calls, and I'm all yours."

Thirty minutes and four million questions later, Tyler relaxed against the stiff back of the chair his office decorator had picked out. She'd insisted it looked regal. He was just glad for the extra support. Despite their time spent laughing over fresh grilled fish on the island, Alberto hadn't taken it easy on him. The man knew his business. Of course, you didn't get to where he was without those qualifications.

"All of this looks good." Alberto rubbed his chin and nodded. "You've got quite a few unorthodox ideas."

It wasn't an exaggeration—but the Ferranti Hotel group was the one for them. "To make an impact, you'll need to stand out."

The older man's face broke into a smile. If it had been a test, then Tyler had just passed it. "I agree, but our board of directors doesn't always concur with me. They can be quite conservative in their approach."

"Please let them know that my approach may be a

bit wild, but my commitment to success is not." Because he always did whatever it took to make that happen.

"That might be enough." Alberto stood and shook Tyler's hand after he'd followed suit. "They aren't like us. They are what you call old money. They have rules and expectations of personal behavior that influence them in business even though the two do not have to overlap. *Mi fanno impazzire!*" He threw his hands up in the air in disgust. "They make me crazy."

"Don't worry, I understand the type well." If he hadn't, he never would have been able to get them to trust him with their money.

"Good, several of the board members will be at the gala tomorrow, and I'm sure they'll be watching you," Alberto said as they crossed to the door.

"I'll be sure to bore them to tears." He'd out–old money the old money if that's what it took.

"An excellent plan. They have no tolerance for passion or excitement, only a devotion to the boring and the profitable," Alberto agreed. "But you won't be bored; you're taking Everly, *sì*?"

And suddenly, his attention veered from imagining disapproving looks to the soft curves and cherry lips of the woman he'd spent way too much time thinking about lately. Not that he'd made any efforts to stop. Fun. It was just until it wasn't fun and it sure as hell was — even with the lack of sleep.

Tyler grinned at the older man. "She finally said yes."

"Good," he said. "The best women are always worth fighting for."

Then, with a knowing wink, Alberto strode out of his office. Tyler gave him a friendly wave as the elevator doors closed before going back into his office. That left Tyler alone to think about Alberto's parting words.

Fighting for a woman? He'd never done that. Not even when he found out his fiancée, a woman he'd thought he loved, had tried to get with his best friend. For him, the fighting had always been about moving up the Harbor City ladder so he could leave Waterbury as far behind him as possible. Did that make him smart or stupid? He wasn't sure anymore.

Chapter Twenty-Three

Helene ran the pad of her thumb over the bottom of her wedding band as the elevator doors closed, taking her and Alberto up to the rooftop ballroom of the Harbor City Grand Hotel. It was an exquisite ring, featuring princess-cut diamonds and a single ruby that had been in Michael's family for generations, which was why she'd told everyone that she still wore it. The truth was, she hadn't been ready to take it off and wasn't sure she'd ever be. Wearing it on a date, though, seemed inappropriate.

"It is almost as beautiful as you," Alberto said, watching her fiddle with the ring.

The unfamiliar feeling shifting her stomach wasn't one she could pinpoint. It was a mix of uncertainty and nerves. "I shouldn't wear it."

Alberto looked at her, the black of his tuxedo jacket bringing out the sparkle in his dark eyes. "Do you want to wear it?"

Want to? She hadn't thought about that. Too much of the past few years had been about what she should do to put others around her at ease. Grief made people uncomfortable. Her stern attitude they could take. But the vulnerability? Only her boys had been able to stand that, and watching them walk on eggshells around her had been what had finally snapped her out of her grief. Whether it was a woman thing or a mother thing, seeing the people she cared about worried brought out the protector in her. She'd gone about expressing it in the wrong way with both boys, but they'd forgiven her natural overbearing tendencies and had shown her by example that life did go on. But her ring? That was her last physical tie to the man who'd helped her make those boys and raise them into the men she was so damn proud of.

"I do want to wear it," she said, her throat raw.

"Then wear it," he said, as if what she wanted was the only thing to factor into the equation.

Not for the first time, she wondered what it was that was wrong with the man. He probably killed kittens in his spare time. "Why are you being so nice to me?"

He stepped closer and cupped her face in his warm palms, looking her straight in the eye. "Because, *bellissima*, second chances don't come around every day, and when they do, you must seize them."

The declaration did something to her, lifted some burden weighing her down that she'd grown so used to that she barely noticed it anymore. It was as much of a relief as it was petrifying. Then he kissed her, a soft brush of his lips, and stepped away. How he'd known she'd need time to process, she had no idea.

Keeping her gaze locked on the floor numbers as they lit up one after the other, she took a deep breath. "You're too nice for me."

"Bah." He waved his hands in the air as the elevator doors opened. "Life is too short to keep what you're feeling to yourself."

Before she got a chance to respond, the elevator doors opened, revealing a colorful swath of dresses and plain black tuxedoes as Harbor City's old money gathered to raise money yet again without actually doing anything to help. Oh, the organizers did the work—and a lot of it—she knew from personal experience, but if she polled the people in attendance, she doubted 90 percent would know the name of the actual charity they were helping. This was her life, the one she'd been raised to conform to, but it was starting to chafe. She wanted more.

Alberto tucked her hand into the crook of his arm and they walked forward, gaining the quiet buzz of attention from the people they passed. They were a sight, she knew. The hard-as-nails society matron and the outgoing Italian hotel magnate. She never would have guessed it would have happened, either, but it felt right. That thought propelled her forward right up until they approached her family, gathered in a knot near the dance floor. Hudson and his girlfriend, Felicia, stood with Sawyer and his wife, Clover, all of whom turned to look with frank, curious stares. At once, her nerves and lingering feeling of betrayal slammed back into place.

Hudson, being the charmer that he was, stepped in to fill the silence. "Alberto, it's so good to see you again." He clapped a friendly hand on Alberto's shoulder. "This is my girlfriend, Felicia."

"Lovely to meet you," Felicia said with a shy smile.

"And you as well. I've seen some of the pieces from Hudson's Wife series and now I see that while he may have gotten close, he did not capture the true extent of your beauty." Alberto took Felicia's hand and, being the outrageous flirt he was, gave it a quick kiss on her knuckles, then turned back to Hudson. "Tell me about this project you're working on with Everly's grandmother's friends. I hear you'll be opening a show at Black Hearts in six months?"

And they were off, lost in their mutually shared world of art, the one Hudson had hidden from her for decades—or at least tried to. A mother always knows. She'd just accepted a glass of champagne from a passing waiter when her firstborn moved in for the kill.

"He seems nice," Sawyer said, his voice as close to

a whisper as possible in the ballroom filled with chatter.

She nodded, wondering where he was taking this. "He is."

"Just be sure he knows that if he doesn't treat you well, I'm not above punching an old man."

Helene blinked away her surprise. Of all the things, that was one of the last she'd expected. "Sawyer Carlyle, I raised you better than that."

He looked her straight in the eyes. "You raised me to stand up for those I love."

Now that was the very last. It wasn't that she didn't love her boys with all her heart or that they didn't love her, but they were a Harbor City family of a certain standing, and bold declarations of love and loyalty weren't their way. At least they hadn't been until Felicia and Clover had come into her sons' lives. It was amazing how much love could change a person. Of course, she wasn't about to give in to the happy tears gathering. She most definitely didn't get weepy in public. Ever. So she fell back on her iron-lady attitude that her children seemed to see right through lately.

"I'm sure temporarily losing Clover because of your own idiotic habits helped you understand that as well," she said, tempering the tart just enough for her non–detail noticing son to realize she was just teasing.

"Without a doubt." Sawyer nodded, looking over at his obviously pregnant wife with a look of total and complete love.

"I'm so happy for you two."

He held up his champagne flute and tapped it against hers. "To happiness—all of ours."

Now *that* she could drink to. Her own happiness wasn't something she'd really considered all that much, even before Michael died. Her life had been a rush instead of an experience. As she sipped the tart, fizzy champagne, she looked around at the people surrounding her and realized that this was exactly what made her happy and she wanted more of it. Alberto was right. Life was too short to keep what she was feeling to herself. She tapped the man in question on the shoulder.

Alberto turned around with an expectant look. "Yes, *bellissima*?"

She set down her champagne on a table. "Let's dance."

A wide smile split his handsome face. "Now *that* is the perfect idea."

It was, and she was going to enjoy every step of it.

Chapter Twenty-Four

Usually these galas were a business opportunity disguised as personal fun. That's what it should have been for Tyler, but then he spotted Everly walking down the stairs that led to the ballroom. She strode in wearing a one-shoulder black dress that followed her figure like a map to the Promised Land. Her hair was pulled back into a sleek, low bun that set off her face, which was all big, beautiful eyes and dark-red lips. And as she made her way toward him, he mentally made a list of every guy who looked a little bit too long.

Tyler? Meet your inner caveman.

By the time they came together on the edge of the dance floor, the list was long enough to merit two pages, single-spaced. This wasn't like him. And tonight was the worst night for him to give in to the testosterone-fed urges gripping him by the balls, but he had to do something. So instead of punching out the finance bro coming their way with lascivious intent in his eyes, Tyler slinked an arm around Everly's waist and pulled her onto the dance floor. She just smiled as if she knew exactly what he was thinking and went along with it, pressing her body close to his as they swayed to the music.

"Good" wasn't the right word to describe how she felt in his arms, but it was as close as he was going to get. As always whenever he was around her, his brain stopped whirring in constant motion as plots and plans came together in his subconscious and all he could do was focus on her.

"You look beautiful," he finally managed to get out.

She gave him a cocky grin that went straight to his dick. "I clean up pretty well for a Riverside girl."

"You clean up pretty well for a Harbor City princess."

It was the truth. Even as part of him knew he should put a few extra inches of space between their bodies according to the rules of polite society and especially because of the extra eyes he knew were watching, he couldn't seem to make himself. Not until the music ended and the band announced they were taking a short break. At that point, holding her was no longer an option. Of course, that didn't mean he didn't let his palm linger on the small of her back as they walked off the dance floor toward the bar and the Carlyles gathered around a table nearby.

"Can I get you something to drink?" he asked.

"A glass of Chardonnay would be perfect. Just let me go say hi to everyone at the Carlyle table real quick, and I'll meet you at the bar." She planted her hand on his chest, leaned up, and brushed a quick kiss across his cheek.

The little display of PDA was all totally acceptable. Her quick ass grab before walking over to the Carlyles? Yeah, not so much, but he wasn't complaining.

Distracted fool that he was, Tyler didn't notice that not only was one of the hotel board members, Gianni Esposito, standing near the bar, giving him the prune face, but Irena was nearby with trouble written all over her. Whatever the woman was up to, he might as well deal with it now before Everly came back over, because he knew exactly what would happen then—Everly, with the best of intentions, would rush to his defense, causing exactly the kind of scene he couldn't have here, and Irena would win. His ex-fiancée hadn't planted herself at the elbow of a hotel board member accidentally.

Making sure to keep a few feet between them at the bar, Tyler ordered Everly's wine and a Scotch on the rocks.

"You know," Irena said, her voice silky smooth and closer than it should be, "I still think of you."

He kept his attention on the bartender. "I don't want to know."

Irena continued as if she hadn't heard the dig or—more likely—didn't give a shit. "On those nights when I can't seem to fall asleep and it's all I can do not to get myself off thinking about how good you were with your tongue as I'm lying in bed next to Carlo."

His stomach churned. How in the hell had he ever thought he'd loved this woman? Were his instincts really that fucked when it came to the opposite sex? "Am I supposed to be flattered by that?"

She flipped her long hair over her shoulder and shrugged. "Just a fact. It doesn't matter what you feel; it never has."

"It's gotta be exhausting to have to pretend not to be such a bitch."

"You should know," she said with a knowing smile.

Now that got his attention. Even though he knew he shouldn't engage—especially because the hotel board member was still watching the exchange with open curiosity; at least he was too far away to hear what was being said—Tyler snapped back anyway. "What in the hell are you talking about?"

"You're just as much of a fake as I am, except at least I'm not faking it for profit like you. I have to play nice because those are the rules of my peers. But you? What do you people do on the other side of the harbor? What am I asking you for? You've been acting like one of us for so long, you probably don't even remember."

Irena's eyes glittered with triumph. She thought she had him—and she almost did. He was holding on to his control with his fingernails. It had all happened as she no doubt had planned. He'd lose his cool. The board members would hear all about it. And Irena would walk away wondering out loud what in the world she could have ever said to have upset the man. After that, the deal would be a bust. Irena may be evil, but she was an evil fucking genius.

"Oh, that face," she said, making a *tsk-tsk* cluck with her tongue as she placed her hand on his forearm, holding on hard enough that he'd have to shake her off to free himself. "I know that one. It's the same one you had on when you watched me stroll out of Sawyer's hotel room the night before our wedding, my shirt misbuttoned and my skirt askew. It's like you're trying to stuff a ten-ton elephant into a soda bottle."

All of the vile words came out pointed and sharp but the sweet, doe-eyed, innocent look on her face never faltered. She really was an expert at this.

"Shut up, Irena." He handed the bartender a wad of cash and picked up his drink with his free hand, hoping she'd take the hint.

She didn't.

"The thing that made me realize that no matter how much money you had or how much you made my toes curl when I came, I couldn't be with you, was a little visit I had with your mom." Her words were as sharp and as deadly as the knife the bartender was using to slice the limes. "You didn't know she'd come to see me, did you? I didn't think so. She was drunk, angry, and looking like she was on the tail end of a lifetime bender. It was a hell of a combination." She smiled so sweetly up at him, it nearly put him in sugar shock. "She told me all about your childhood, about your dad, and about how she was responsible for that scar on your eyebrow. Ten stitches? That must have been some aim she had with your Little League baseball trophy."

Tyler held himself perfectly still and filled his veins with ice. This was how he'd survived that night and a million more, by learning what everyone who'd ever faced down overwhelming odds before had—to never let them see what was really going on inside. Once he was sure he was there, he lifted his glass and took a drink—not too big, not too small. It was deliberate to show her words had no impact.

Instead of quieting her, though, it only emboldened her. She threw back her head and laughed, a cheery tinkling noise like the sound of a bell attached to an antique shop's door.

"That elephant still won't fit in that bottle, will it?" She leaned forward and lowered her voice. "You know what else won't fit? You. No matter what you do or how well you pretend, you'll always be the kid from Waterbury with the parents who beat on each other for entertainment and beat on you when you tried to stop them. You don't belong here. You don't belong with Alberto's business..." Something over his shoulder must have caught her eye because the words died on her tongue. Unfortunately, she didn't lose her track of thought for long. "But her? Oh yeah, she's definitely your speed."

He didn't need to look back to know who Irena was talking about, and judging by the satisfied look on her face, Everly was heading their way like a woman on a mission. He shot back half his Scotch in one swallow, trying to dull the feeling that came along with knowing she was coming here to defend him—something very few people had ever done before. God knew his parents never had. But by the time the alcohol burned its way down to his belly, the logical side of his brain had taken over. Everly didn't give two shits about causing a public scene, which Irena had to be depending on and why she'd made sure to deliver her little speech with an uptight hotel board member nearby. Tyler couldn't afford to let that happen, though, if he was going to make the deal that was big enough and sought-after enough to make everyone in Harbor City forget where he'd come from. How in the hell he was going to stop her, though? He had no fucking clue.

Everly knew Irena's type. Rich. Insecure. Bitchy. That combination led to a pain-in-the-ass, high-maintenance customer at the gallery and a woman in dire need of correction in other circumstances like this one. She didn't need to see Tyler's face or hear their words to know Irena was up to the same bullshit she'd pulled out on the street the other day. That shit would not stand, not when it came to someone she loved. She nearly tripped in her favorite four-inch heels as the realization struck. It was the only explanation for the fury burning her from the inside out and the overwhelming urge to fight for Tyler when he wouldn't fight for himself. You didn't do that for fuck buddies. You did that for the people you loved.

Shoving the thought aside to be dealt with later when she wasn't on the warpath, she put on her best don't-fuck-with-me expression and stopped next to Tyler.

"Having a good time?" she asked, picking up her wine from the bar.

"Of course," Irena said, flashing a brilliant smile that was about as real as the diamond studs in Everly's ears. "We were reminiscing about the good old days."

Tyler pressed his palm against the small of her back and said, "Everly, let's go."

"Yes, you really should enjoy this experience while you can," Irena said. "It's not like you'll be getting more chances to attend events like this. People like you two may get a peek in at what happens upstairs, but you'll always just be downstairs staff."

Tyler flinched beside her. It was only minimal and most people wouldn't have caught it, but she did. Everly had met plenty of people like Irena, where their entire self-worth was based on what others thought of her, and any threat to that opinion was met offensively. She was probably striking out before Tyler could put her down, discredit his words. It was a good strategy, but it was unnecessary. What was she, afraid he'd let everyone know what a bed-hopping fiancée she'd been? Clearly she didn't know Tyler as well as she thought, because this man would never say anything publicly that might make him look classless. But that didn't give her the right to take him down a peg. And she was going to do something about it.

Irena was a slimy bitch—one Everly had had more than enough of. Ignoring Tyler's none-too-gentle push against her back, she stood her ground. He might feel like he had to play within some arbitrary rules of society, but she didn't.

"You say that like it's a bad thing to work for a living."

"Oh no, I understand many people have to do it," Irena said with a casual shrug.

In another situation, this would be an attack kind of moment, but a solid punch to the nose was too good for someone like Tyler's former fiancée and, let's face it, she'd never been a physical fighter when her words were much better weapons.

"You spoiled hag," Everly said. And it was past time that she and the others like her heard it. At that point something clicked inside her that usually only went into fighting fury mode when it came to defending art or her family. She could quiet that loyalty urge, but only for so long in the face of someone like Irena, and time was up.

Tyler took a step away from the bar, his hand at the base of her spine steering her along with him. "This isn't the time or the place."

She turned to him, unable to understand how he could put up with even another second of this shit. "Exactly when is it, then?" she asked, her voice loud enough that heads turned. "You cannot let this woman get away with it anymore."

"Get away with what?" Irena asked with mock innocence. "I'm just telling the truth."

"Everly," Tyler said, his voice full of warning. "Let it go."

That wasn't happening. She turned back toward the other woman. "Tyler and I may not have been born with a silver spoon in our mouths, but we've gained everything we have through hard work and determination. All you did was be born—and look what you've accomplished with your life because of it. Nothing. Unless you count turning into the kind of woman who tries to cheat on her fiancé on their wedding night as an accomplishment."

Tyler's hand slipped from her back, taking his warmth with it. She was so caught up in the moment of finally putting Irena in her place on Tyler's behalf that she barely noticed.

Blotchy red spots exploded on Irena's cheeks. "How dare you talk to me like that!"

"Easily. Of course, it's not your fault you turned

into such a crabby bitch; it's not like you had access to the best education, travel, and opportunities to better yourself." Everly let out a dramatic gasp as fake as the crocodile tears filling Irena's eyes. "No, wait. You did! You just have such a big oak tree stuck up your ass that you've never realized how lucky you were."

"You two deserve each other. Why don't you get out of here and go have some white-trash babies who'll just end up sucking off the public teat," Irena said, her words quiet enough that only Everly could hear them. "That's what you people always end up doing."

Everly's wrist flicked before she realized what she was doing, and the wine from her glass landed with a splash against Irena's face, the liquid running down her cheeks along with her mascara.

Irena's jaw dropped, and she let out a squeal loud enough to get the attention of everyone around them. The crowd's focus jumped from Everly to Irena, who gaped at her like a fish tossed onto the shore.

"How could you?" Irena asked, her voice filled with false confusion. "All I did was ask about your gallery." She turned to an Italian man at the end of the bar who was one of the hotel board members. "I'm so sorry you had to see that. Please know it's not a reflection on Alberto or Carlo."

The men in question hustled toward the bar. Ever a Riverside girl, though, Everly clocked their position in her periphery and kept her focus on the lying bitch who'd done so much damage already. Carlo handed his fiancée a napkin from the bar. She smiled up at him like a woman who'd been horribly wronged.

"*Tesoro*, is all well?" Alberto's question to Everly was soft, but the concern in his tone boomed. "This is not like you to get so passionate about something other than art," he said. "Are you feeling all right?"

All right? No, she felt fucking amazing, as if she'd conquered— She turned her attention to Alberto, and her internal answer died out along with that triumphant feeling. There was a small crowd around them, all of whom were pretending not to listen while taking in every word as if they were court reporters. The Italian man at the other end of the short bar was looking straight at her, distaste plain in his hard gaze. Closer to home, Carlo stood next to Irena, who may be a horrid bitch, but she was still his fiancée. The expression on his face was a mix of confusion and anger. Pivoting just a bit, she got her first look at Tyler since she'd mounted her vigorous defense. "Thunderous" would be a generous description of the look on his face. Worst of all, beneath the fake tears, there was no missing the victory in Irena's eyes. *Shit. Shit. Shit.* What did Nunni say about doing the wrong thing for the right reasons? She couldn't remember at the moment, but no doubt it would come back to her soon.

"Actually, yes. I do feel a little out of sorts." And at the moment it wasn't a lie. Her stomach was in knots and her throat was tight enough to make getting the words out difficult.

"Is that what you call such rude behavior where you grew up in Riverside?" Irena asked, balancing the ire with hurt in her voice. The woman really had missed her calling.

There was nothing she wanted more than to tell Irena to go fuck herself, but she couldn't. She'd fucked up enough as it was by forgetting the audience around them as she fired away at the other woman. "I have no excuse; please accept my apology."

"Of course." Irena offered her a weak smile that didn't reach her still watery eyes and held out her hand. "Where would we be if we couldn't forgive?"

She took the other woman's hand and shook it, ignoring the shiver of revulsion that spilled down her spine. "That's very kind of you. Now, if you'll excuse me."

Irena gave her a regal nod before turning to Carlo and whispering to him not to worry. It was just low blood sugar on Everly's part or something that caused all the fuss.

Grinding her teeth to keep from saying anything else, Everly strode away from the bar. She made it two steps before an unmistakable awareness spilled over her as Tyler fell into step beside her. He was mad. She could accept that, but the fact that he was with her now confirmed the hope she hadn't even realized she was harboring until this moment—that he'd stick with her no matter what, that he wasn't like her father.

Once outside the ballroom doors, he turned left and led her to an empty alcove away from the chattering crowd. Holding her tongue until she looked around to make sure the coast was clear—who said she couldn't learn from her mistakes—she let out a deep breath.

"My God, can you believe that woman?" Everly asked, taking a step toward Tyler, wanting nothing more than his arms around her at that moment.

"Her?" He evaded Everly's touch. "I can totally believe that Irena would set up a public scene like that. What I can't believe is that you fell for it and fucked everything up, possibly permanently."

It was taking everything Tyler had not to let loose the last frayed strings of his self-control. Frustration and fury blasted his gut and singed his lungs as his brain spun, trying to find a way out of this hole Everly had dug for them both. If he didn't, then the deal he needed so fucking badly would fall apart. The truth of that was in the look of disgust on Gianni Esposito's face and the concern on Alberto's.

"What in the hell are you talking about?" Everly whisper-shouted, getting right in his face. "I stuck up for you, which was more than you were doing for yourself."

"Do you really think what that woman thinks of me matters?" No, what he'd been doing was playing the game, just like he always had. That's what she failed to understand, what she'd always failed to understand. "Do you really think I care about her at all?"

She let out an angry huff and threw her hands up in the air. "You don't have to care about what she thinks to have some pride in yourself and not let other people treat you like shit."

"Is that what you think I was doing? Just bowing down?" Is that what she thought of him? That he was just some kind of wimp?

"That's what it looked like," she shot back.

Jesus. He'd filled his veins with ice in order to learn how to not respond to every jibe, not to give in to the so-called friendly ribbing that was anything but, not to react to the questions about his abilities because of where he was from. He was playing chess, watching the pieces and always thinking six moves ahead. That's how he'd survived his home as a child and how he'd managed to make a name for himself in Harbor City. He sure as fuck hadn't accomplished anything by allowing himself the luxury of letting his emotions—justified or not—determine how he reacted to a situation.

"I always have a plan," he said, keeping his voice low and as neutral as possible. "My ex-fiancée was just goading us with the specific intent of getting a rise out of me and making me lose my temper to show the hotel board just how unsuitable I am. I didn't do that, but you sure as hell did. You let her get your Riverside up and let loose calling her a whore and doing the one thing I didn't think anyone could do, make Irena look sympathetic."

"How is that even possible with all she said about you?" she asked, matching his volume despite the heat in her words.

And there it was. That was the brilliance of Irena's plot to fuck him out of this deal.

"Because no one else heard that part, only we did." Gianni Esposito from the hotel board certainly hadn't. "The people who *matter* only heard you."

"The people who m-matter?" she sputtered. "You sound like Irena."

"And in there, you sounded like my parents before the dishes started shattering." Fuck. That was not where he'd wanted to take this conversation. Refusing to give in to the fire burning in his belly, he exhaled a deep breath. "You're smart, talented, and passionate about the things you care about, but you don't understand these people like I do. I've spent my life trying to prove to them that even though I'm an outsider, I'm more than just some kid from Waterbury. It has been the only thing I've focused all my attention on since I got that scholarship to prep school. Since then, every day has been about moving forward, strengthening my reputation, and always knowing what to expect next—until I met you and the unexpected became an everyday part of my life. It's a distraction I can't afford if I'm going to convince the board to pull this deal back from the edge—and I have to maneuver them into that decision, which is going to be that much harder because of what you did in there."

Her lip trembled as an angry flush swept up from her chest and she took a step back, smoothing her hair and raising her chin a few inches. "Do you have any idea how it feels to never be good enough for the people in your life that you—" Her voice cracked as she seemed to nearly choke on the emotion turning the tip of her nose red and making her chin tremble. Then, she took a shaky breath and continued. "That you care about when all you want is for them to accept you for who you are and they don't?"

Was she joking? Had she not heard what he'd been saying about the precariousness of his position and the value of this deal in finally solidifying his place in Harbor City? "Every fucking day, which is why it's so important that I go back inside and fix this massive fuckup."

He expected more fiery emotions, more verbal explosions. Instead, he watched—almost in a slow-motion perspective that shredded him from the inside out—as all the emotion drained out of her eyes and she went perfectly still. He knew that look. He'd fucking mastered it. It was the one that said there was nothing left in her veins but ice and that whatever had just happened didn't matter because she no longer cared. She'd shut down—no, she'd shut him out.

Panic flared in his chest. "I'm sorry. I didn't put that well," he said, his words coming out in the same frantic speed as his heartbeat. "But this is the only way to make everyone see past where I've come from and to where I'm going. I *have* to make this deal."

She looked him dead in the eye. "You know, no one judges you for your working-class roots as harshly as you do yourself."

Heat blasted through his body. How many times had he heard the taunts at school, the whispers in the boardrooms? *But when was the last time that happened?* a small voice inside him asked. He pushed the doubt aside. Throughout his life there'd been one thing motivating him and moving him forward—proving everyone wrong. He wouldn't let go of that now. He couldn't. Without that fire, who was he?

Everly continued, pressing against that wound of his that never seemed to heal. "Your parents may have started you on that self-loathing route—and God wouldn't I love to tell them to go fuck themselves for doing that to a child—but you're continuing to march down it of your own volition. At some point in time you have to take responsibility for the path you've chosen. You can't blame all of it on where you've come from."

"That's bullshit. You don't know anything about me. And for someone who talks the talk, how much are you really walking the walk? Care to share more about your daddy issues with the class?" he asked, his snarly voice loud enough to make the waiter passing by on his way back to the kitchen flinch. *Dammit. Cool it down, Jacobson. Causing another scene is not going to help anything.* Heart still racing but his voice lower, he continued. "Everly, I—"

"Don't bother," she interrupted as she pushed past him. "Whatever you're gonna say next doesn't matter anyhow. We're done here. Only until it's not fun anymore, remember our agreement? Well, this isn't my definition of fun."

Stunned, he didn't have a response beyond saying her name as she walked out of his life. Once again, she'd done the unexpected. This turn of events, though, was a steel knife through the chest. He wanted to scream, to rant, to rave, but he couldn't. The lessons he'd learned came rushing to the forefront—never let anyone see your emotions because it gave them too much power. So while the caveman inside him screamed at him to fight, he did the opposite. He swallowed the razor blades and stayed frozen to his spot. Her footsteps hesitated for the briefest of moments, but when he made no move, she went on without him while he listened to the distinctive *click-clack* of her heels as she marched across the marble floor.

Chapter Twenty-Five

Tyler spent the next four days almost exclusively at his office. That meant his back ached from sleeping on the couch, he was out of fresh clothes kept in his executive bathroom, and he hadn't shaved in days. He'd reached out to every member of the Ferranti Hotel group's board who was in Harbor City and did his best to smooth things over. It hadn't worked. Oh, they hadn't said that outright, and his pitch meeting was still scheduled in three weeks, but he knew a polite brush-off when he experienced one. He smelled like shit. He looked like shit. He felt like shit. So it was pretty much the trifecta of shit in his life.

So why was he sitting at his desk scrolling through old text messages from Everly? Because that was as close to fun as his life got anymore. God, he was fucking pathetic. Just as he was about to put the phone down and continue the exercise in futility known as putting together a hotel expansion presentation that wasn't going to go anywhere, it vibrated in his hand.

EVERLY: *No need to hide out any longer. I left my keys with the super.*

What the fuck? Where in the hell was she going? Hiding out? He'd been working his ass off. There was a difference. Anyway, why would he hide? She was the one who'd told him to fuck off. He stood up so quickly that he sent his desk chair flying back behind him and it *thunk*ed against his credenza.

"That can't have been good news," a familiar deep voice said.

Sawyer Carlyle stood in his open office doorway, holding a white paper bag. It had been a rough few years between them. At first, there'd been only a cold silence with Tyler plotting to make the other man's life as difficult as possible. However, his heart was never really in it and cracks in the ice had started to form when Sawyer fell for his now-wife, Clover. Something about seeing the other man so completely at a loss about what was going on in his life thanks to the whirlwind that was Clover had brought the two of them back together. By the time Hudson Carlyle had made a public declaration for Tyler's friend Frankie Hartigan's little sister, Felicia, he and Sawyer had started to rebuild their friendship. Now? They weren't in each other's pockets, as Mrs. Hartigan had said repeatedly when he and Frankie were growing up, but they were friends again and it felt good—just not right now, when it felt like an iron hand was squeezing his lungs shut.

"She's leaving," Tyler said, his attention dropping again to the phone screen.

"Who's leaving?"

"Everly." He grabbed his chair and flopped back into it.

"The gallery owner?" Sawyer asked, walking over to the pair of chairs in front of Tyler's desk and sitting down, setting the bag on the floor between them. "Yeah, Hudson said she was opening up a new place on Aucoin Avenue."

What the fuck? Why was he just hearing this now? "She can't."

Sawyer snorted. "Oh yeah, why's that?"

"Because she signed a lease with me." That sounded lame even to him.

"One that according to Hudson you let go to a month-to-month without any notice requirements." Sawyer shook his head. "Rookie mistake, Jacobson."

No shit. And one he couldn't fix at the moment—if ever. God, this fucking sucked. And to top it off, the happily-in-love jerk in front of him just sat there grinning like a man about to enjoy ice cream and beer for breakfast. The rat bastard. If they really weren't friends again, Tyler would be showing his smug ass the door.

"How do you know this?" After all, that kind of intel was usually *his* bread and butter.

"Because my little brother is all sorts of pissed at you because of Everly, and he felt like yammering while I was working out this morning," Sawyer said. "So tell me, what in the hell did you do to her?"

Act like an asshole. "Nothing."

Sawyer lifted an eyebrow. "Really?"

"She did it to m-me," he sputtered, remembering the ice in her eyes when she told him it wasn't fun anymore, so different from the fiery avenging-angel look she'd had going while handing Irena her ass—if it hadn't been for the fact that Everly had fallen right into the other woman's trap, it would have been a sight to behold. Instead it had been like watching everything he'd worked for implode. "She caused a huge scene at the gala and more than likely sank the Ferranti Hotel group deal, and then she told me that she didn't want to see me anymore."

"So she broke up with you," Sawyer said, distilling Tyler's hell into six one-syllable words.

"We weren't going out." He shoved his phone away so it was half-hidden under a stack of papers. "It was just fun."

Sawyer nodded. "Sounds like it."

"Fuck you."

Sawyer just laughed in response. "Can't imagine why a girl would go running from you when you're such a nice, cheerful guy."

Tyler all but growled at his friend, but the other man didn't even flinch, which just amped up Tyler's already raging temperament that had his blood pressure jacked sky-high. "She had a great deal in my building. Any other person in Harbor City would have jumped at the chance to keep it. Why can't she ever do what's expected?"

"Because then you wouldn't be moping around your office instead of at our previously scheduled lunch."

"Shit." He glared at his laptop screen and the calendar reminder in the top right-hand corner alerting him that his lunch was supposed to start forty-five minutes ago. "I missed that?"

"You did. Lucky for you…" Sawyer grabbed the white bag next to his chair and plopped it on Tyler's desk. The smell of bacon and cheese and an unholy amount of greasy goodness wafted out from it. "Vito's has takeout. I drank your shake on the way over."

Tyler didn't miss appointments. He certainly didn't miss ones for lunch at the best diner in Harbor City. He thought he'd been coping well with the whole Everly thing. He was wrong. Obviously. "I'm so fucked."

"Pretty much," Sawyer agreed. "But not on the Ferranti deal, from what I heard."

Tyler froze in the middle of pulling out the aluminum-foil-wrapped burger from the bag. "What?"

"Yeah, word is the old man stuck up for you at the board meeting. Something about brilliant ideas and fiery commitment."

That didn't make sense. Alberto was firmly Team

Everly on anything and everything. If she was pissed at him, Alberto should be, too. Why couldn't these people make sense? Or, more likely, what had being with Everly done to his ability to know what moves everyone was about to make before they made them?

"Why would he do that?" he asked, taking the burger the rest of the way out and unwrapping it on his desk as he tried to unravel the riddle.

Sawyer shrugged and settled back into the chair. "Because he probably saw the same thing I'm looking at."

Tyler glanced down at his lunch. "A double bacon cheeseburger with extra mayo?"

"Jesus, you're dumb." Sawyer leaned forward, propping his elbows on his knees and giving Tyler a you're-a-complete-moron look. "An idiot in love and going about everything in exactly the wrong way."

And he thought Sawyer might actually be onto something. Instead, he was just busting his balls. "Fuck off."

The other man took the curse in stride. "I'll take that as confirmation, and if you know what's good for you, you'll go after Everly."

Yeah, right. Even if she were the kind of woman he wanted in his life, which she wasn't (*uh-huh, whatever you say, buddy*), Everly had absolutely no interest in him. "She made it pretty clear she doesn't want to see me. Anyway, the hotel pitch meeting is next week, and I have to finalize this presentation."

Sawyer muttered something that sounded a lot like "clueless asswipe" under his breath and stood up. "For a smart guy, you sure are a moron sometimes."

Tyler, the burger stopped halfway to his mouth, watched his friend stroll to the door. "You're not eating with me?"

Pausing in the office doorway, Sawyer looked back at him. "After your no-show, I made a lunch date with my wife. Amazing how being around a woman you love will make your schedule open up and make you become more flexible. You should try it sometime."

"Oh yeah, and next thing you know I'll be fixing up flea market finds."

"Don't knock it until you've tried it, buddy," he said. "Especially if it involves watching my wife paint in a bikini—not that you'll ever get to see that vision."

With a sickeningly sweet smile stapled to his face, Sawyer offered a quick wave and walked out of Tyler's office, leaving him to stew about what in the hell was going on with his life and what he needed—not wanted—to do next.

The new Black Hearts Art Gallery was relocating in a month to the former industrial building that some investor had renovated into a kind of art mecca with several galleries sharing the street level and the next three floors housing art studios. Above that there were typical Harbor City small apartments at outrageous rental prices. She hated it, but she was determined to sign the lease. It wasn't the space's fault it didn't come with an infuriatingly sexy know-it-all. Now it was her apartment's turn. Yeah. There was nothing in the world as fun as unpacking hastily packed boxes that weren't even labeled because she'd been too pissed to remember the basics of moving.

Kiki sliced through the duct tape (it was the only kind Everly had had in her old apartment) holding a large box closed to reveal kitchen stuff. Great. It was just the reminder she needed of what had gotten her here.

"Forget that one. I'll get to it later."

Kiki carried the box the six steps to the other room and left it sitting on the three feet of counter space (total) in the galley kitchen.

"So you know I'm gonna kick your former downstairs neighbor's ass, right?" Kiki said as she made her way through the maze of boxes in the living room/dining room/bedroom combination.

"He has a name." *And his head up his ass.*

Kiki scoffed. "As far as I'm concerned, it's Dead Man."

She couldn't lie; the image of Kiki going after Tyler made her smile in that deep, dark, fuck-you-and-the-horse-you-rode-in-on kind of way. It was the first thing to knock the been-hit-by-a-crosstown-bus look off her face since she'd used every ounce of pride and Riverside bluster to walk out of the gala as if her heart hadn't just been put through a garbage disposal.

"Thanks for the offer," she said as she shoved another book onto the shelves the moving guys had put next to the single window. "But I made the call to end things, not him."

"Why are you being so nice about this?" Kiki sliced open another box, this time revealing the shoes Everly had just thrown in there. Her friend looked around the sparse surroundings. "Where do you want these?"

"There's a shoe rack hanging on the inside of the closet door." She'd sacrifice space for her winter coats for her babies. "Anyway, I can be cool about it because"—she was too numb to feel anything but the occasional flash of anger or sadness—"none of it mattered. I've told you eighty billion times already that it was just for fun."

"And that's why you had to hotfoot it out of his building where you had twice the space for almost the same price?" Kiki asked as she loaded a fourth pair of black shoes onto the shoe rack.

Okay, that hadn't been her most brilliant moment, but she'd needed space away from Tyler more than she needed space in her apartment. "I was month to month, and this place is in the heart of the art district for the same price. How could I not grab it? Gotta think with your head not your heart."

At least, that's what she was telling herself. Repeatedly. Day and night. Maybe even in her sleep.

Kiki crunched the now empty box and added it to the pile the super would cart away tomorrow. "Solid life advice there."

Yeah, if only she could follow the wise words she spouted. Needing to move and to change the direction of this conversation before she confessed that she hadn't stopped thinking about Tyler since the gala—sometimes it was fantasies about laughing as he groveled at her feet and sometimes it was banging him against the wall after he'd sufficiently groveled— Everly stood up, pressed her palms to her lower back, and arched. God, that felt good. Hauling boxes sucked. Then, she took the four steps over to her bed where her purse sat in the middle. She grabbed her wallet from the bag and fished out the check she'd written this morning thanks to the return of her outrageous security deposit from her old super.

"Well, the good news is that because of the move, I can finally give you this." She handed over the check to Kiki. "It's everything I owe you for the catering you've been doing at the shows."

Kiki took the check, looked at the figure written on it, and immediately tried to hand it back. "You know there's no time limit on this. With the move, I know things have to be tight right now."

"Friends don't take advantage of each other." She shoved her hands in her pockets. "You helped when I needed it, and now I can finally pay you back. That was our agreement, and I'm sticking to it."

"You're good people, Everly," Kiki said. "That asshole didn't deserve you. Especially not with the crap he pulled about that Irena chick. That was a ginormous load of crap."

"True." Of course, that didn't make the hole in her chest close up any faster.

"You know you matter, right?" Kiki enveloped her in a hug, squeezing tight before letting her go. "To the people who count, you matter, and we'd fight right beside you even if it meant causing a scene in the middle of some crazy Harbor City high-society event because you're worth fighting for."

Everly pressed her lips together and fought to make her chin stop trembling. "That's the nicest, most unhinged pep talk anyone's ever given me. I just wish I didn't need it." Cue the waterworks. Damn, she hated not being able to stop the tears and for having tears for him. "I fell for him. I knew I shouldn't have. I didn't mean to but…" The rest of the words wouldn't come.

"Oh honey," Kiki said, hugging her again.

Everly just let the tears that she'd been holding onto for the past four days fall. It wasn't a pretty cry. Her nose ran. Her face went flush. It was an ugly cry over a man she never should have been with anyway. One who thought she didn't matter because she was a Riverside woman through and through.

"So much for just being about fun," she said, once she could finally form words again. "I fell for him. I thought he was different. I made the exact same mistake my mom made even though Nunni warned me almost every day growing up to watch out for men like Tyler."

"I'm gonna kill him." Kiki grabbed the open bottle of wine sitting on the end table still wrapped in plastic next to the couch and poured a good measure into a red plastic cup and handed it to Everly. "For you, I'd wear orange."

"But if you go to jail, who would cater my next gallery show and provide the horrible wine?" she asked as she downed a gulp of the wine that may not taste great but it had alcohol in it and that would make things temporarily better.

"Shit." Kiki poured herself some wine. "Looks like we have to let him stay breathing." She held up her glass. "Up with good friends and down with assholes."

Everly cracked a smile and tapped the top of her plastic cup to Kiki's. She would drink to that—probably all night long. And tomorrow, when she woke up with a mouth full of cotton and a head full of aches? Well, she'd deal with what came next then, even if she had no idea how.

Chapter Twenty-Six

A last-minute call from Alberto a week later had Tyler scrambling. The Italian was still rooting for him to get the consulting job and figured the best way to help make that happen was a do-over meet and greet with the board, which was how Tyler had ended up outside Helene Carlyle's penthouse for an informal pre-wedding dinner with a guest list that just happened to include several key members of the Ferranti Hotel Group board who'd crossed the Atlantic to attend Carlo's wedding.

One knock and the door opened wide, revealing Helene and Alberto holding hands and looking like they'd been together for years and settled into that kind of bonded happiness he only ever saw on TV or when he'd go over to Frankie's house as a kid and see Mr. and Mrs. Hartigan interact.

"Finally, you're here," Alberto said with a wide grin.

"Alberto, darling, your mother was asking for you right before the doorbell buzzed; do you mind checking in on her?" Helene asked.

"Of course." He gave Helene a knowing look.

Spidey sense tingling, he felt his gaze follow Alberto through the large living room until he stopped next to a tiny woman who had to be eighty draped in black lace and another woman who he'd know in a zero-visibility snowstorm let alone a semi-crowded Harbor City cocktail party. His pulse kicked it into high gear and every sense went on alert. Everly. She was here. He couldn't look away. She was wearing a familiar black sheath dress. He knew the feel of that dress, knew how it looked crumpled into a ball on his bedroom floor next to her sky-high heels and scraps of lace she called panties—if she was even wearing any that day. The memory immediately had him wondering what was under that dress tonight.

That was bad enough. What was worse was the unraveling of the tension wrapped around him like invisible barbed wire as soon as he saw her. The disappearance, for the first time in five days, of the biting tightness that had worked its way down to his bones was as much of a relief as it was a shock.

"Don't feel bad; it happens to us all," Helene said, the sincerity in her voice genuine.

Ignoring the urge to rush over to Everly, Tyler turned his attention back to his host. "What's that?"

"Falling in love."

What the— "Why does everyone keep saying that?"

"Because you have no poker face when it comes to Everly." Triumph lingered in every cultured syllable.

The pieces fell into place. The board members were there—along with Hudson, Felicia, Sawyer, Clover, and an unsmiling Irena and Carlo who, judging by their body language, were having about as much fun at the dinner in their honor as Tyler was—but his gaze kept going back to Everly, who hadn't stopped glaring at him since he spotted her. "So this was a setup."

"Did you really expect anything else?"

Well, he shouldn't have, but his instincts had been all fucked up since the first time that Ms. 3B decided to stomp-walk across his ceiling. Not that he'd admit that. "Alberto said this was a chance to redeem myself after the gala and that the entire board would be here."

Helene shrugged. "It is and they are."

He scanned the room, confirming that Alberto was mixing and mingling among all the board members, stopping occasionally to make eye contact with Tyler and wave. That was where his attention needed to be. Not on the woman across the room who was sipping a glass of champagne and gesturing wildly with her hands while she talked with the old lady in lace. It was where his attention *would* be.

Mind made up, he mentally promised not to pay her any attention—and immediately found himself watching her again. *Pull your head out of your ass, Jacobson.* "I don't like being manipulated."

"Who does?" Helene asked. "But a schemer like yourself should understand that eventually the tables are going to get turned on you. Take a lesson from a kindred spirit—love is too valuable to throw away. If you're lucky enough to find it, you fight for it."

Everly must have felt his gaze because she glanced over at him and gave him the kind of glare that didn't need words to say "fuck you" and then returned to her conversation with the woman who had to be Alberto's mother. A kick in the balls with one of her pointy-toed shoes would have felt better.

"She doesn't want me here."

Helene made a noise that if it would have come from another woman he would have called it a snort. "Good thing it's not her home, then."

With that, Helene wandered off toward her sons and their significant others. Alberto was already there. Seeing the group of them laughing and chatting away made Tyler's stomach burn with the bittersweet knowledge that that could have been him with Everly. If he had different priorities or she'd been a different woman, they could be like the other couples—happy. Instead, they were on opposite sides of the room. It wasn't right. He should say something, anything, to smooth this over. Before he got a chance, though, Helene announced dinner was served. Not surprisingly, he found himself sitting next to Everly. It was now or never and even though he didn't have a plan, he jumped on it anyway.

Lowering his voice so only she could hear, he said, "I just want to apologize."

She shook out her linen napkin and draped it over her lap without looking at him. "I just want it to never get below sixty degrees."

Okay. That went over about as well as the idea of no second breakfast to a hobbit. Still, he hadn't gotten this far in life by giving in when things got tough. "I shouldn't have said what I said, the way I said it, at the gala. I'm sorry."

This time Everly did turn and look at him. He expected to see heat, anger, hurt, anything. Instead her face was completely neutral.

"But you meant it. Every word, don't try to act like you didn't," she said, her voice quiet, calm, and thick with her accent. "Us Riverside girls can smell bullshit from five miles away."

Thank God Helene wasn't serving steak or Everly would be tempted to use the serrated blade on Tyler's thigh. He just wanted to apologize. What a load of crap. He wanted to make things look good in front of Alberto and the board members. That's what men like him did. They sure didn't cause a scene. So what if the bags under his eyes were getting bags and the scruff on his jaw looked more than a little scraggly, she still should have run over him in the parking garage when she'd had the chance.

"Everly—"

"Don't." Just the sound of her name on his lips had her wanting to give in. It was ridiculous. "We're both adults here, and there's no reason to make this messy, especially not here."

Making nice with Irena was hard enough; she couldn't play pretend on two fronts. The other woman had done the whole kissy-face, we're-the-best-of-friends thing and she'd played along for Carlo's sake. For whatever reason, he'd picked Irena to be his wife in name only and who was she to judge? It wasn't like her love life was anything to brag about. Exhibits A–Z were sitting right beside her and making her nerves jittery and her body electric. In his dark-blue suit that set off his gorgeous though tired eyes and only made his already broad shoulders look even stronger, he didn't even have the common courtesy to look like the scumbag he was—even with the edgy energy stringing him tight. It wasn't fair to still want him after what he'd done, but she did, and it just pissed her off more than she already was.

"We need to talk." He paused, his hand coming to rest on her knee under the table and sending a jolt of awareness through her. "Please."

Not melting under his touch took all the energy she had at the moment so she could get out was a single word. "No."

The vein in his temple throbbed, and his gaze grew heated. "That's it, just no?"

The possessiveness in his voice made her thighs clench. Dammit. She was smarter than this. She knew what was at the end of this path. He only wanted to be with people who mattered. She was just fun. Like mother like daughter, except she wasn't going to end up like her mom, devastated and broken, so she gathered the anger still burning in her veins.

"Yeah." She plucked his hand off her knee and let her working-class, not-the-kind-of-person-who-matters accent deepen. "That's it."

Then she turned to Carlo's nonna and switched to Italian, freezing out the man on her left—or at least doing her best to ignore his every movement that she seemed to catalog anyway. Why? Because life wasn't fair, and her heart was still making a case for the schemer who would only break her heart again and again because no matter what, she'd never stop being Riverside through and through. It was who she was, and if he couldn't accept that, then Kiki was right and he didn't deserve her even if she was already in love with him. Happy endings were just BS.

After dinner, instead of turning left onto Marlowe Avenue, Tyler merged onto the bridge leading to the one place he always seemed to find his way back to no matter how hard he ran in the other direction—home. Traffic lightened up once he passed over the bridge and got off the parkway at exit nine. People were bundled up on the sidewalk on their way from the train station to the commuter parking lot. Farther on, he turned onto Brookside Avenue and drove past the shop windows with snow spray-painted on the windows and the couples strolling down the sidewalks to one of the many restaurants that punctuated groups of shops like commas in a sentence that didn't end for blocks and blocks.

It wasn't Harbor City's famed shopping paradise with elaborate Christmas windows that went up right after Halloween, but it also wasn't as dependent on appearances or the need to strive to be bigger and better and more astounding than the display next door. The library he'd hung out in as a kid was two blocks to his left, right past the middle school he'd attended. The house he'd lived in was four blocks in the other direction, and as he drove past it, he spared it only the briefest of glances. A new family lived there now. Hopefully a happier one where a kid getting a scholarship to a prep school across the harbor was cause for celebration instead of derision.

He drove past the park where he'd had his first beer in the shadow of the spiral slide and the high school where he'd lost his virginity while parked in the football stadium's shadow. Three more blocks with a four-way stop sign on each corner and he pulled to a stop in front of Frankie and Finian Hartigan's two-story bungalow. Their parents were a few blocks to the north. The other siblings were scattered around in a ten-block radius, all except Felicia, the ant scientist, who'd fallen for Sawyer's younger brother Hudson and was the only Hartigan to ever leave Waterbury. They were all smart and outgoing, able to take on bigger things, and yet they'd stayed in this working-class township so close to Harbor City they could see its skyscrapers' lights twinkle in the distance.

His phone vibrated in the car's cupholder. He hit talk. "Yeah?"

"You gonna stay in your car like some weirdo stalker or come inside and have a beer?" Frankie asked.

Tyler looked toward the house where Frankie stood in the open front door. "Is it good beer?"

"It's free beer; is there a better kind?"

Ten minutes later and he and Frankie—Finian was on duty at the firehouse—were sitting out on the deck as close as possible to the fire pit in a failed attempt to stay warm as the pre-winter night gave them a preview of what was ahead in the next few months.

"Tell me again why we're out here instead of inside where it's warm?" Tyler asked, already halfway done with his first beer.

Frankie grinned at him, a little bit of that Hartigan crazy sparkling in his eyes. "Because we're men and we're tough."

The number of dumb plans he'd agreed to when they were teenagers because of that line were too numerous to count, and also some of his favorite memories. "There is something wrong with you."

"Nothing I can't live with." Frankie sipped his beer and looked out at the yard. "So what has you on our side of the bridge twice in one month?"

Shit. He must look rough if Frankie was asking him in dude code if he was all right. "Just got in the car and ended up here."

Silence punctuated by the snap and crackle of the burning wood in the pit filled the night air. There were too many streetlights around to see any stars in the sky, but they both stared upward anyway. Looking at each other would just be too weird.

"You should have brought your girl along," Frankie said, breaking the silence. "She makes you more fun."

He took a swallow of beer that suddenly tasted like sawdust and chalk. "She's not my girl."

"Dumped your ass already?"

"Pretty much." He downed the rest of his beer.

"That sucks, man," Frankie said, and handed him another.

No "I'm sorry." No "what happened." Just acknowledgment and moving on. It was exactly the reaction he'd expected from one of his oldest friends who knew without being told that Tyler didn't want to talk about it. Not that Frankie was the kind to push for details anyway—at least not of the bad-news variety. He'd always kept his life simple and easy. Tyler kind of envied him for that—especially when his own self-made complications fucked up his world.

"Why didn't you ever leave?" The question just sort of popped out before Tyler had a chance to consider how to phrase it.

Frankie snorted. "Why would I?"

"Because you could," he said, still staring at the invisible stars. "Despite the show you put on for people, you're smart. You could make more money. You could be more than just some guy from Waterbury."

"See, that's your problem." Frankie twisted in his chair to face him, his jaw tight and his shoulders tense. "You're the only one I know who worries about that shit. I *like* being from Waterbury, where people make eye contact with you when you pass them on the street. The town is filled with people who work hard for what they've got and they appreciate it. I'm a blue-collar guy, and I don't need to pretend I'm anything else."

Tyler's spine snapped straight and he turned on his friend. Pretend? He didn't need to pretend. He needed to forget—to make others forget. "Are you saying that I do?"

"Fuck yeah," Frankie said, not giving an inch.

"I have my reasons for wanting to leave this place behind." The two main ones being the people who contributed to his gene pool.

"Yeah, I know. Your parents were shit." The other man took a long swig of beer. "We all knew it, but there wasn't a thing we could do about it short of kidnapping you and hiding you in our basement—an option Finian and I brought up with our dad."

"I bet he had an answer for that."

"Sure did." Frankie looked him dead in the

eye. "Where do you think the invite to apply for a scholarship for that fancy-ass prep school came from? One of the guys in his firehouse was married to a woman whose sister taught at that place."

"He did that?" That sucked the shitty attitude right out of Tyler, and he sank back against the knockoff Adirondack deck chair. "I had no idea."

"There's a lot you don't have a fucking clue about." Frankie was on a roll and he leaned forward, elbows on his knees, and got right in Tyler's face. "Remember that first Thanksgiving you spent with the Carlyles?"

"Yeah."

"That happened because my mom spotted Helene Carlyle heading out of your house with your mom watching her go from the window, a half-empty vodka bottle in her hand. Well, Ma all but grabbed Mrs. Carlyle and forced her into our kitchen. It was a madhouse, what with all of us trying to get out of there in time to catch the bus to school, but that woman stuck it out and listened to Ma explain about your parents and tell her that you were different. That you could really be something if you could just get away from the bastards who birthed you. Of course, she used nicer language than that, but that was the gist."

It was like someone had turned out all the city lights, and the stars started appearing one by one in the night sky. "So that's how I ended up spending so many holidays and vacations with them."

"Yeah, and when you couldn't be with them, you were at our house adding to the bedlam there," Frankie snarled, sitting in his chair and turning his face back to the sky. "That's the blue-collar community that you find so horrible. We watch out for one another here in Waterbury. It may not always be visible and we may not always brag about it or hold fancy parties to raise money for things, but we make good things happen. You wanna know why I stayed? Because I want to contribute to that, but you've been trying to put as much distance between you and where you grew up for so long that you can't even see all the good stuff. And every time you try to hide who you are and where you came from you're telling us—and Everly—to fuck off."

Jesus. What in the hell did he say to that? Every possible response evaporated like so much nothing. How had he missed all of this? For a man who prided himself on always knowing what someone was going to do before they did it, this revelation had his brain buffering for signal. And in the darkness, he saw the one thing he'd always missed before. That he wasn't running away from where he was from, he was running away from himself. He'd been a complete asshole who'd been fighting so hard to avoid becoming his bitter, paranoid, always-ready-to-screw-over-people-before-they-had-a-chance-to-screw-you-over parents that if he wasn't careful, he'd end up being just like them anyway.

He drained his beer in one gulp and set it down on the deck next to his other empty soldier. "You're right."

"What?" Frankie turned and looked at him with a smug grin. "I must have gone temporarily deaf. Can you say that again?"

Tyler flipped him off. "Fuck off, you heard me."

"Yeah, I did. So how about you tell me the real reason why you ended up parked outside my house like the world's saddest multimillionaire dickhead in desperate need of a cleanup because man, you look fucking rough."

"Everly." Because she'd seen through it all right from the beginning.

"You mean the woman who's not your girl even though you love her?"

"I don't love her." He just couldn't figure her out when it appeared that she had his number. The first time they'd met most likely.

Frankie laughed. "Lie to yourself; don't lie to me."

Heat rushed through him along with the sneaking suspicion that he was full of shit. "I'm not."

"Okay." Frankie shrugged and nodded. "Then say it. Say, 'I don't love Everly Ribinski, the hottest girl who ever told me to fuck off and die.'"

"She didn't say that." Delay? Him? Never.

Frankie just shook his head. "Stop stalling."

He wasn't stalling; he was just stupefied. He wanted to say it. He needed to say it to get his know-it-all best friend off his ass but...he couldn't. The words turned to ash on his tongue. There was only one reason for that. He loved her. Like a complete moron, he'd fooled around and fallen in love. Hell, he had probably already been halfway there when he'd decided the best idea in the world was to sit on a lounge chair in the parking garage and wait for his bitch queen of an upstairs neighbor to come home. And when she'd gone toe to toe with Irena at the gala, that hadn't been her being unable to control her temper. That had been her defending him, something he had so little experience with—or so he thought—that he hadn't been able to identify that feeling of gratitude so he'd freaked out and had pushed her away.

"Shit," he said, ramming his fingers through his hair. "I've fucked it all up."

Frankie just raised an eyebrow, so Tyler gave him the whole story from the parking spot coin flip to the gala blowup to the way Everly had cut him to the quick at dinner.

"Damn." Frankie chuckled. "I like that woman. If she hadn't already fallen for you, I would be shoving you out of the way to make my move."

"Go for it." Misery sunk like an anchor in his gut. "She told me to hit the road, wouldn't even let me apologize tonight at dinner."

"If I even believed for a millisecond that you meant that, I would. I might be the one who runs into burning buildings for a living, but you're the true idiot," Frankie said. "Everly is one of us and, unlike some douchebags, doesn't need to try to hide it."

"You got that from one poker night at your house?" Tyler wasn't disagreeing, but that didn't mean he was accepting it with grace, either.

"I'm a people person." He shrugged. "Look, here's what I'm telling you. Everly is a woman who wears her heart on her sleeve. If she wanted to put you on blast, she would have, and smoke would still be wafting from your charred-beyond-recognition ass because of the chewing out you got. But she didn't. You want her, you gotta fight for her."

Yeah, it was the kind of thing that made sense on paper, but how in the hell he was supposed to actually make it happen when she wouldn't even talk to him was a whole other thing. "How?"

"You're the fucking evil-genius plotter who's in love with her—you go figure it out," Frankie said, and gathered up their empty beers as he stood. "Just do it quick because if I have another one of these touchy-feely conversations anytime soon I might throw up."

"Such a softie." Tyler stood and walked back toward the house with Frankie.

"Trust me," his friend said. "'Soft' is not the word the ladies use to describe me."

Tyler may have been laughing again by the time he walked out to his car, but his brain was going at supersonic speeds. Frankie was wrong about the love thing—there was no way he'd fallen for the exact opposite of the kind of woman he needed in his life—but he wanted her, missed her, needed to be around her. Some might say that was the same thing, but he'd seen love up close and personal with his parents. They fought. They said I love you. They fought some more. That wasn't what he needed in his life. But he did need Everly because he…well, because he did. So like the schemer he was, he spent the drive home going through options and prognosticating outcomes, because this was one plot that had to go according to plan.

Chapter Twenty-Seven

On the best of days, Everly wasn't a fan of weddings—especially not fancy, five-hundred-guest weddings at the most sought-after church in Harbor City—but today was even worse. She hated love. Love sucked donkey balls dipped in rancid mayo. Love was a lie. Yeah, the timing of her moving through the heartbreak stages from sad but numb to hurt and pissed had coincided with showing up to the chapel to watch Carlo say "I do" for business purposes only to that evil hag Irena. Wasn't she just the luckiest? Even worse, she had to pretend to be happy about being there. The irony of having to act like a member of Harbor City's elite wishing the couple well after what had gone down with Tyler wasn't lost on her.

And speak of the devil, he was heading straight toward where she and Nonna were waiting in the vestibule before they walked down to their assigned seats in the front row. The man looked like hell. His tie was askew. His shirt wrinkled. His scruffy beard had moved straight into the lost-in-the-wilderness stage. And the jerk was still hot enough to make her girlie parts sit up and say, "Hello hottie." God, she hated him.

"What is he doing here?" she mumbled to herself as he made a beeline over to them.

"*Lui è molto carino*," Nonna said, patting Everly's forearm.

Cute? Yeah, despite the fact that his black tux seemed to hang on him a little more than it had before, it still made his blue eyes stand out. Of course, that wasn't what she needed to be thinking about right now. Wishing there were more people than just her, Nonna, Alberto, and Carlo in the vestibule to add cover, Everly turned her attention to the closed door leading to the chapel because watching him wasn't doing a damn thing to make the swirling emotions inside her subside.

It was a mistake. Diverting her focus just meant she didn't see his final approach until it was too late.

"Everly," Tyler said, tucking an errant hair behind her ear. "We need to talk."

Hating how her body instantly responded to him with a yes-please shiver, she refused to look at him. "I'm busy."

"Everly." His voice deepened. "I want you. I promise I can make it fun again, just like it was before."

She whirled on him. "What did you say to me?"

He just stood there, so close she could literally lean over and brush her lips across his jaw, looking like a man who'd been through the wringer and still managed to be the hottest person she'd ever seen in her life. It wasn't fair. And now he told her he wanted her? Not needed her. Not loved her. But wanted her. After radio silence for weeks? After he'd watched her walk away at the gala without even trying to go after her. After his lame attempt to apologize last night? The spark of anger in her belly grew into a flame, and she held onto it with both hands, not caring if she got burned. Really, it was too late for that anyway.

"I want it to be like it was before," he repeated. "Fun."

Alberto, Carlo, and Nonna all stared at the live show of Everly's humiliation, their mouths agape. Scratch that. Carlo's mouth was agape. Nonna smiled placidly and Alberto had the smug expression of a man who had all the answers.

When she didn't say anything—she couldn't—he kept talking. "I know I was slow on the uptake. Turns out I'm good at reading other people's motives and shit when it comes to knowing my own. And my motive, from the first moment you almost killed me with your boxes but spared me when I put my foot in my mouth, was to be with you. I'm miserable without you. You look miserable without me."

She raised an eyebrow in an oh-really reaction because she'd seen herself in the mirror today but couldn't promise the same of him. "So you want me and that means that I should just fall to the ground overwhelmed with joy? Do you know how many times my dad told my mom he *wanted* her? Do you know how many times she *believed* him? Every time right up until she put that rope around her neck. I deserve more than someone who *wants* me. I deserve someone who loves me. Can you say that? Can you say those words?"

Tyler didn't say anything. He didn't have to. The panic in his eyes round with shock said it all.

It wasn't fair. It wasn't even close. Emotion turned into a lump in her throat, and no matter how many times she swallowed, she couldn't get past it. And worst of all, she wanted to believe him because those were the only words she'd been wanting to hear from him since that night she'd come home to find him on a lounge chair in the parking garage. Giving in would be easy... and beyond a risk she was willing to take. Just having fun was one thing, but she wanted more than that from him. She wanted love.

"Everly," he finally managed to get out—but it was too late.

She held up her hand, silencing him because she couldn't stand to hear the words. How often had her mother made herself believe only to end up broken because of a man? Taking a deep breath, she glanced at the others in the vestibule with them. None of them bothered to hide their curiosity because they didn't need to. They knew who they were and what they wanted. Unlike Tyler, they weren't pretending. Using up her very last bit of control to keep herself from falling apart, she turned back to Tyler and did what she had to do, what her mother should have done.

"Please." He reached out, but she evaded his touch. "We can go back to what it was."

Yeah. That wasn't going to happen.

"It's too late for that. I want someone who knows that I'm worth fighting for, not someone who is fighting to forget who I am…" She leveled a glare at Tyler that should have fried him right down to his toes. "Or who he is. I want someone who loves me as much as I love him." *As much as I love you…*

Before she could say anything else, the chapel doors opened and an entire church full of wedding guests turned in their direction. She slammed her mouth shut and slipped her arm through Nonna's. The older woman looked at her, then over to Tyler, and then back again.

"*L'amore ti fa matto*," she said, and held out her free hand to Tyler.

Nonna couldn't be more wrong in her assessment of the situation. Love may make some people crazy, but it just fucked up Everly's world.

Together, she, Nonna, Alberto, and Carlo walked down the aisle into the church, leaving Tyler behind, just like she needed her heart to do.

Tyler stood dumbfounded in the vestibule as the minister began explaining to the wedding guests seated that the bride would be reading from her favorite sonnet behind the closed vestibule door before walking down the aisle.

L'amore? Love? Why did people keep saying that? It wasn't love. Love was crazy and out of control and overwhelming to the point where a person could lose themselves completely. He scrubbed his palm against the nearly three-week growth of beard that he hadn't meant to grow and caught a glimpse of himself in the glass case of church mementos. It was impossible to miss the meals he'd skipped with how his tux hung on him or the more than a hint of wild desperation in his tired eyes. Crazy? Yeah, he looked a little bit that way. Out of control? He was going with yes. Overwhelmed? That was affirmative.

"Fucking A," he said, too shocked to care that he was talking to himself. "I love her."

"Do not even think about it, Tyler Jacobson." Irena's snotty tone was like taking a dull knife to the eye.

He turned to see her flanked by attendants as she marched from the waiting lounge straight toward him. She was in a poofy, overdesigned monstrosity of a wedding dress, a mic in one hand and a piece of paper crumpled in the other. There was an unhinged fury in her eyes that at any other time would have made him head for cover. Right now, though, he was still too stunned about the fact that he'd fallen in love with Everly to give a shit.

"You and that low-rent tramp had better not even be considering stealing my thunder. This is my day. Mine." Irena raised the hand holding the mic and pointed it at him, her thumb brushing the power button. "I am the bride and you shouldn't even be here. Neither should that social-climbing gutter rat. Why Alberto insisted, I have no clue beyond the nearly unbearable Pollyanna attitude of that man, but I swear to God if either of you do a single thing to mess up my day, I will make it my life's mission to put you two back in the slums where you belong."

His gaze slid from the little red light on the mic to the closed doors between them and a church full of wedding guests. In half a heartbeat he knew exactly what he needed to do. It was time to let his Waterbury hang out.

"You could try," he said, making sure his voice was loud enough to be heard clearly through the speakers in the church. "You might even be able to do it, but I'll tell you something, Irena, a single broke Everly in a run-down tenement is still worth more than three hundred of you." He took a step closer to his ex-fiancée, determined that the only person he cared about on the other side of the doors would catch every word. "Do you want to know why? Because she knows who she is. She's earned what she has. She doesn't fight to keep other people down, she fights to protect them. You're deluded if you think you could ever take anything away from Everly."

Irena rolled her eyes. "Thank God I'm not actually in love with Carlo because that sentimental bullshit was almost enough to make me puke."

"For once you're right about something," he said, all but dipping his head to be close to the mic. "I love Everly. I can't imagine life without her."

"Yep." Irena made a gagging face. "I definitely just threw up in my mouth a little."

After everything the woman had put Everly through, he should draw out the moment more, but all he cared about was getting to the woman he loved as soon as possible. "You want to know something that will really send you over the edge?"

"What, you want her to have your babies?"

"Someday, but that's not what I was going to say." Of course, the image of mini Everlys filled his head. "I was going to tell you that your mic is live and everyone inside that church heard every bitchy little word you just said. After the pain in the ass you've been over the years and all the shit you've pulled, that should be the best thing about this whole exchange, but you know what?" He grabbed the mic from her hand while she stood there blinking rapidly, her mouth hanging open. "The only thing I care about anyone hearing is this: I don't just want you, Everly Ribinski. I love you. So much so that I'd tell all these big-money assholes exactly what they can do with their hotel deal if they don't want to give the consulting position to a scholarship kid like me. Because even a lifetime of being accepted by them doesn't mean anything compared to spending just five minutes with you."

And with that, he dropped the mic, yanked open the doors leading to the church, and marched inside, determined to find his woman.

That wasn't going to happen right away, though, because the place was total chaos, with football-offensive-lineman-size ushers plugging up the aisle, not letting anyone through—with one exception.

Carlo rushed past him out into the vestibule. No doubt he had something to say to Irena regarding the catty line about his dad that had gone out on the hot mic, but Tyler didn't care. She didn't matter. Most of the people in the church didn't matter. The only one who really did was sitting with Nonna near the front. She was the only person there who wasn't transfixed by the Irena and Carlo show going on behind him. He had to get past the ushers and get to her.

"What do you mean, you can't go through with it?" Irena yelled loud enough that they must have heard her across the harbor in Waterbury and pulled Tyler's attention behind him. "That you were wrong to think it could work? There is an entire church full of people waiting for us to get married."

Carlo shrugged. "We both know this whole marriage was just a business arrangement, and with that performance piped in over the speakers, you know it's not going to work out anymore."

"So you are leaving me at the altar?" Irena asked, all pretense of the Harbor City sweetheart part she played to a T gone and the actual harpy she was on full display.

Carlo glanced back at the chapel, relief apparent on his face even from where Tyler was standing.

"Technically," Carlo said, "you're in the vestibule."

"And you think that matters?" She grabbed her voluminous skirt with both hands. "You…you…Italian asshole."

With that, she stormed off, her attendants scurrying after her. Everyone in the church sat watching as Carlo made his way back up the aisle to the halfway point where Alberto was waiting, a huge smile on his face. The two men conferred for a minute before Carlo strode up to the front of the church and the minister waiting there, his hand on his Bible, and turned to address the crowd.

"I'm sorry to tell you that the wedding is off," Carlo said, his voice sounding happier than Tyler had ever heard it before. "Thank you all for coming."

The church erupted with chatter. Irena's family marched out, their chins high and their gazes locked straight forward. Everly and Nonna marched up to Alberto and Carlo in the front, offering their support and solidarity. Tyler remained standing near the back, desperate for a plan to appear in his mind fully formed as to how he was going to get Everly to listen to him plead his case. The place was deafening with everyone talking at once. No doubt those with friends who weren't there were busily texting them to let them know what had just happened at what was supposed to be the society wedding of the year. It was exactly the kind of gleeful reaction at someone else's expense that he'd dreaded being at the center of for as long as he'd been around these people. It almost made him feel bad for Irena. Almost. And it reminded him that in Waterbury, this wouldn't be happening. Oh, people would be having a shit fit, but there'd be a lot more sympathetic faces than those he saw in the church.

Damn, he'd been lucky to find the Carlyles. He never would have made it in this piranha pit without them. And he couldn't make it — anywhere — without Everly.

There was no way either of them was leaving this church without settling things between them. Life without Everly wasn't one he wanted to lead and he didn't care what kind of public fool he had to make of himself to get her to understand that.

"Hey, 3B," he hollered over the buzz of the crowd, loud enough to silence them. "You still interested in that parking spot?"

Everly turned in slow motion, hands on her hips, a queen-of-not-putting-up-with-your-shit look on her face. "What are you talking about?"

A Harbor City man would have run from her don't-fuck-with-me attitude, but he was from Waterbury and he had stones the size of watermelons. He pushed through the ushers and started to make his way up front. "The closest to Mrs. MacIntosh's Chevy — even though I'm sure no one can afford that ding insurance."

She cocked her head. "I don't live there anymore, remember?"

"Oh, that's right." He halved the distance between them. "Guess I need to sweeten the deal. How about you get the whole building? It was my first, you know. The one I love more than any other, so it's only right that the woman I love should have it." Taking advantage of her shocked silence, he grabbed his wallet from inside his tux jacket and pulled out the grubby quarter that he'd had since he was twelve. The one he'd used to take the emotion out of decision-making, the one he'd let guide his life for way too long. "Flip for it?"

Oblivious—or more likely not giving a shit—to their rapt audience, she strutted over to him, all badass woman from the tips of her black heels to her ebony hair pulled back in some kind of fancy bun. "Are you trying to buy your way back into my pants with a building?"

"No." He wanted more. He wanted all of her.

"Thank God," she said, the hard upward curl of her lips looking nothing like the smile she'd given him the first time he made her pasta. "I thought you'd—"

"I'm trying," he said, cutting her off, "to worm my way into your heart by making a complete and utter ass of myself in front of the most powerful people in Harbor City, the ones I've spent my life trying to get to see me as something other than I was."

She blinked in surprise, and there was no missing the nervous way she razed her bottom lip with her teeth. "Oh yeah, and what's that?"

"A fool." Yeah, that about summed it up.

She let out a shaky breath, and there was just enough interest in her gaze to give him hope.

"Keep talking," she said.

"You were right."

"About what?"

The only answer he could give was the real one, the one that cost him everything. "It all."

She didn't say anything. She just stared at him without blinking. His hands turned clammy and a line of sweat slid down his back. Then something changed. Her face softened. Her chin trembled. And her mouth—that lush red mouth that did such dirty, dirty things—curled up on one side.

"You're so infuriating," she said, her voice trembling just the slightest bit. "And you can't cook."

"Not true. I can make pasta," he said, pulling her in close. "You drive me nuts, too, with your loud clomping shoes and love of German painters when I like paintings of dogs playing poker."

"Your taste in art is atrocious," she said, relaxing against him. "How could I have ever fallen for a guy like you?"

"I'll let you know as soon as I figure out how I fell in love so hard with the most stubborn hard-ass woman in the world. I had to rethink everything about my life until I realized that the only thing I could do was admit to myself that I loved you—the woman you were, the woman you are, and the woman you're going to be. I love all of you. Forever. So let's do it; let's get married." And now he meant to be hers as much as she was going to be his. He adjusted his stance so that his hand with the quarter was free and angled his thumb for the best odds just like he'd practiced for years, not realizing that it was all for this moment. "So let's flip for it. Heads you say yes."

The coin went flying into the air and he held his breath because everything was riding on the outcome. Everly snatched it out of midair.

She handed it back to him without looking. "Heads."

Cupping her face, the one he wanted to be the first one he saw every morning and the last one every night, he moved in to kiss her, stopping just short of heaven. "You told me once that you don't believe in happy endings. I didn't, either, until I met you. I love you, Everly Ribinski from Riverside."

There was no missing the emotion in her eyes. "I love you, too."

Kissing her like it was the beginning of forever— because it was—he lost himself in the woman who'd sent every plan and plot he'd ever made on its ear. By the time they broke apart, everyone in the church was clapping.

"I guess there's only one thing left for us to do," he said, unable to take his gaze from Everly's beautiful face.

"Get married," Carlo said. "You have the minister here."

Everly threw back her head and laughed before giving Tyler some prime, grade-A Riverside smack talk. "No way—you're gonna have to work to get me in white."

That was his girl, never one to take the easy route without offering a challenge of her own. "Oh, believe me, I'll come up with the perfect scheme to make that happen."

"Well, *bellissima*," Alberto said from somewhere behind them. "It seems it's up to us to take advantage of having a church full of family and friends."

Dumbfounded, Helene turned to Alberto. This was not what they'd discussed. A quiet courthouse wedding and then waiting for the right time to break it to Hudson and Sawyer.

"We can't just get married now," she said, looking around at everyone watching them, her gaze stopping on Hudson and Sawyer standing in the fourth pew with Felicia and Clover, all four of them looking completely and utterly shocked.

"Why not, *bellissima*?" Alberto asked, picking up her hand and kissing it. "I know we were planning on having your judge friend do the ceremony and then breaking it to your boys when the time was right, but the minister is here. We have a license. And I love you."

Torn, Helene looked around at the church filled with the people she'd spent most of her life with, those who helped her with fund-raisers, those who'd seen her through Michael's funeral, those who made her grit her teeth and remind herself that it wasn't polite to tell them to go shove off, and—most importantly—her boys, who didn't look angry or offended at the idea. They looked…hurt.

"Mom," Sawyer said, striding forward to where she stood holding Alberto's hand. "You were going to get married without us?"

Mommy guilt—it never went away no matter how old her children got—twisted her stomach into knots. Her job was to protect them. To keep them safe. To see them into adulthood and help them become the men she knew they could be. Did that job end? Shouldn't that be her first and only priority? And they both had loved their father so much, she hadn't wanted to make them think they had to divide their loyalties.

"I was waiting for the right time to tell you," she said in a rush, for once floundering for the right words to say. "I know it will be hard, and your father, what would he say?"

Hudson walked over, a soft smile, so much like his father's, on his face. "That he's so happy you found love again."

"Exactly what we would say," Sawyer added.

And for once when the tears spilled down her cheeks she let them flow, unashamed and owning them fully.

"*Bellissima*." Alberto wiped away her tears. "Say yes."

The three-letter word was on the tip of her tongue, but she couldn't say it without making certain. She looked over at Hudson and Sawyer. "Are you sure you'll be okay with this?"

"On one condition," Hudson said, his face turning serious. "We get to stand up with you. I'll be your maid of honor, of course, since I'm prettier than Sawyer."

Her eldest snorted. "And so much more of a pain in the ass."

"Boys," she said, her tone the sharp one of rebuke that every mother used on occasion. Then she smiled. "That would make it perfect."

After that, it happened quickly. She stood up at the front of the church saying "I do" to a man whom she loved with all her heart and who had taught her one of the most valuable lessons of all. A new love didn't mean forgetting who came before, it only meant remembering that there was always more to come.

Everly loved weddings. Loved them. How could she not after that? Walking toward the church doors with Tyler, their hands intertwined, behind the newly married couple, her heart fluttered in her chest.

"I can't believe all of that just happened," she said.

Tyler chuckled. "People are going to be talking

about it for years."

Her steps faltered. "And you're okay with that?"

He jerked to a stop and turned to her, his face serious. "I couldn't care less about what they say. You're the only one who matters to me, and I promise to spend the rest of my life showing you that."

What could she say to that? Nothing. So she kissed him, a soft brush of her lips across his that promised so much more—an eternity of more. She broke the kiss and they started down the aisle again. Just as they were about to walk out, though, Tyler pulled them to a stop. He took his wallet out and plucked the quarter from the little pocket inside where he always kept it. Then, without the slightest hesitation, he dropped it into the poor box by the door.

"But that was your favorite quarter," she said, trying to figure out what in the world he was up to.

"That's what I thought. But it wasn't really. It was just a quarter I filched off my dad's dresser the day I decided I'd never be like him, and I kept it as a reminder. I used it to take the emotion out of decisions—at least that's what I told myself—but it turns out it was more than that. It brought me to you." He looked sheepish as he turned to face her, his gaze not quite meeting hers. "I have a confession to make. Now, I know that what I'm about to say might end in my physical pain, but all I ask is that you keep an open mind...and remember, I never used my power for personal gain."

She narrowed her expression as she tried to pull the truth from him. If he ruined their perfect reunion with another idiotic stunt... "Then what *did* you use this *power* for?"

"Funny you should ask. Umm... It's entirely possible that I know how to finagle a coin toss to put the odds in my favor." *She is going to kill me.* "But let's think of all the good I did with each coin toss. I carried your bags in the rain, I cooked you oatmeal, I even saved your car from Mrs. MacIntosh's ding jobs by leaving you only the one spot. Hell, I even bought a Harley I can't ride for you. All of it for you—even when I didn't realize it yet."

She shook her head. The man was demented. He'd been tricking her all along with a cheat coin toss. It was bad, of course, but then why did the fact that this man, who was all about appearances, completely risked looking bad just to win more time with her make her want to grin ear to ear? They were both totally demented.

"So let me get this straight. You bought a bike—which apparently you don't know how to ride—just so I wouldn't park my Helga next to Mrs. MacIntosh?" She raised one eyebrow at him, daring him to deny it.

When he nodded while side-eyeing the exits, she knew she would love this man forever. This impossible, ridiculous, foolishly head over heels in love man from Waterbury. "Well, you know now there's only one thing you can do to make it up to me, right?"

He brushed a stray strand of hair from her face and looked down at her with such love it took her breath away. "Anything."

"You know, I've always had a thing for hot guys on Harleys…with tattoos," she said, her eyes twinkling.

His eyes widened. "Oh hell no."

She *tsk*ed. "But you said 'anything'…"

Well, he'd said "anything" and he'd meant it. Today. Tomorrow. Forever. Whatever it took to keep that smile on the face of the woman he loved.

Epilogue

Three Years Later…

The Carlyle penthouse had been transformed. Oh, it still looked like the home of the über-rich Helene Carlyle, but it was different from the place that he'd first walked into as a scholarship kid in prep school because the people laughing and drinking and celebrating together in it. In addition to Sawyer, Hudson, and Helene, there was Sawyer's wife, Clover, and her parents, who were cracking up on the couch; Hudson and Felicia, who had made the younger Carlyle wait for years before she agreed to marry him; and Helene chasing toddler Michael by the family piano where Tyler stood on the opposite side. Alberto and his son, Carlo, were catching up in the corner after the elder Ferranti's latest trip with Helene to the French Alps. No doubt they were talking business; Carlo had become a bit obsessed since he'd broken it off with Irena at the alter—a fact that Alberto and Helene had both decided needed to be taken care of and soon. Those two, they were schemers after his own heart.

"Plotting again?" Everly asked, her voice a tickle on the back of Tyler's neck.

Turning so that his back was to the piano, his breath caught. The woman was as gorgeous as the day she'd first stomped her way across his ceiling and into his life.

"Busting my chops again, sugar?" he asked. "I'm beginning to think that and my mad bingo skills at Nunni's are the only reason you married me."

"It's true," she said with a wry grin before leaning closer so that only he could hear her. "You figured me out. But you know what I love more—even more than my name you got tattooed over your heart to celebrate getting your motorcycle license?"

He knew what his answer was and it would be happening again tonight. "What?"

"You."

And there it was, the unexpected answer from the woman who always managed to surprise him. "Are you getting soft on me, Ms. 3B?"

She laughed, the sound joining in with the joyful chaos around them. "You can't call me that anymore, since now we're Mr. and Mrs. Penthouse."

"We need a monogram." And maybe matching tattoos. Was it wrong that he wanted to mark her permanently as his? Too bad if it was, because that was just the kind of guy he was. Anyway, he knew the perfect Waterbury tattoo parlor to get it done. Now all he had to do was hatch a plan to get Everly to think it was *her* idea.

"I'll just take your parking spot instead."

"We do have an affinity for parking garages." And getting naked in them. He had all the camera angles mapped out in the new building so he always knew the best spot to park in.

"I can't help myself," she said, her voice turning husky as she trailed her fingertips up his arm. "It reminds me of how all this started."

"Believe me, I'm not complaining." Never. Not a single quickie time.

"Well," she said, her voice turning serious. "There are consequences for that kind of behavior."

"Jail for public indecency?" He had money for bail, and causing a scene just didn't seem to be a problem for him anymore.

She shook her head and then whispered in his ear. "Babies."

His brain fizzled. Literally. He could smell the burned wires and hear the sizzle. He scrambled for something to say. Anything, and all that came out was, "When? How? Boy or girl?"

This time Everly's laugh wasn't quiet and everyone in the room turned to look. Not ready to share this bit of news, Tyler grabbed Everly's hand and hustled her across the room and into Helene's gourmet kitchen, which was as untouched as it was gorgeous. For once, though, he didn't have eyes for the subzero refrigerator or the restaurant-quality gas stove. He couldn't stop staring at his wife and her belly and her smile that went almost from one ear all the way over to the next. Baby. His baby. Their baby.

"As for when, about seven months," Everly said, walking him through this because she obviously knew just how much she'd blown his mind. "In answer to how, all I have to say is that you were there so I'm hoping you understand the mechanics of that. And when it comes to boy or girl, I want to wait until the baby's born to find out."

Wait and be surprised? It sounded…perfect. Pulling her into his arms, he kissed her with enough heat to remind them both of just how this baby thing had happened. When he finally broke the kiss, Everly's lips were swollen and her eyes hazy while he was wondering just how soundproof the walk-in pantry was.

She raised her hands to cup his face, tears of joy balancing on her eyelids. "I love you, Tyler Jacobson."

"And I love you."

Today, tomorrow, forever, and definitely enough to sneak her out the service entrance at the back of the kitchen and down the elevator, because he was either getting her home to celebrate in private or they were going to christen a new parking garage. What could he say, he was a schemer. It was just that now his plots all centered on getting Everly naked and showing her just how much he loved her and always would.

Did you love this book from Entangled's Amara imprint? Check out more of our titles at entangledpublishing.com!

Acknowledgments

A huge thank-you to Kerri Carpenter for sharing her stories about her nunni, who loved romance books, and for letting me use her grandmother's nickname in *The Schemer*. xoxo

Discover more Entangled titles...

STRAIGHT UP IRISH
a Murphy Brothers novel by Magan Vernon

I need a wife if I want to help save my family's billion-dollar pub empire. There's just one problem: I never plan on marrying. So, I need someone who understands that this is just another business deal. I don't do commitments. And my brother's beautiful executive assistant, Fallon Smith, fits that bill. A fake wedding and a whole lot of whiskey. What could go wrong?

CINDERELLA AND THE GEEK
a British Bad Boys novel by Christina Phillips

I'm not looking for love or a Happily-Ever-After because I know how that ends. I just need to concentrate on my degree and look after myself. But there's something about my boss, Harry, I can't resist. It's crazy since he's so hot and smart it should be illegal. But I'm off to pursue my dreams, and he's taking his business to the next level. There's no way this fairytale has a happy ending, but that doesn't keep me from wishing for it.

PLAYING HOUSE
a Sydney Smoke Rugby novel by Amy Andrews

Eleanor is content with her boring life—mostly. She's even fine being the quirky sister in a bevy of beauties. So imagine her surprise when one of her brother's Sydney Smoke mates hits on her at an engagement party. Bodie is shocked the next morning to find the soft, sexy virgin who seduced him with corsets is his best friend's little sister. If he could kick his own ass, he would. Two months later, he's in for an even bigger surprise…

DIRTY GAMES
a Tropical Temptation novel by Samanthe Beck

Quinn Sheridan suddenly has half the time she anticipated to turn herself into an action hero for the role of her career. Luckily, her agent calls in a secret weapon, but the demanding, drop dead gorgeous hardass fails to understand *she's* the client. She has no problem taking direction, but Luke's definition of cooperation feels more like complete and utter submission. And she's tempted to give it to him....

AMARA
an imprint of Entangled Publishing LLC